"I'm not accepting any new clients."

Not even if she was the daughter of the richest man in town and he could use the business. Will walked around the dog and held the door open for them. "And I'm too busy to make small talk."

Sarah put her hand on the dog's head and looked down at him for a minute. Will was pretty sure he was going to win this encounter. It was a weird feeling. At seventeen, he'd been happy to escape her notice. Now he wanted to see the expression on her face while she digested that bit of information.

She straightened her shoulders, smoothed her red dress and shifted in the sky-high heels. Her red lips curved up and she tilted her chin. "Come on, Will, won't you even give me a chance to tell you how much I need your help?"

Dear Reader,

Ever since I met a beagle puppy named Jake, I've been dog crazy. Back then I was cute enough to convince my parents that dogs sleep *in* the house and *on* the bed. Today I'm lucky to have a writing partner named Jack, a stray I met in the middle of the road. I believe in rescues. Old or young, purebred or indeterminate mix, shelter dogs (and cats) change lives. Rescue work is a challenge due to hard stories, limited resources and the unending, disheartening turnover. The flip side is the serious joy of successful adoption and proof that second chances happen every day.

In *Heart's Refuge*, Sarah Hillman is already falling under the spell of a shelter dog named Bub when she corners Will Barnes in his office. Sarah gave Will a hard time in high school, but she's determined to save Paws for Love and she needs Will's help. I've loved spending time with Will and Sarah and the animals that change their lives, Bub and Jelly. I hope you will, too!

If you'd like to know more about my books and what's coming next, enter fun giveaways or meet my dog, Jack, please visit me at cherylharperbooks.com. I'm also on Facebook (CherylHarperRomance) and Twitter (@CherylHarperBks). I'd love to chat!

Cheryl Harper

HEARTWARMING

Heart's Refuge

—

Cheryl Harper

H HARLEQUIN® HEARTWARMING™

Recycling programs
for this product may
not exist in your area.

ISBN-13: 978-0-373-36746-7

Heart's Refuge

Printed in U.S.A.

Cheryl Harper discovered her love for books and words as a little girl, thanks to a mother who made countless library trips and an introduction to Laura Ingalls Wilder's Little House stories. Whether it's the prairie, the American West, Regency England or Earth a hundred years in the future, Cheryl enjoys strong characters who make her laugh. Now Cheryl spends her days searching for the right words while she stares out the window and her dog, Jack, snoozes beside her. And she considers herself very lucky to do so.

For more information about Cheryl's books, visit her online at cherylharperbooks.com or follow her on Twitter, @cherylharperbks.

Books by Cheryl Harper

Harlequin Heartwarming

Visit the Author Profile page
at Harlequin.com for more titles.

To everyone who calls a rescued dog or cat a member of the family, and the volunteers who keep these animals safe until their new families find them, thank you.

CHAPTER ONE

WILL BARNES STRAIGHTENED the pad of paper so the bottom was perfectly aligned with the edge of his desk. Next, he hit Play on his voice mail. For more than a decade, every morning had started the same way—voice mail, email, crisis management. Whether he was in a Dallas high-rise or his quaint new office in downtown Holly Heights, his clients, the ones who'd stuck with him, had come to expect quick answers.

People liked to know what was happening with their money.

And dependability mattered. Especially now that Will had left the practice he'd helped build to step out on his own. Proving he was the same guy who'd protected his clients' futures—minus the slick city office— was critical.

Only his daughter, Chloe, could convince him to walk away from what he'd built, the partnership he'd been chasing, for the unknown.

Since she was currently clearing every one of his shelves and restacking the books to her liking, he wasn't sure he was off to a great start. Entertaining a twelve-year-old girl for a whole summer would tax his creativity.

Neither of them was certain he could do it.

When the last message started, Will realized his day was about to take a sharp downturn.

"Will, I'm sorry to do this to you, but I won't be in to work today." His secretary, Ann, cleared her throat. "Actually, I won't be in again. Ever. Life is too short to spend it filling out forms. Six weeks is enough to convince me of that." Even the click when she hung up sounded agitated. That didn't surprise him. By the end of almost every day, Ann herself had been pretty agitated.

"Great." Will carefully pushed the button to end the call and tried to ignore the headache building right between his eyes. "Another assistant bites the dust."

Without someone to answer the phone and follow his procedures, the whole balancing act had just gotten more difficult. If he'd been juggling watermelons before, now he had a chain saw in the mix.

"No more Ann? *Now* who will feed me?" Chloe shoved his binders in the bottom shelf, her pink stripe of hair—the one that still gave him indigestion—flashing.

Remember it clips in. It's only temporary.

"You can feed us both. Brenda's down at the diner. Go see if she's got any work you can do, and bring back lunch when you get hungry." Will shifted to pull out his wallet. "Here's a couple of extra dollars. Put my initials at the top of the old Galaga machine."

Chloe snatched the bills out of his hands, folded them with a crisp crease in the center and slipped them in her back pocket. "If you'd get me a tablet, I could sit quietly." Chloe shook her head slowly. "Might save you money in the long run."

The upward curve of her lips reminded him so much of her mother, but Olivia would have been dumbfounded at the idea of wasting her time on an old video game.

In April, she'd listened to him rant for a full five minutes about the hair before she explained it wasn't permanent. Then she'd flipped the script, saying that if he'd pick up his daughter or come for her soccer games or school awards ceremony, they could discuss Chloe's fashion phases and things like pierced ears.

Which his daughter also had. Today she was accessorizing with gold stars.

At the rate she was changing, tomorrow she'd be driving, the next day she'd go off to college and by the end of the week he'd be a grandfather.

And he might not know her at all.

Olivia had moved his daughter to Austin, but he was the one who'd let work take over his life.

One conversation. He'd changed his whole life after one conversation.

Quit his job. Sold his house in a nice Dallas subdivision. Hired movers.

Taking the risk of going into business for himself had been a big, scary step, but he'd done it.

For Chloe.

His daughter perched on his mahogany desk, one sneakered foot thumping against the drawers.

Will gave her the most ferocious frown he could.

Then he grabbed her, pulled her close and tickled her until she couldn't breathe. When her beautiful giggles finally died down, he said, "Yeah, smarty-pants, a tablet might save money except you keep dropping them. Shattered screens don't keep you occupied for long."

Chloe was wiping her nose and panting, but he was happy to see the bored stare replaced by something else.

"Trust me, Dad. I won't drop it again." She put one hand over her sequined tank top to make this solemn vow.

"Go help Brenda and we'll see. I'm calling to tell her you're on the way. Don't talk to strangers on the sidewalk. Don't *dawdle* on the sidewalk. Don't leave the restaurant without calling me to tell me you're coming back. Order me a hamburger. And don't talk to strangers on the *sidewalk*."

"Got it. Talk to every stranger I see, get in random cars and bring you tofu." Chloe waved a hand as she disappeared.

He trailed behind her and peered out the window to make sure she made it the four doors down to the diner. If she caught him watching, she might actually bring him tofu.

If Sue Lynn's Best Burgers had tofu.

He had his doubts but no time to check. Revising the employment ad yet again had reordered his to-do list. In Dallas, any time a job opening was advertised, he'd had plenty of experienced candidates to choose from. Recent finance graduates were willing to work long hours in order to move up the ladder.

But very few candidates wanted to drive from Austin to Holly Heights every day.

Ann's previous experience had been running a hotel front desk. He'd thought that would mean discretion, good time management and an ability to follow procedure. Finance and investments and the paperwork that came with it must have been a boring change.

Will opened the employment ad he kept on his desktop. "Maybe 'financial administrative assistant' isn't the right title." The leather executive chair that fit the expensive atmosphere of his office was silent as he twisted back and forth and flipped through the possibilities. "Assistant financial planner. Junior finance agent. Salesperson with a flair for investments. Person who can use a checklist and answer the telephone."

He didn't understand the difficulty. He yanked the three-inch three-ring binder off the shelf and dumped it on his desk with a thud. "Everything is in here. All I need is someone who will follow these directions step-by-step." He flipped the pages and read, "How to answer the phone, what to do with the mail, when to take lunch and breaks…"

Reworking the employment ad would be a waste of time, so he emailed the Holly Heights classified editor and the newspaper in Austin to run the ad as soon as possible. This could be the time he found a UT Austin finance graduate who'd always dreamed of a small-town life instead of a hefty paycheck.

When the phone rang, he waited for someone else to answer it and realized it was going to be a long week.

"Barnes Financial. This is Will."

"The man himself. What happened to the assistant who answered the first time I called?" Rebecca asked. Will could hear the smile in her voice. That's the kind of person Rebecca Lincoln was. Her sunny personality made bad days better. "And are you already hard at work finding good places to send my money?"

"Not yet. I start by finding ways to *make* you money. It's kind of my thing." Will waited for her to laugh. When she did, he relaxed in his seat. "I've got some good leads, too, so whenever you have a minute, I could present them to you and Jen and Stephanie." Was it cowardly to ask Rebecca to arrange things with his stepsister? Possibly.

"Jen's insistence that I'll be robbed blind without your help is insulting," Rebecca muttered. "I've managed to keep the lights on all by myself for some time."

"Sure, but now you're going to be a juicier target." Will grimaced. *Juicier* wasn't a word he should use in conversation with a client.

"I guess." Rebecca sighed. "And even if I want to give it all away, I would like to make sure the money has an impact."

Will didn't understand Rebecca's urge to donate that much money, but he could still help Holly Heights's lottery winners make good decisions. "If we use some of your winnings to make more money, that means more help to spread around." As well as a solid payday for him.

"You and Jen, you're stuck in the same loop. But I agree. All of us together, we're going to make Holly Heights better and change the world. This is about more than finding places with the best financial returns. You're sure you know what I want?"

He wasn't sure he agreed with her, but the client was always right at Barnes Financial.

Unless he couldn't stomach how wrong they were.

"How about I present you with some options? I know you've already earmarked funds for the hospital's mentoring program, and I've made donations in your name to the short list of causes you gave me when we started. Now we can talk investments and other programs closer to home. You let me know what works with your schedule, and I'll have a few things to show all three of you."

"Sounds good. Stephanie passed along the check I wrote to HealthyAmericas, but we might want to send another donation. Daniel's identified five students to sponsor through the university in Lima, so he'll need funds for tuition. Please add them to your list," Rebecca said.

"Okay." Will jotted a reminder to study the financials of the medical charity Rebecca's brother, Daniel, worked with in South America. Researching not-for-profits was going to be a new direction, but the process should be similar.

Not that it mattered. Rebecca's brother and her best friend, Stephanie, were doing good things in Peru. Stephanie's blog was a record of how money and dedicated, passionate people could make amazing progress that would impact generations.

It would take some serious mismanagement to turn Rebecca and Stephanie away from HealthyAmericas. His gut said it wasn't a problem.

"We'll have a dinner party to send the lovebirds back to Lima. I'll give them the check before they go." Rebecca sighed happily. "By then, my new kitchen will be finished. And you're coming." The long pause indicated she was waiting for his answer.

"I wouldn't miss it." Almost everyone he knew in Holly Heights was a part of Rebecca's crowd, but there might be a few networking opportunities.

"You need to call your sister," Rebecca said. "She's making some big decisions. It would be nice if she had some advice."

He'd tried that once. She'd ordered him to go shove his head in the lake. Loudly.

They'd always mixed like orange juice and toothpaste.

"I will call her. I promise." But not today. Tomorrow, definitely.

"I'm going to hold you to that. Aunt Jen would like to know your Chloe." She hung up and he wondered if this would be the way he and Jen communicated now that he was in town. Rebecca would get tired of being the middleman sooner or later.

And Chloe and Jen and Brenda—his stepmother—together were the reason he was taking this risk in the first place.

But his plate was pretty full at the moment.

First, he needed some leads on organizations Rebecca would love. Jen and Stephanie were mainly along for the ride.

"Who could I call to find out about local organizations? Somebody at the chamber of commerce?" He scrolled through his list of business contacts, saw the name of his leasing agent and decided that was a good place to start. Real estate agents should have plenty of inside information on all the businesses in town.

Before he could dial the number, he heard the front door open, thanks to the chime he'd had installed after his first secretary left him in the lurch. The how-to binder had been much smaller then. He'd learned a lot from that three-week stretch.

Had Chloe even tried to follow his orders?

He put the phone down and rolled the chair back, ready to either lecture his daughter on safety or explain to his visitor that he wasn't seeing clients that morning, but he'd be happy to make an appointment, when he heard a dog bark.

Inside his office. There was a dog inside his office.

He hurried around his desk and paused in the doorway to the reception area. His ears hadn't deceived him. There, standing on the rug he'd bought because it matched the room's tone of somber wealth, was...a dog. Big. Brown. Hairy. And happy, if the lolling tongue could be construed as an emotional display. The dog barked again and the woman—who had absolutely no hope of stopping it if the creature decided to make a break for it—shushed him. "Bub, be quiet. Use your inside manners."

"Or better yet, take whatever manners you do or don't have right back outside and away from the very expensive furnishings." As soon as Will spoke, the woman and the dog both turned to stare at him. And both of them made it pretty clear what they thought of his directive.

The dog sat. The woman propped one hand on her hip. Will waited.

"Bub is well-trained, an obedience school graduate." She ran a hand over the dog's head, and Will was pretty sure he saw the dog wink.

Of course the dog didn't wink. They didn't teach winking in obedience school.

Did they?

Will shook his head. "Doesn't matter. This is a place of business, so unless he's a service animal, please take him out."

"You were chased by a dog as a child, weren't you?" the woman asked. Then Will realized who was invading his office with a canine in tow as if she had every right to do so. Sarah Hillman, homecoming queen and queen of mean to every outcast at Holly Heights High. He should've known—his junior year he'd developed a sixth sense to warn him when she was in the vicinity. Obviously, if he didn't use his Hillman radar for more than a decade, he lost it.

"I'm not accepting any new clients at this point," he said. Not even if she was the daughter of the richest man in town and he could use the business. Will walked a wide circle around the dog, who hadn't moved a single inch, and held the door open for them. "And I'm too busy to make small talk."

Sarah put her hand on the dog's head and looked down at him for a minute. Will was pretty sure he was going to win this encounter. It was a weird feeling. At seventeen, he'd been happy to escape her notice. Now he wanted her to look right at him while she digested that bit of information.

Then she straightened her shoulders, smoothed the skirt of her red dress and shifted in the sky-high heels that made her legs look as if they belonged on the silver screen. The brands weren't important. If Sarah Hillman was wearing it, it was expensive. And now that Will wasn't afraid of social suicide, he could see the way her face changed when she was about to hit him with the full force of her personality.

Her red lips curved up and she tilted her chin. He watched her lick her lips and run a red nail around the curved neck of her dress. "Come on, Will, won't you even give me a chance to tell you how much I need your help?"

For a split second, he imagined he knew what the snake charmer felt when he stared into the beady eyes of a cobra. Except her eyes were a beautiful, warm brown. That probably made her twice as dangerous. Then he realized the unfamiliar feeling warming him from the inside was pleasure that she'd remembered his real name.

He shook his head and looked out the door. The dog stood up and peeked around the door frame as if to check on whatever Will was watching and then sat back down.

"Don't you remember me? We went to high school together." She reached over to tug on his sleeve. "You have time for an old friend, surely."

Instead of jerking his arm away, Will snorted. That wasn't the most elegant or dignified answer, but it was honest. And it surprised her. Another win.

"Sarah Hillman. I remember. What surprises me is that you can recall my real name. Beanpole Barnes would roll more naturally off your tongue." She laughed as if it was the funniest thing in the world and unbelievably Will wanted to laugh along with her. In high school, the nickname had been an embarrassing insult, but no one would think to use it now.

"I thought you'd go with Barn-door Barnes from that time you spent most of lunch with your zip…"

"Why are you still here?" Will asked. This walk down memory lane had already gone on for too long.

"We were kids. That's what kids do." She walked her fingers up his sleeve. "You're no beanpole now. Time's been good to you, Will Barnes."

"Yeah, my sister's doing pretty well, too. Maybe you remember her? Red hair? Lots of freckles? Cried more than once when you pointed them out?" He crossed his arms over his chest and the office was silent except for the chime of the door closing. "Raggedy Jen. Was that because of the red hair or her secondhand clothes, too?"

Sarah blinked and the calculations taking place in her brain showed in narrowed eyes and tightened lips. Then she ducked her head, folded her hands in front of her and said, "That was all in *fun*. You've got ten minutes. For me?" She stuck out her lower lip as she looked up at him.

"No." The dog drooped to rest his chin on Will's polished loafers. Two pairs of puppy dog eyes were nearly impossible to withstand. The second no was harder to get out, but he managed. Then he stepped around the dog. "Please leave."

Will walked back into his office and closed the door firmly. He didn't have to worry about Sarah Hillman running off with his carefully chosen knickknacks. He'd been trying to give the impression of good taste and old money. She *had* the old money.

He pressed his ear against the door to listen for the chime that would signal her defeat and retreat. Instead, he could hear angry muttering. He wanted to crack open the door to see her disappointment in living color but didn't want to restart the conversation.

And he had work to do. Will had to admit, Sarah Hillman could probably help with that... Holly Heights was filled with signs saying Sponsored by Hillman Luxury Autos. Little League teams, the local stadium, the Fourth of July fireworks displays and every Christmas parade had been funded by Bobby Hillman. She'd be able to come up with a list of contacts.

But Will would go door-to-door through every street in the downtown area begging for recommendations before he asked for her help.

With a firm nod, he moved back around his desk and reached for his phone. Before he could dial the numbers, Sarah Hillman shoved open his door and followed her dog into his office.

His clean, orderly office now had a dog in it. And a beautiful brunette who was no longer begging in an attractive, manipulative sort of way. Now she was determined.

"Listen, I'm sure keeping track of Daddy's money is exhausting, but I will not help you. Head over to Austin. There are lots of choices for portfolio management and you can add in lunch and a shopping trip. I'm sure there have to be spas somewhere."

Instead of carefully considering the right

face to try, Sarah marched over and planted her hand in the middle of his shiny desk.

"Don't be that guy, Will. You have a chance to be the bigger person. Come on. Don't you want to feel superior to me?" Nothing about her said she was faking or flirting or manipulating.

"If I wanted to feel superior, I wouldn't have to try hard, Sarah." Instead of the satisfaction he'd expected to feel at finally winning a verbal sparring match with her, he was almost instantly sorry for what he'd said, even if it was a pretty good last word.

"Well. You have done some growing up, haven't you? Learned how to throw a punch." She eased back. "Make sure you don't go too far, kicking a girl when she's down. Might make you a bully."

He snorted. Again. He'd need to get a better handle on reactions like that.

"I'm sure you're amazed that something isn't going your way, but let's call it my gift to humanity. You can take your dog and go. And I'll get back to work." He pointed at the computer. "You know what these are for, right?"

She pushed her shoulders back and propped

a hand on her hip, using her curves and crazy-long legs to her advantage. It almost worked.

"Don't bother. I can see through the manipulation now. That's the gift of your high school education."

Instead of turning away to stare at his computer screen as he wanted to, he watched her hands tighten into fists. "Fine. I heard about the lottery win and whoever is answering Rebecca's phone refuses to let me talk to her. On the last call, they told me to come to you with any requests, so here I am. Could you please give me ten minutes to make a case for an appointment with Rebecca?"

"So, what? You want Rebecca to float you a loan until Daddy's allowance arrives?" He swept a glance from the top of her shiny hair to the ridiculous shoes. "Doesn't look like you need handouts."

His inner nice guy was telling him he had ten minutes. That was the easiest way to get her out of his hair, pretend to listen.

Sarah ran her hand over Bub's head. "No, but these guys do. Ten minutes, Will."

Bub stretched forward to rest his chin on Will's formerly spotless desk and sighed.

Sarah had given up on manipulation to go for honesty, but Bub's skill was impressive.

Will knew he was making a mistake, but sometimes mistakes were inevitable. "The clock is ticking. Make your case."

CHAPTER TWO

SARAH COULD SEE the no on his face. Bean-pole Barnes—Will—had grown into an attractive man. His starched dress shirt, silk tie and perfectly pressed slacks made it easy to believe he could be trusted with a fortune.

She couldn't imagine what he thought of her own outfit. Only desperation could have convinced her to put on the best dress she had left, even if it was years out of fashion, to face someone who'd be happy to shoot her down while she held her hand out for money. *Begging*. The sour taste in her mouth made it difficult to maintain her pageant smile.

But she had to do something or the animal shelter she'd funded for the past year would close, leaving innocent dogs and cats without a safe place.

Sarah could relate. As of this week, she'd moved her own suitcase into the shelter office.

The police had torn up her father's house

looking for evidence of embezzlement. Since she'd answered phones at Hillman Luxury Autos for years, and had seen no shady dealings, she knew they'd come up empty-handed.

But sneaking her father in—or herself out—while under the police's watchful eye would be difficult. Until the Austin detective making her life miserable tracked her to the shelter, she had some breathing room.

And no one would care if the shelter was her home for a few days. After her father skipped town, the shelter's manager had walked off the job. Donations had stopped. So had her paycheck and the payments her father made on her condo in the city.

Before long, her father would come for her, explain the misunderstanding, and her life would go back to normal, even if the new normal was a country with sandy beaches and no extradition. Sarah wanted him to be innocent and did her best to believe it. The longer her trials lasted, the harder it was to hold on to that dream.

The eviction notice had been a wake-up call. It had clarified how quickly her situation was deteriorating.

"Thank you for your time." Sarah sat in the leather chair across the desk from Will.

She rubbed Bub's silky ear for encouragement. But Will had frowned at the adorable stray, a dog she'd roped in at the last minute to seal the deal. If Will Barnes wasn't an animal lover, her job had gotten much more difficult, but if he was hard-hearted enough to withstand Bub's tricks, she was doomed.

The shelter was broke and closed to new animals.

Will checked his watch. "Five minutes. Go."

Okay, she could do this. "Paws for Love is a no-kill shelter that I started supporting a little over a year ago. Now that... Well, as head of the organization, I've committed to raising funds for the shelter's improvement, but it's not easy."

"Could be something to do with your beautiful personality," Will muttered.

The idea that this man, who'd been one of the gangliest math nerds to ever come out of Holly Heights, could hurt her, even if he was speaking the truth, was almost unbelievable. But this was what her life had come to: begging for help from people who'd much rather enjoy her misfortune.

How could people hold her past actions against her when she was trying to do something *good*?

"Since the funding has stopped, the shelter manager disappeared. I'm doing my best with the volunteers to keep the doors open, but Paws needs investment and soon." She almost told him about the overdue bills but decided that might smack of poor management to numbers-man Will.

Without fast cash, she wouldn't be able to afford the basics—food and electricity. Even the local vets who'd been donating time and services would pull their support if she couldn't keep the lights on. Juggling the bills had become her latest obsession.

"How much?" Will asked as he stared over his shoulder at his computer. Apparently, even five minutes of *undivided* attention was asking too much.

"A lot. Anything would help. I've got an event planned for next month, so if I could get enough to pay the bills for this month and next, I'll have more options." For reassurance, she scratched the spot right above Bub's tail and listened to his tail thump the floor. His happy sigh bolstered her resolve.

"What happened to the other donors?" Will leaned back in his chair, one elbow braced against the armrest. If he was distracted before, his focus now was intense.

"They are...unhappy with my involvement. Some of my father's business decisions aren't popular." There. She'd tiptoed around the truth.

Will raised an eyebrow and waited. The silence between them stretched until Bub shifted to sniff under Will's desk, breaking Will's concentration and giving her a chance to breathe.

"You know you'll need something more concrete than 'a lot' to convince me to spend any of Rebecca's valuable time. Budgets for this year and next, salaries, staffing, capital improvements needed, the percentage of the donation that could go to overhead versus the animals. You aren't ready for fundraising. Come back when you are." He didn't shy away but met her stare head-on.

"And you'll refuse to see me then, too." Sarah shook her head. "I'm surprised, Will."

"I'm not. Of course you thought you could

walk in here and everything would be forgotten because you wore your prettiest dress and red lipstick. That's the Sarah I remember." He braced both hands on the chair's armrests, prepared to...defend himself? Battle? She wasn't sure.

"Another thing hasn't changed. I always get my way." She eased back. "Bub and I are going to stay right here until you agree to at least visit the shelter. I'll jump through your hoops, but I want you to see what we're doing when I get my proposal done. Come to the shelter or Bub is staying put." She tapped her fingers on the arms of the chair. "And you do not want to know how long it's been since he's had his walk. He's a big, thirsty dog. Could have a mess pretty soon."

She surveyed his office. "Walnut bookcases polished to a high sheen. Leather furniture." She squinted at the lower shelves. "Are those first editions down there? Bub really likes books." Was that true? Who knew? Bub played his part like a master, ambling over to nose around the bottom of the bookcase.

Will straightened in his chair, both hands held out as if he were about to spring into action. Would he carry Bub out himself or use his body as a shield to protect his belongings?

"Fine. I'll come out to see the place, but that's as far as I'm taking this. If you don't leave right now and take your dog with you, I'm going to call the police."

Sarah couldn't help the pout that had gotten her through a lot of harder discussions. "Aw, you don't want to do that. Wouldn't look good for your business to toss people out, would it? And Bub can howl on command." She'd grab some treats and teach him to tonight, just in case. She held out her hand and the dog moved to stand by her side.

"Don't expect me to change my mind. I won't waste my client's time on any business that's so poorly run it's about to close." He tilted his head. "And when she finds out it's you asking, I'm pretty sure she'll thank me for running interference."

"I was never mean to Rebecca. What's she got against me?" The waver in her voice was an unwelcome surprise. The shelter's survival depended on Rebecca, her cash and her friendly disposition. If Rebecca was an enemy, too, where could she go for help?

Sarah wished she could take the question back. Showing weakness would never do.

Bulletproof. That's the only way to live in this town. Remember.

"My stepsister Jen's one of her best friends. We talked about her already, didn't we? Jennifer Neil. Tall, thin…good with numbers, like me. Hit the lottery. Maybe her last name threw you off." He raised an eyebrow. "Ring any bells?"

Don't panic. You can work this out, Sarah.

"Vaguely. But none of us are in high school anymore."

Will crossed his arms over his chest. "Well, *she* still is. Teaches there every day. Probably keeps the memories alive." His lips were a tight line as he studied her face.

The hole he'd punched in her hope made it difficult to stand straight and tall. *Flash him a smile, grab the dog and live to fight another day.* "I'll be excited and grateful to show you around the shelter. Thank you so much for your valuable time."

She didn't think her fear or discomfort could be heard in her voice, but her gritted teeth didn't much resemble a smile. Still, she calmly, slowly led Bub out of the office, working the dress, the heels and her best features until she stepped back out on the sidewalk. As soon as she passed his window, she collapsed against the brick, closed her eyes and fought back tears.

"That was harder than I thought it would be." Bub licked her hand and she remembered why fear, frustration and her own embarrassment didn't matter.

At this point, she was out of options. Difficult was the only way.

Until her father came back for her or she tracked him down.

She fished her phone out of her handbag. No missed call. No text. Nothing to indicate that her father was on his way.

"Time to get back to work. These shoes are beautiful but deadly."

Bub stood, too, happy to go wherever she was going, but a woman coming down the sidewalk called Sarah's name before they could take two steps. The dread was nearly immediate. Running into any old "friend" was bound to be another lesson in humility.

Why was it these lessons were coming so often lately?

"Hey, Cece, it's good to see you." Lying

through her teeth was one lesson Sarah had learned a long time ago. She gave Celia Grant's cheeks the expected air-kisses and stepped back.

"How long has it been? Three months or so?" Cece asked, and placed a hand on her shoulder. "I loved this dress, too. I finally had to let it go, though. Needed the space in my closet." She leaned forward. "You didn't pick this up at the consignment store over on First, did you?" Then she twitched her shoulders as if she was being a naughty scamp.

So turnabout was fair play.

For years, they'd traded similar exchanges. Cece must still be annoyed about Sarah's comments on her green Armani. But there was no room for argument. Sixty-year-old Deborah Simmons had worn it better and *first*.

"Ah, no, and I'm certain this dress isn't yours." Sarah stepped back and studied Cece's gorgeous outfit. "I'm pretty sure we're still different sizes. Yours would positively swim on me." She smiled sweetly.

Although it was a direct hit, Cece didn't give her the pleasure of wincing. "Always such a funny girl. How's the family?"

"Oh, you know how hard it is to stay in touch sometimes, but I'm doing well." Sarah navigated all of Cece's land mines and then changed the subject. She'd been moving in the shark-infested waters of society for a long time. "Are you and Doug moved into your new house on the golf course yet?"

As Cece droned on and on about the challenges of building a five-bedroom custom design in a small town like Holly Heights—not to mention the lack of solid contractors—Sarah weighed her options for escape. On one hand, this couldn't go on indefinitely. On the other, her feet were about to walk away and leave the rest of her stranded on the sidewalk.

When Cece wound down, she pointed at Bub. "What sort of dog is that?"

Bub cocked his head at her and seemed to give a disapproving expression.

"Mutt. Rescue. The best kind." Sarah ran her hand over his head and realized that this encounter was meant to be. The Grants were wealthy enough to have spare cash lying around. They could be the ones to keep the lights on.

"Of course. Pedigrees are expensive, aren't they, darling?"

Sarah studied Cece's eyes. In high school, Cece had been one of the crowd that circled Sarah, always ready to take advantage of her father's wealth. There wasn't much friendship showing in her eyes now, if they'd ever been real friends.

"Actually, it's wonderful to run into you. I'm planning a fund-raiser next month for the shelter and I'd love to include you on the list." At Cece's reluctant nod, Sarah got a jolt of energy, which made it easier to press for more. "We're always in need of donations from caring people like you and Doug, so don't wait for a formal invitation. Stop by and see the shelter sometime, won't you?"

"It does seem you could use cash right now. Doug's always got more requests than money to give, but I can persuade him to visit. I'd love to find out more about your little hobby. But there won't be any actual animals there, right? They make such a mess." She was shaking her head as she pulled out her wallet and removed every bit of cash she had. "Here. This should buy some dog food and…things."

Feeling a bit like a panhandler, Sarah swallowed her pride and accepted every wrinkled bill. "Cece, you've made a big difference for Paws for Love. I won't forget your generosity." She riffled through her purse until she found a pen and an old grocery receipt, then scribbled the amount and signed it. "Here. For your records." Then she put the cash in a ragged, empty envelope and jotted down the date, Cece's name and the amount.

It wouldn't be enough to keep the doors open, but this month's dog food was now paid for. That was a relief.

Cece awkwardly pinched the wrinkled paper. "I'll make sure to pass it along to Doug. What are you doing here? Hiring Will Barnes as your financial adviser?" Bub picked that minute to turn on the charm and batted his eyelashes at Cece like a starlet. She took a step back, but the corners of her mouth turned up.

The dog was magic.

"Adviser? I thought he was some kind of accountant." Sarah studied the facade of Barnes Financial. She should have asked more questions about what Will did. That might have been the polite thing to do, and it would have given her a better concept of his donation potential. If he was drawing

Holly Heights's upper crust, he could write a check, too.

"According to the gossip at the club, he's some kind of investment guru. He was part of a big firm in Dallas until he moved to town to open his own office. I keep telling Doug that we might want to find someone local to help with money management, but you know how husbands are." Cece stopped and patted Sarah's arm. "Oh, sorry, darling. You *don't* know how husbands are."

Good one. Cece had gotten sharper.

The near-smirk and warm glow in her eyes suggested she knew it, too.

"Maybe you should try the patented moves on Will…" Cece winked. "As I recall, no boy was immune once you turned on the charm. Of course, he's not a boy, is he? Maybe they're too weak for men."

Do not mention my inability to catch a husband again or I'll…

Bub leaned against her leg, distracting her from plotting mayhem. Woman's best friend obviously.

Cece was right. Beanpole Barnes had blushed three colors of red if she so much as glanced at him. Will had met her head-on and cut right through her tried-and-true moves. If things were different, that would have doubled her determination. But now she wasn't sure she could conquer him even with her old wardrobe and her father's money.

A small part of her understood that the challenge made Will a prize worth winning.

"If you've got the time…" Cece held out her hand. "Come to lunch. My treat."

Sarah wanted to. The chance to sit down at a nice restaurant, eat a meal prepared by someone who knew how to cook and not worry over how she'd cover the bill was seductive. But she had Bub. And these shoes were a torture each second she stood there. "I can't. I've got so much work to do at the shelter, but I meant what I said about stopping by. I'd love to catch up."

Cece wrapped her arm around Sarah's shoulders. "I will. I wish there was more I could do to help with your *situation*."

Sarah tapped her purse. "You've already helped so much. Watch for your invitation in the mail."

"I'll warn Doug to start saving his discretionary funds, darling." Cece blew her an air-kiss and walked away.

"Good news. We're going to have water for a few more days." Sarah scratched Bub's neck, dodged his tongue and enjoyed the brief instant of relief. "Let's go home."

He woofed in response and followed her to her car, a sporty black convertible that had been perfect for the heiress to a car fortune. Now it was too small to do what she needed and too paid for to get rid of. Her single suitcase would fit neatly in the backseat when the time came.

"Load up."

Bub jumped into the passenger seat and Sarah fastened his seat belt in his harness. Shelly had almost had a fit when she'd loaded Bub into her car that morning and nearly forgot the harness. Animal safety was a Big Deal for Shelly. And now that she knew better, Sarah could understand the commitment.

Still, if he was riding shotgun often, Bub was definitely going to need a cool pair of sunglasses.

He could be the shelter's celebrity spokesdog, cruising around town in a convertible and shades.

Temporarily. Until he was adopted. Until

her father came back to Holly Heights. Or she made her escape.

Sarah slid into the driver's seat with a grateful sigh and thought about taking the shoes off to drive barefoot. Then she imagined the picture she'd present to the policeman who pulled her over. Convertible hair would not be conducive to flirting her way out of a ticket.

The drive to Paws for Love was quick, but when she reached the sign pointing the way to the interstate, she paused and considered her options. It would be so easy to hit the road, but she had no idea where to go. So, it was better to stay in uncomfortable but safe Holly Heights. Her foot eased off the brake, and before she'd managed to leave behind all the bad energy from her run-ins with Will Barnes and Celia Grant, she was carefully negotiating the gravel parking lot in high heels behind a determined Bub.

"Hey, boss, I'm so glad you're back." Shelly met her at the door and danced back and forth, agitation clear on her face. "I left some messages on your desk. I'm afraid they're bill collectors." She whispered the last two words as if it was a big secret that the place was broke.

She wiped her eyes and Sarah wondered if she'd been crying again. "Fine, Shelly. But I've told you not to call me boss, haven't I? We're coworkers." Sarah didn't pay Shelly, although she certainly deserved more than Sarah's cheap yet undying gratitude.

Unfortunately, that's all she had to give.

"Oh, right." Shelly smoothed her shirt down nervously. "Got time to help with the dogs?" She cleared her throat and tacked on, "Sarah."

What she wanted to do was say no. Shelly could handle the noise and mess of overly excited dogs while Sarah stretched out on the couch and dreamed of dinner in Austin.

But she'd watched Shelly struggle that morning.

This was something she could do.

"Sure, I know you need to get home on time tonight." She offered Shelly the leash. "Could you let Bub out for me?"

"Oh, I'm in no hurry. Nothing there for me but sitcoms and leftovers." Shelly buzzed around her with fluttery hands to take Bub's leash. When she and Bub walked away, Sarah ran her hand through her hair. Helping Shelly recover from a divorce was not one of her skills.

Right now she had her hands full helping dogs and cats. She'd add encouraging lonely people after she conquered that. Though she was learning more and more about being lonely and discouraged every day.

Sarah jammed her shoulder against the door to the shelter's office and winced when the warped wood squeaked. "Something else to add to the list of things that need attention."

First, the shoes. They had to go.

"Don't knock over the piles." Sarah scooted between the files on the floor and on the desk to drop down onto the ragged office chair held together with tape and goodwill. Her gusty sigh as the shoes came off could probably be heard miles away.

But the minute she caught her breath, all she could think of was Will's face and Cece's cash. "What a morning." She dug around in the suitcase behind the desk and dragged out her favorite jeans.

At one point they'd been pretty stylish. Now they were comfortable.

Once everything she was wearing was washable, she scooted back around the piles, rolled her shoulders to ease some of the tension and jumped into Shelly's whirlwind. Two hours later they had all the dogs walked, every animal had been fed and Shelly was on her way home to fall apart in private. Bub was snoring loudly from the couch when she sat down and pulled out the cash Cece had handed her. "Electricity or groceries. Which should it be?"

The image of her father sitting on a sunny beach somewhere, a cold drink in his hand, floated through her brain. The haze of jealous bitterness followed before she could stop it.

As soon as possible, she'd head off for a restorative spa day and then book a flight to St. Barts.

But what sort of life would she have living on stolen money?

Her old, normal life was a dream.

Reality was being covered in dog hair and worse while trying to decide whether she wanted to eat or see.

People like Will Barnes sneered at her.

And her friends had disappeared like the money.

"Bub, you'll never leave, will you?" She

ran her hand over his side and ignored his annoyed kick.

"Two choices, Sarah. You can either sit here and have a pity party. Or see if you can come up with the stuff Will wants and prove him wrong." Pity party was an attractive option, but she'd spent a lot of time at that particular one-woman show lately.

Sarah brushed the hair off her pants and maneuvered back to the desk.

She was fully capable of starting even if she couldn't do it all on her own.

CHAPTER THREE

WILL PULLED UP in front of the dilapidated building and parked in the gravel lot. A worn sign said Paws for Love out front. "This is not quite as…fancy as I expected Sarah would demand."

His passenger had absolutely nothing to say.

He should be getting used to that. Chloe's bored expression made him think of his stepsister. Which was crazy, as they didn't share a single drop of blood.

"It's an animal shelter," Chloe drawled. "No doubt it'll be educational."

Sarcasm. She and Jen spoke the same language, too. When he slanted a watch-your-tone look at his daughter, she held both hands up. "It's Saturday. We could be doing something fun."

Will couldn't argue with that.

He studied the building through the windshield. The place was tired, needed to be landscaped and given a new paint job at the least. Even to his amateur eye, the roof was sorely in need of replacement.

Instead of exaggerating the shelter's needs, Sarah might have been downplaying them. Could he walk away and get the petty revenge he wanted when it was clear this place and the animals it saved needed real help?

Could he play with the puppies and not pull out a checkbook?

"All right. Fifteen minutes, twenty tops. Then we'll do something fun. You can pick." Will opened his door and slid out. Chloe hopped out, as if this might have been the promise she'd been waiting for.

"Good. The lake. We're going. We'll swim." She pointed a finger. "No phone calls."

"We could rent a boat. Pick up lunch." He saluted her to acknowledge the excellent plan. "You should be in charge every day."

She held up her hand for a high five, something she'd picked up on the soccer field. He smacked her hand, grabbed it and pulled her close for a squirmy hug.

"Twenty minutes…and go." Squaring his shoulders, Will walked over to the door, held it open and stepped inside right behind Chloe. "Hello? Anybody here?" The place was unexpected on the inside, too. Clean, if ragged, with a nice pine scent.

Bub ambled around the corner first, followed by Sarah. "Sorry, we were out back cleaning up the yard now that the animals are inside."

The surprises kept coming. Instead of ridiculously expensive clothes and seriously hot shoes, she was wearing denim and cotton and the kind of black boots he imagined farmers wore to milk the cows. Even in weekend casual jeans and a polo, he was overdressed for this tour.

Sarah fidgeted with her ponytail, waiting for him to say something, but he was stumped. Then he realized she was wearing no makeup, no lipstick, no nothing. The only hint of the seductress was in the red nails that tapped on the scratched linoleum counter.

"Introduce me to the rest of the committee?" Sarah pointed to Chloe, who'd stopped as close to the door as she could.

"This is my daughter, Chloe. We're on our way to the lake." When he felt a weight on his foot, Will glanced down to see Bub perched on his sneaker. The dog sighed as he leaned against Will's leg and glanced up at him, tongue dangling out of his mouth.

Should he object? Unseat the dog? He glanced up to see both Sarah and Chloe watching him.

Moving Bub could wait.

Chloe stepped forward to shake Sarah's hand.

Like an adult. A serious, fully grown woman.

Except she was wearing pink shorts and black sneakers that squeaked with each step.

For a brief second, Sarah's lips flattened, but she pasted on a smile. "It's a beautiful day out there. I won't take much of your time."

"Twenty minutes." Chloe motioned over her shoulder. "He promised. The guy works all the time. It's *Saturday*." The exasperated expression on her face was a carbon copy of his ex-wife's.

He'd heard similar complaints from Olivia regularly.

Sarah clasped her hands in front of her and nodded seriously. "Sure, but does his work always include cute cats?"

"No, that's new." Chloe pursed her lips. "Where are they?"

"Ah, someone who likes to cut to the chase. I wonder where you get that?" When Sarah's eyes met his, he could see she was teasing him.

They weren't friends. Maybe they weren't enemies, either.

Sarah pointed at the hallway. "Follow me?"

"Show me your cats." Chloe marched around the corner, pulling Sarah and Will along in her wake.

Giant miscalculation, Barnes. A kid, surrounded by cats and dogs ready for adoption. What are you going to say when she finds the one that has to come home with you?

He'd say no. When Chloe was in Austin, he would be working. All the time. No animal would be happy or healthy with a setup like that.

He was a *person* and didn't really enjoy it.

But it was too late for sound judgment now.

"Realizing you didn't think everything through?" Sarah wrinkled her nose, the teasing glint in her eyes returning. "Kids love pets."

Will nodded. "Yeah. Let's get on with the tour."

Sarah saluted. "Bathroom. Cramped conference room." They paused in front of a door with a large glass window. Inside he could see concrete floors, cinder-block pens with chain-link gates. Everything was fresh and clean. "Prepare yourself. There will be barking."

She was right. Inside the room, conversation was impossible. He walked down the line and read the cards. "Good with kids. Needs special care. House-trained."

Sarah motioned them to follow and then stopped in front of a large window. The room on the other side held a few smaller cages, an interesting jungle gym and cats of different colors and sizes. "Cats don't cause much fuss," she said. Where the dogs rushed their gates to speak to him, the cats sat back and eyed him coolly.

Chloe immediately stepped close to the glass, her breath fogging the window.

Sarah shot him a sympathetic glance. "You can go inside if you like."

"No" burned on the tip of his tongue, but Chloe's pleading eyes made it impossible to say. He waved a hand at the door. Chloe slipped inside so fast that she missed him say, "Don't get too attached. We aren't taking one home."

He shoved his hands in his pockets as he watched Chloe carefully approach a fat orange cat. They stared at each other for a long minute before Chloe reached out slowly to run a finger over the cat's head. A dog would have probably knocked her to the ground and licked her from head to toe at this point.

"I think I must be a cat person." He appreciated the quiet and reserve. "Although Bub is nice, too."

Sarah blinked at him for a minute. "I did not expect you to say that. Better take a look at your pants before you commit."

He glanced down to see the white hairs dotting his pants. "How does a brown dog leave white hairs?"

"Unsolved mystery," Sarah said.

"Time to clean the litter boxes," a small, older woman sang as she came down the hall.

No one should be that happy about cat litter.

Sarah's lips were twitching as she said, "Shelly, can you keep an eye on Chloe?"

"You got it, Sarah." Shelly slipped inside.

"Shelly's one of the volunteers keeping the doors open." Sarah led him into another room. "Food, treats, toys, everything we might need for the cats or dogs stays in this room and we keep a careful inventory." Sarah pointed at a long line of bowls. "Shelly's getting ready to feed the cats next."

"All by herself?" The cat-to-person ratio seemed high.

"Usually I help." Sarah led him back to the hallway. "The vets who volunteer sometimes use these exam rooms. We take the animals to the clinics for anything out of the ordinary, but the van isn't running. Needs a new battery." She shoved open a heavy door. "And this is our exercise yard."

Will stepped out behind her to see that this part of the shelter was also immaculate. Beyond the fences was another grassy area but it was overgrown. "What do you use that for?"

Sarah studied the fence. "Well, if we could repair the fences, we'd use it as another exercise yard. The shelter has room to grow, so we could increase our capacity, but not without more volunteers and some improvements."

And that was the critical point. They both knew it.

"Come back to the director's office. It's cramped, but if you have a minute, I'd appreciate your opinion on the information I worked on last night. If I'm on the right track, I'll keep going." Sarah rubbed her forehead. "You will let me meet with Rebecca, won't you? If I have to, I'll wait for her at the grocery store and spring out from the frozen foods. I need this."

His steely reserve was faltering. This was not a big surprise.

"Show me what you've got." Maybe he was going to cave, but he wouldn't make it easy for her.

Sarah's fist pump of victory was premature, at least as far as she knew, but he enjoyed the way she lit up. Today she was young and honest and completely trustworthy. It was too bad they hadn't met today for the first time.

She moved back through the building at twice the speed of the tour. Will stopped in front of the cat room to check on his daughter. Chloe had worked her way across half the room. She and Shelly were discussing a black cat perched high in the corner.

When he got Chloe's attention, he pointed in the direction of the office, and she nodded quickly to dismiss him.

Is the lake enough to get her out of here without a cat?

He might have to throw in the new tablet, too.

"Come on. My twenty minutes are up." When Sarah hit the door to the office and it refused to budge, she muttered under her breath. "Stupid warped door. Cooperate with me this once."

A loud squeak brought Bub running, and all three of them walked into the office.

Sarah motioned at the couch. "Move Bub out of your way. He's staying in here with me until we reopen to surrenders. Have a seat." He watched her shimmy between two tall stacks of files and pick up a notebook from a pile of papers on the desk.

Sarah wedged herself in next to him to keep from disturbing Bub. He'd rolled up into a tiny ball and was watching the action through drowsy eyes.

At this close range, Will could see that Sarah was tired, worried and still so pretty it was hard to think of her as Sarah Hillman, high school terror.

Like a drowning man grasping for a rope,

Will studied the papers in her hands. "What have you got to show me?"

"Well, now that you've had the tour, you know the list of things the shelter needs is extensive. The most critical items are written down in order." She pointed at a handwritten list. "Sorry. No computer. I think the last manager took the laptop with her."

Deciphering the words took some work. "Utilities. Staff. Repairs." He couldn't argue with her rankings. "Do you have numbers? I'm sure you know plenty of guys who can help you do the math."

"Help me do the math? Nice zinger, Will." Sarah snatched the notepad away.

It had been an easy shot. Since he'd been her designated math nerd in high school, on call for homework answers and class notes as needed, he knew how she operated. So why did taking the easy shot feel so mean?

Sarah pointed at the messy desk. "I will definitely get the numbers. I've started sorting everything to come up with a yearly estimate for all the utilities. I'll add in a manager's salary and coordinate the volunteers myself. The rest of the staffing can come at some later point. As far as the rest, we need to clean up the lobby and make repairs on the van we use to transport animals to adoption events and the vet."

Will worked the paper out of her fist and flipped through her outline. What she'd come up with was pretty impressive. She had a long way to go but her plan was solid. Just as surprising was that she'd done every bit of the work by herself. She was anxiously watching his face, and he wondered why she *hadn't* enlisted reinforcements.

"I could have something ready to go next week, if you'll promise me a chance to meet with Rebecca. Otherwise, I'll be wasting a lot of time outside your office, me and my howling dog."

"Fill in the blanks and I'll make sure you sit down with Rebecca, Stephanie and Jen. That's all I can do." Even though the logical voice in his head was telling him he should have stood his ground, Will couldn't. Whatever her faults were, she had a good cause. This fit the criteria he'd been given: the shelter made Holly Heights a better place. Rebecca would make her own decisions.

Sarah's head dropped back and she closed

her eyes, some of the tension melting away as he watched.

"This isn't a done deal, though. My sister, in particular, has a long memory and—"

Sarah threw her arms around Will's neck quickly enough to cause a thoroughly relaxed Bub to grumble his discomfort. "Thank you, Will Barnes. Without this shot, I don't know what I'd do."

She rested her head on his shoulder without letting go of him. And the sad truth was she didn't feel like a villain pressed against him. She felt so right. Cotton and denim and messy hair might be her alter ego but it worked. His hands landed gently on her back and he slid them up and down, enjoying her weight against him until she sniffed in his ear.

"Are you crying?" Will urged her back, worried at how reluctant he was to unwrap her arms from his neck.

"Little bit." Sarah laughed and wiped the tears from her eyes before she met his stare. He had no idea what to say to that anyway, so he waited.

"I'm so relieved." She wrapped her arm

around a concerned Bub and kissed his head. "No worries, Bub."

"You don't have any money yet." Tears. If only she'd known how well they'd work against him, she could have started there.

"I know, but this was the part I was really afraid of." Sarah shook her head. "Asking for help."

"Try being…" He wasn't sure what the right word was.

"Nice? I wasn't sure you thought I had it in me." She blinked and sniffed again over a shaky smile.

"Honest. Let's go with that. Don't play games and I'll see what I can do to help."

Whatever she had to say in response was lost as the lights went out. A faint yowl sounded from the cat room. Will could hear footsteps pounding toward the office.

"Boss! We've got an injury." Shelly and Chloe rounded the corner into the small room, Chloe's arm held out in front of them. "Jelly took exception to the sudden darkness."

Sarah hurried over to the desk and pulled out a first-aid kit. "Oh, no. I hope you and Jelly are both okay, Chloe."

Be cool. It's a scratch. She's had worse.

"Let me see." Will took Chloe's arm and pulled her closer to the window before opening the blinds. Long red scratches ran down her forearm. Bumps, bruises, even a sprained ankle—she'd gotten them all on the soccer field, at one time or another. But Chloe loved soccer. She hadn't even wanted to come with him today. "Looks like Jelly hates the dark almost as much as you do."

He never should have dragged her here.

Chloe didn't laugh, so Will studied her face. She wasn't crying, but her cheeks were pale.

"You don't leave kids unattended with the animals, do you?" He yanked the disinfectant out of Sarah's hand and applied it carefully.

"No, I don't." Sarah offered him a tube of antibiotic.

"I was with her." Shelly stood in the doorway, her hands tangled together. "I'm sorry."

Will gritted his teeth. Snapping wouldn't accomplish anything. And it was a scratch, nothing major. Even if Chloe hadn't said a word yet.

No need to worry about saying no to adopting a cat this time. Jelly had handled that all by herself.

"Animals can be unpredictable," Sarah murmured.

Chloe nodded when Sarah patted her shoulder. Then she took the large adhesive bandage from Will and covered the deepest area of the scratches herself. "I'll wait for you outside, Dad. Time's up, I think."

Will stood and watched her go.

Shelly covered her face with both hands. "Sarah, I'm so sorry. I wasn't even using the outlet that flips the breaker this time."

Sarah crossed the crowded office and squeezed Shelly's shoulder. "No, I know. The electric company finally caught up with us. And the thing with Jelly was an accident. Go ahead and feed all the animals. I'll get everything straightened out."

"I can drop the payment off on the way home." Shelly peeked at Will and said, "I'm really sorry. Please let Chloe know she was such a big help."

Proud of himself for not overreacting to the injury, Will tipped his chin. He would pass the words along. Someday. Probably not today. Not until he was sure they were safely out of cat-adoption territory.

Sarah waved Shelly on. "I'll take the cash

I have on hand and put some sugar with it, see if I can buy more time. But thank you for offering." Her smile was bright, and even though it didn't match the worry and defeat in her eyes, Shelly bought it. She gave Sarah a thumbs-up and left.

"We better get you out of here. Ten minutes on the lake on a day like today will fix Chloe's world. Whenever my daddy took me out on the lake, I had a hard time holding on to my teenage angst." Sarah moved to the doorway and motioned regally as if escorting him out of the cramped office.

"Hoping a quick exit will keep me from getting mad about the cat and taking back my offer to help?" Sarah blinked slowly. What made him think that was more for effect than actual surprise?

"It was an accident. Chloe and Jelly were probably both startled when the lights went out. And both of them are fine." Sarah smoothed her ponytail over her shoulder. "You see that."

She didn't follow up by saying, *Any reasonable person would.* But he could hear the words all the same.

"How much cash do you have? Enough to

catch up?" Even as he asked, he wasn't sure why he wanted to know.

"No, but if I go and make my case..." Sarah led him to the door. "I'll give it my best shot."

Will sighed. "Let me see what I can do. I know some people over at the electric company." He'd already called on every single executive and member of the board of directors. The instinct to start there had been solid. One of his two new clients could help. "I'll find out the minimum they need and see if I can get the lights turned on fast. Animals need electricity, right?" He'd have to do it while Chloe was distracted. No phones. That was the rule.

"I'll take care of it. You've already been such a big help." She opened the door and stepped back to let him pass.

"Try it your way, but if that doesn't work, let's see if I can't come up with a solution." To please her, he stepped back into the lobby. From here, he could see Chloe leaning against his truck, her cell phone in one hand. If she was taking a photo for social media, he was going to be in so much trouble. Olivia would have plenty to say about that scratch.

Will pulled out his phone and started checking his online accounts before scrolling through his contacts. Get the shelter situation settled. Distract Chloe. That was the plan for the rest of the day.

"Why would you help? Two days ago you were ready to call the cops. Two minutes ago you wanted to let me have it because your daughter got hurt. But you'll call in favors for me? I don't get it." Her eyes were bright with tears, red and swollen to match her nose. Her T-shirt was covered in hair of every color imaginable.

"You need my help. That's why." It was as simple and complicated as that.

"I do," she said, and then sniffed. "I really do."

Her breakdown didn't last long enough for him to figure out what to do about it. She straightened her shoulders and said, "Thank you, Will. That's all I can say right now. Someday I hope I'll be in a position to help you or someone else the way you've helped me already."

"Okay. Fine. Come into the office on Monday and we'll take a look at what you've got."

Sarah trailed him to the parking lot. Bub

peered out at them through the shelter's glass door.

"You okay?" he asked as he turned the key in the ignition.

Chloe grunted. "Yeah, but you better not be going back on your word. That was more than twenty minutes." She waved her bandaged arm. "And I have the wound to prove it."

"One call. That's it. Then we hit the lake. Hard." He pulled out his cell phone and flipped through his contacts until he landed on the vice president of operations at the local electric cooperative. When John Garcia answered, they made small talk about the weather and golf games. Then Will said, "I've got a big favor to ask. I have a friend who's behind on the bills for the animal shelter she's running. Is there any way I could come by and make a payment and you could get the lights back on this afternoon?" When John agreed, Will said, "Great, I'm on my way."

He ended the call and counted down to Chloe's angry outburst.

Instead, she said, "One stop. Then we hit the lake. Hard." When she held up her hand, he high-fived it and then rolled down the windows. One stop and he'd put Paws for Love and Sarah Hillman out of his mind.

CHAPTER FOUR

AFTER WEARING HERSELF out making lists of things to fix and people to call, Sarah closed the washing machine door and jammed it shut with the table knife stored on top. A towel was already on the floor to catch any drips, but she nudged it closer before she twisted the knob to start the wash. Doing laundry every day was a drag.

Doing laundry *at all* was a drag. And getting the beat-up machine in the shelter's cramped supply closet to work took real engineering. Every day, about this time, she remembered fondly the space-age shiny washer and dryer in her sweet condo.

Oh, well. In her new place, she'd have fancy machines with all the bells and whistles, but this time she'd know how awesome her washer and dryer were.

Someday. This whole experiment in taking care of herself had started as a way to make sure everything seemed normal. One day her dad was there. The next he was gone and the police wanted to know where, when and why.

Playing dumb had been easy enough. All her father had said before he slid into his Cadillac was "Take care of business."

At the dealership, that had been his way of telling her he was out to lunch and she was in charge.

Mainly, she'd been in charge of telling people when Bobby Hillman would be back.

Now she wished she had a clue.

Every day, her situation got a little more serious. Selling everything she loved, except for the convertible, was about as low as she could go.

Or so she'd thought. Now she was daydreaming about fancy laundry equipment—a sign her life had taken a drastic turn.

She hit Start and stared at the knob when nothing happened. Then she realized the electricity was still out. She'd been squinting at the notepad in her office for so long a wrinkle was forming over the bridge of her nose, and now she'd tried to start the washing machine. In the dark. Like an idiot.

"So many talents I never knew I had. None

of them are worthwhile without electricity," she said with a sigh, and glanced over at Bub. He was patiently carrying around his plastic bowl. He would continue to do so until she'd crossed every single item off the to-do list. "Good idea. Let's eat."

Bub, the smartest person in the room, knew exactly what she meant. His wagging tail shook his whole body when she took his bowl and filled it with dry dog food. "Such a good boy you are." She wasn't sure he could hear her over his own crunching but surely he got the gist.

Bub's fortunes had been a roller-coaster ride. First, he'd been abandoned at the town's landfill, then rescued by some well-meaning types who didn't know what to do with a puppy. Since he'd been surrendered, he'd bounced from one foster to the latest one who'd brought him back to the shelter, intent on ending her association with Paws for Love due to the unsavory Hillman connection.

Sarah had made Bub her roommate. Temporarily. When the shelter was staffed and reopened to surrenders, Bub would go back into the general population. For now, she was his foster.

Living out of a suitcase and sleeping on the office's couch.

Poor Bub.

Finally, instead of a rampaging beast intent on carnage, Bub was a normal dog again. He'd reached the point in his meal where he could sit and savor. Sarah pulled down the loaf of white bread and the peanut butter jar to make her thousandth sandwich.

Bub licked his lips slowly.

"Peanut butter would hit the spot, huh?" She shook her head at his mournful expression. "Not today." The jar had to last her a long time. Sarah reached into the cabinet to grab a treat. "Have one of these instead."

With her sandwich in one hand, Sarah went back into her office to grab the notepad and then led Bub through the shelter to the play yard.

Shelly was watering the pitiful row of plants along the fence.

"What are you still doing here? I thought you went home." If she'd known Shelly was still around, she'd have... Sarah wasn't sure. At the very least, she'd have given up on the budget sooner.

"I wanted to wait until the electricity came

back on." Shelly shut off the hose. "Besides, I like it here."

As Sarah ate her sandwich, she considered that—preferring to spend time at the shelter instead of home. "How long has it been? Since your divorce?"

"Six months. I'm over it." Shelly's lips trembled a little but the smile was nearly convincing.

"One hour." Sarah set the timer on her phone. "If the lights aren't on in one hour, I'll suit back up and head into town. Electricity is nonnegotiable."

The cash Cece had given her would be enough to buy time.

She shouldn't have given Will the chance to intercede.

The list of things she had to fix, pay for, hire and manage ruffled in the breeze.

Rest. Just a minute. Close your eyes and rest.

"You're doing a good job, you know?" At Shelly's encouragement, Sarah's eyes snapped open. "Don't give up on us. Not yet."

While she fussed with her drooping ponytail, Sarah said, "You run this place single-handedly. If I didn't come in tomorrow, these animals would be in good hands."

Shelly waved a hand to brush Sarah's answer aside. "I mean it. Don't give up, Sarah. This place needs you. I need you. I did run the shelter by myself for a week or two and it was…overwhelming. I need support, some company." Shelly rubbed Bub's ears as he trotted up, obviously satisfied that all the new smells were acceptable. "Actual, live people. Having someone to talk with while I work makes everything easier."

"Okay. I'll keep trying." Sarah wished she was the kind of person who knew the right thing to say. She had plenty of practice with snarky set-downs. Encouragement was out of her comfort zone, but whatever Shelly heard, it was enough.

Somehow, making the promise gave Sarah a tiny boost of energy. Lately, she'd found herself swinging from justified doubts to the crazy certainty that she could handle whatever came up.

But Shelly was here, working with her.

Bub went to stand patiently by the door. He was ready to go back inside apparently.

"He's so well-trained," Sarah said. "What

is he doing in a shelter?" Sarah sighed as she and Shelly stood.

"It never gets easier to see smart, well-mannered pets staring out through chain link." Shelly held the door open for Bub. "That's why we do what we do."

Being included in Shelly's "we" felt right. At some point, Paws for Love had changed from a whim to a...cause.

Life wasn't fair. Not for people, not for pets, but somewhere in the world was the person who deserved Bub and who would give him the love he should've had from the beginning. All she had to do was keep the doors open. They'd find each other eventually.

"Late in the day," Shelly said. "Do you think the electricity is coming back on?"

The thought of a long night in the dark filled Sarah with dread, but she tried for a carefree shrug. Shelly couldn't change a thing. There was no sense in adding to her worry.

Closing the door on the late-afternoon sun was easy enough, but when Sarah flipped the light switch and nothing happened, she was reminded how dark it could get without electricity. Sunset always made her less brave, more afraid of the future and what it might hold.

Sarah shook her head and forced herself to laugh along with Shelly. "Habit." She pulled out her phone to check the time just as the whir of the shelter's systems kicked in. Bright light illuminated curious kitties and ruthlessly clean floors before she moved on to the dog room. Instead of a loud celebration, she got a few curious head raises and then everyone settled back down.

Late afternoon was nap time. The schedule never changed much here.

"Oh, good. Everything can get back to normal. Giving meds in the dark would have been difficult," Shelly said with a relieved sigh.

If Will Barnes had been standing with them under the bright lights, Sarah would have kissed him.

"Go home. The morning walks will come way too early." Taking a chance, she hugged Shelly quickly. "We're making progress. Tomorrow will be another good day."

She watched Shelly get in her car and waved before she closed and locked the door.

All alone. Again. Sarah walked back to her

office and pulled out her phone to check for missed calls. She dialed her father's number, fingers crossed that this time he'd answer, and listened to the rings. When his voice mail picked up, she said, "Hi, Dad. I wanted to... check on you. I'm worried. Please call me."

That's all you can do. Immediately, images of her father hurt or worse flashed across her mind. *Just stop. There's no reason to think the worst.*

Her peanut butter sandwich turned into a lump in her stomach.

Work was still the best distraction. Sarah grabbed the phone book. "Bids. The first step is finding out what a new roof and fence cost. Easy enough." The yellow pages fell open to the page she'd turned to most often. "All for Animals." The overcrowded Austin shelter would be *her* animals' only hope if she walked away.

When she was stretched out on a beach somewhere, would it bother her that she'd let them down?

Her stomach lurched.

Bub gave a happy sigh. Somehow, he was stretched out the full length of the couch, all four feet in the air. Her response, a weird mishmash of amusement and concern, answered her question.

Paws for Love was hers. Leaving it without funding would haunt her. If she could turn the shelter around, she'd have something of her own to be proud of.

No one could say this had been given to her.

And when Holly Heights was nothing more than dust on her tires, she could enjoy the freedom.

"Sure wish I'd chosen business school, Bub." She shifted in the broken-down office chair and studied the mess on her desk. At some point, she was going to have to get organized.

Since that would let her put off the hard work of identifying how much she didn't know, Sarah started rearranging the stacks of overdue bills. "Food. Gotta pay for that first." Or should she give the vets a portion of the cash? Sort of a good-faith gesture that she wasn't going to leave them holding the bag.

She was adding up the costs of the most recent vet visits and cursing her lack of a computer when she remembered the bids she'd planned to gather first.

Her brain had always worked this way. In circles.

"Slow and steady, Sarah. Do one thing at a time." She picked up her cell phone, hoping the calculator could help, when the shelter's phone rang.

Had her father tracked her here? Was he calling the shelter to avoid the police?

"Paws for Love. This is Sarah." Too late, she remembered her plan to avoid answering the phone. Nice bill collectors would hesitate to leave a message. And the rest? Well, they'd definitely leave a message, but she certainly didn't want to talk to them.

Fingers crossed, she added, "How can I help you?"

"It's Will. Are your lights back on?"

Sarah pressed cold fingers to her cheek, grateful that Will Barnes couldn't see the flush that instantly covered her face. She was amazed at this ability to blush when she never had before. Her high school behavior, ambushing kids like Will and his sister, Jen, who hadn't done much to deserve negative attention, hadn't embarrassed her a bit. Now she was a little uncomfortable with the memories. "Uh, hi. Yes, we have lights. What did you do?"

He cleared his throat. "Made a call. You'll have a month or so to make another payment. By then, you'll have a better plan in place and some funds to set things right."

Unable to answer at first, Sarah stared at the stack of bills on her desk. "If I can come up with the right information for a certain meeting, I definitely will."

She tried a smile as she answered, but something about the fake, flirty tone made her feel worse than knowing she hadn't been able to accomplish this on her own. "Sorry. What I meant to say is I appreciate you getting me more time. And I am hopeful that Paws for Love is on the right track."

Neither of them said anything for a minute. For good measure, she added, "Thank you." Why did it sound as if she was choking on her own tongue? "How's Chloe?"

"Sunburned. Eating her third piece of pepperoni pizza. Seems to be happy for the first time since she came for the summer." Will cleared his throat. "But you were asking about her arm. The bandage is gone. I think the trauma is, too."

"Trauma? I'm so sorry, Will."

"Maybe that was just me." Will sighed. "At some point, the accident became my fault because she's never been allowed to have a pet. So she doesn't know how to handle them."

"Wow. This visit has *not* been easy, has it?" Sarah propped her elbow on the desk. As a teen, Sarah's mood swings had been epic. Her dad had learned to toss the checkbook into her bedroom and slam the door closed again.

Will was actually spending time with Chloe. He must be brave.

"It really hasn't. But I'm willing to agree with part of her argument."

"Does that mean you want to adopt a cat?" Sarah asked, the corners of her mouth twitching.

Will grunted. "Not if I can help it. And if I catch you planting the suggestion, I'll have to devise a devious form of payback for you and Chloe both, something involving a mall but not me." But he wouldn't sabotage her shot at funding. Because Will Barnes was a good man, with integrity.

She tried to imagine him bailing on Chloe, even for her own good, and the picture wouldn't form. Maybe he had trouble in small, day-to-day things, but Chloe could count on him for the big stuff.

Once, Sarah would have said the same thing about her own father.

"Your threat lacks some sting." Sarah would dance through the racks at Neiman Marcus given a chance and a credit card. "Malls are wonderful."

"The last time Chloe and I shopped for jeans, I was pretty sure someone had replaced my baby girl with an evil imposter. One who cried. A lot." Will's gruff voice suggested he could have handled almost anything but that.

"That's your problem. Many women cry when they try on jeans."

His chuckle made her grin so hard her cheeks hurt. And the blush filled her cheeks again.

Why was she enjoying this conversation so much? She'd flirted with doctors and lawyers and men with yachts. Talking with Will about his daughter filled her with a warm glow of comfort. Laughing with him convinced her life was about to get easier.

"I know you want to get the adoptions going again. Just don't count on Chloe and Jelly to start it off," Will said.

"This time next month, things will be different. I know it." She straightened in her chair. "And it'll be thanks to you, Will."

She jotted a note to add a thank-you card to the shopping list. Squinting at the note made her realize that he wouldn't be able to read her handwriting anyway, so she almost crossed it out again.

"So, I'll be ready on Monday. How about early? Eight?" Sarah bit her lip. She hoped she could be ready by then.

"Uh, sure."

"Is that a problem? Do you have clients scheduled?" Sarah traced the number eight over and over at the top of her pad. She'd have to get a predawn start so that Shelly didn't have to feed and water all the animals by herself.

Predawn start? What kind of crazy talk is that? Feeding and watering the animals is Shelly's job.

"I didn't picture you as the early-bird type," Will said. His voice had lost some of its warmth.

"Oh, I'm not. Never have been." Sarah sighed. Living in the shelter's office meant fewer hair products and cosmetics. An unlikely silver lining. "But I can make it if you can."

"I'll see you at eight, then."

Before he could hang up, she blurted, "Will, without your help, I'm not sure... Well, you'll get as many tail wags as you like here at Paws for Love. Free dog hair for life, okay?"

Then she wrinkled her brow. *Stupid. You're trying to convince him you've got a solid businesswoman inside. That sounded like you routinely put a heart over every* i.

But his quiet laugh eased some of the disappointment that was making her shoulders droop. "Good to know. A little dog hair now and then is exactly what I need."

Sarah hung up the phone and stared over at Bub, who was blinking at her from his perch on the couch. "Don't get up. I've got this taken care of."

He licked his lips and then shoved his nose back under his tail.

"Some assistant you are. Better watch out. I'll replace you as soon as I have the chance." Although spending time with a real, live human who answered her would take some getting used to.

"All right. New list. Estimates I Need. Fence, roof, signage, flooring, paint…" Everything about the place needed an overhaul. Four months ago, she'd had visions of a new, fancy, streamlined lobby with interactive videos and digital boards that would be updated as dogs and cats came and went. Now she wanted electricity.

"Just the first round, Sarah. Focus. There'll be plenty of time for dreaming big later."

The cash register sound signifying a text snagged her attention. She fumbled the phone before gripping it tightly enough to make the plastic creak.

Take care of business.

The number was unfamiliar. But her father's favorite exit line—the one he'd always delivered on his way out the door of Hillman Luxury Autos—was so familiar.

He was okay. Somewhere, her father was able to text.

From a number she didn't recognize.

Where are you?

Sarah chewed her fingernail while she waited. Ten minutes of glaring at her phone was enough to give her a headache.

"Business. Take care of business." Sarah carefully set the phone down and turned back to the mess on her desk. That text was enough to keep her going for a few more days. She could count on her father to fix everything. All she had to do was hold on a little bit longer.

CHAPTER FIVE

WAKING UP AT the same time she used to fall into bed had been a shock, but Sarah might be getting the hang of it. Instead of dealing with wolf whistles and offers to buy her a drink, she worked to clean up the pens, but grateful, goofy dogs were their own reward.

Coffee would be better.

Especially since this meeting with Will Barnes was going to require all her focus. "I'll help you with the meds as soon as I get back, okay?"

"No worries, boss," Shelly said. "You've already done so much. And now you look like a corporate raider. There's no way you can fail in heels like that."

Sarah checked her black heels, one of the three pairs she'd refused to sell on consignment. They made her legs lethal. And the dark suit had stayed in her closet on the understanding that there would be occasions when she'd need to impress rich men with her business aptitude.

She'd never seriously planned to *get* the aptitude.

That might have been a better place to start.

"We'll work with what we've got." Sarah stacked her neat pile of file folders with the few estimates she'd gathered and her ragged notepad. No matter how many times she rewrote her figures, consciously doing her best to use her best penmanship, she still had a difficult time reading her own writing. "You don't happen to have a laptop, do you, Shelly?"

A nice spreadsheet would have been the perfect accessory.

"No, sorry," Shelly said. "Martin took his when he moved out."

"That's fine. Maybe…" She wanted to say she'd buy one. That was the Hillman thing to do. Go out. Swipe the card. Simple.

But the cards were overloaded and overdue.

"There's always the library," Shelly said helpfully. "We could take your notes in, work something up. I know they've got people who will help. We could go before we let the dogs out this afternoon."

Tempted to hand everything to Shelly, Sarah studied her coworker's hopeful face.

Shelly was excited about a field trip to the library to work on the computer.

With Sarah.

Why was that flattering?

She'd been surrounded by people who were excited to be with her…in the VIP section of the hottest club or enjoying Sunday brunch where a Hillman credit card covered the tab.

Shelly needed to get out more.

For that matter, so did Sarah. These shoes pinched her toes like the worst torture device and they were at least two inches shorter than her dancing shoes.

"Shelly, you're the best. I don't know what I'd do without you." Sarah studied the scribbled writing on her pad to avoid eye contact. "But this is a job I should do myself."

Shelly's grin faded, but before she could smooth things over, Sarah added, "Instead, I think this afternoon we should…" What did women bond over other than shopping and lunch?

"Talk. We should definitely talk." Sarah

nodded confidently and watched Shelly process her weirdness. "Meanwhile, keep your fingers crossed." She straightened her shoulders. "Bub, keep an eye on the place."

He woofed and then meandered into her office to jump onto the couch.

"Les is coming in this morning. Anything you need me to pass along?" Shelly tugged the bottom of her shirt and then fussed with the gray hair at her temples. "He wants my opinion on paint colors. He's repainting his house."

Les, the retired vet who went above and beyond for Paws for Love... Was Shelly into him? The mention of his name certainly brought color to Shelly's cheeks.

If so, Sarah knew exactly what they'd be talking about. Finding something in common, other than dogs and cats, would be a struggle, but men were always a solid topic.

And encouraging a budding romance? Fun, fun, fun.

How to throw them together?

"Ask Les if he'll examine Socks, make sure his eye is healing as it should, and take out Scamp's stitches. Please do what you can to help." Sarah tried to add to the list of reasons

Les and Shelly needed to spend more time together, doing a mental walk-through of the shelter.

Shelly straightened her shoulders. "We'll take care of it. Les said I'm the best assistant he's ever worked with."

I'll just bet he did.

Sarah nodded. "He's so good to the animals. And tell him I'll have a check for him… soon." That was the best she could promise.

"Not to worry, boss. Les is happy to help." Shelly smiled slowly. "He's one of the good ones."

"He is. You two make a great team. With the *animals*." Sarah crossed her fingers and waved both hands. "Think positive things."

On her way to Will's office, Sarah was impressed again with how pretty the morning could be. All those years of sleeping until ten had meant missing cool dawn air with birds singing and the fresh appeal of a brand-new day.

Dancing until last call was nice, too, but the next day was always less fun.

It was hard to say which was better, but with enough breathing room to keep the shelter's doors open, she wasn't sure she'd go back to the way things were.

Not that her friends would still welcome her to the VIP section, anyway.

"Fake it till you make it, Sarah," she murmured under her breath as she parked. One quick swipe of lipstick and a few nervous adjustments of her hair and she was sliding out of the car, her hands clenching the files so tightly that her fingers ached.

Pushing back her shoulders made a confident strut easier. Yanking on the door to find it locked almost turned that strut into slapstick. She bobbled her files and cursed under her breath.

"You're early. I didn't expect that." Will and Chloe were standing behind her. "We got a late start. Someone had to stay up until she'd finished storming the castle."

Uncertain how to answer, Sarah held her paperwork like a shield, but Chloe muttered, "Saving the princess is important work, Dad." She glanced at Sarah. "Round Table Realm. It's a game. There are swords. He's not very good at it."

"I would be worse," Sarah said. Video

games had never been her thing. "Are you a knight?"

"Better. A magician." Chloe shrugged. "If I had a tablet, I could be a wizard by now."

"And if I tell your mother how much time you spent playing that game over the weekend, you could be grounded from the game. Forever," Will said.

Chloe slid into the chair behind the receptionist's desk and immediately started clicking. Before Will could say a thing, she held up a hand. "Facebook. Email. Just the usual."

Instead of arguing, Will turned to Sarah. "Do you make coffee? I know, I'm the worst. But if you could, you would be a lifesaver."

Determined to ignore her sudden awareness of Will Barnes, his deep voice, broad shoulders and entirely too intelligent daughter, Sarah nodded. Finding the kitchenette with the industrial coffeemaker wasn't difficult. Getting the coffee going took two false starts but eventually what dripped out could be called coffee.

"How's the arm?" Pausing in front of the receptionist's desk seemed the polite thing to do. Apparently, it was her day to start awkward conversations with people for her own good.

Chloe frowned up at her, the question clear on her face.

"The scratch. Everything okay?"

Chloe immediately glanced down at the pink stripes on her arm. "Oh, yeah, it's fine."

"You seemed a little shaken when you left." Why was she even bringing this up? Will had let it go. She should definitely watch it float away in the breeze instead of catching it with both hands.

"Yeah, I mean…" Chloe studied the computer screen. "She surprised me. I was half a second from telling my dad we were taking Jelly home. Then she attacked."

Sarah sipped her cup of coffee and thought about that. Will had threatened her with his idea of a terrible punishment if she planted the adoption idea.

He really should have thought that through.

"*Attack* seems a little strong. Jelly was afraid. She hurt you, but she was only doing her best to protect herself." She knew very well what that was like. High school had been one big experiment in the best way to keep people from hurting her. An occasional swipe now and then was a good defense.

"Maybe. Or I just don't know how to handle a cat." Chloe shrugged a shoulder. "I didn't hurt her, did I?"

Ah, so it was more than the scratch.

Sarah snorted. "Come on. Jelly? To handle Jelly, sit still. That's it. She'll be wrapped around your neck like a scarf five minutes later."

Chloe glanced at her. "She's pretty sweet. Claws excepted."

"I saw her this morning, staring down the hall. She's a people cat."

Chloe tilted her head.

"You know, like a people person. She wants to be around people. Give her another shot."

Will's swift finger-across-the-neck motion caught Sarah's attention and ended her conversation.

If Jelly and Chloe were meant to be, she'd done the best she could.

Les and Shelly. Chloe and Jelly. Maybe Sarah was meant to be a matchmaker.

When she set the mug in front of Will, his glare was loud and clear.

"You wouldn't want her to be scared of dogs and cats for the rest of her life," Sarah said as she eased into the chair across from him.

"No." Will sipped his coffee. "I don't want that. I also don't want a *cat*."

Sarah held up both hands. "Then we're on the same page." For now.

"I'm behind schedule. Show me what you've got."

Go time. You can do this. You've been over and over the figures. He wants to help because he's a good guy. Don't panic. Charm. You've got this.

When Will slid the stack of her work across the desk instead of waiting for her to answer, Sarah understood that trying seduction at this point would be the easiest, fastest way to destroy all her chances. So, like it or not, she was going to have to take her chances with her brain.

"I had already gotten a few quotes. The roof, repairing the fences. With those big-ticket items addressed, my focus would change. We'd bring all the utilities up to date, pay our standing accounts and have a fresh start. That's part one of the plan."

Chin resting on his hand, Will squinted at the itemized list she'd made.

"And the bottom line for those necessities is…" He flipped to the next page. "Your handwriting is some of the worst I've ever seen. And I specialize in helping medical professionals with their finances."

"Yeah. Sorry." Sarah tried to imagine what might excuse terrible handwriting, something that would earn some sympathy, but nothing came to mind.

"Thirty thousand dollars. That seems… conservative." Will stretched back in his chair. "Does that even cover the new roof? That place needs at least twice that much in physical improvements."

"Right. I think so, too." Sarah had gone back and forth over her figures all weekend. Asking for more would mean she could afford a broader scope of improvements, but keeping it to the bare minimum strengthened her chances of getting an agreement.

If she whipped out a secondary plan at the meeting, one that would get the shelter back up to full speed at a somewhat higher price tag… Well, maybe Rebecca, Stephanie and Jen would think she was an expert planner.

And once she got them inside the shelter, the warm fuzzies would make it easier to write a bigger check.

Will slid the notepad back to her, folded his hands over his stomach and stared up at the ceiling.

After a quick check to make sure he wasn't looking at something horrifying, like a hairy spider, Sarah tried to settle comfortably in her chair to wait.

"Why not get your dad or one of his cronies to write a check?" Will's chin dipped down. "Wouldn't that be painless?"

Sarah studied his face. There was no way he hadn't heard about her father's escape, not in a town this size. Even if his stepsister hadn't passed the juicy, satisfying gossip along, surely someone else had.

But why pretend otherwise? A test to determine what her answer might be?

Their eyes locked while she tried to figure out how to pass it. Then she got angry.

Sarah stood to pace in front of his desk, but after one lap, she had to kick off her heels. Apparently, spending a few months out of the shoes had ruined her ability to enjoy them.

But pacing barefoot, even on his carpeted

floor, lacked some of the punctuation she wanted.

"He's gone, accused of embezzlement. That's why the shelter's donors bailed. Believe me, if I could do this without asking for help from the people of this town—who seem almost gleeful at my current situation—I would." She scrubbed her hands over her face. "If I could leave it all behind, I might. But someday soon, he's coming back with an explanation. Life will be normal again." Those shoes that pinched her toes would fit like a dream, she'd be able to talk her way out of tight spots and Paws for Love would be out of trouble. Normal.

"But you've got friends, don't you? What about your mother?"

Sarah rubbed at the ache in her chest. It wasn't Will's fault that he couldn't remember her mother had died while she was in high school. She'd been the furthest thing from a friend to him at that point.

"She's been gone for years. Without Dad, I'm on my own." Telling this guy, who had a good reason to hate her, that she had no friends to count on was humiliating. "I took a position as the director of the shelter—"

she crossed her arms to prevent herself from using air quotes around the word *director* "—because I was bored. Now I can't walk away." She dropped back into the chair. "Think this is karma coming around?"

Sarah grimaced. More than anything she wanted to rest her head on his desk and cry out the tension and fear that made it hard to sleep at night.

But she needed his cooperation.

Will Barnes was not the kind of guy who'd let emotions influence his decisions.

He didn't answer her right away.

Oh, don't be silly. Everyone does things they regret when they're kids. Everything is going to work out.

Wouldn't it be nice if that's what he said? But no.

"What you've got here is a good start. From this point, you need to collect more bids, demonstrate financial due diligence." He shook his head. "And I'll set up a meeting with Rebecca."

Sarah clasped her hands under her chin, the wave of relief almost overwhelming. She'd managed to avoid tears so far, but her defenses were failing. Fast.

"But your presentation will need some work. Fire up your computer. They're going to have to be able to *read* the proposal." He wagged a finger at her. "And whatever you're thinking about what happens next, make sure it goes in the request. Try honesty."

The corner of his mouth turned up.

Sarah thought about pretending shock. She could brace one hand on her chest and blink wide eyes at him in protest. Honestly, she *was* surprised he'd anticipated her bait-and-switch idea.

"Okay. All the cards on the table, one gamble for the whole high-dollar total. I can do that." She picked up her files and notepad while she slipped her shoes back on, somehow reluctant to leave now that she'd gotten what she'd come for.

"Chloe seems a little young to be manning the receptionist's desk." She shifted from one foot to the other while she evaluated the best way to make a breezy exit.

"The last one quit unexpectedly," he said.

That might explain why the door had been locked and the coffee unmade.

"Maybe Jen can help you find a replacement." The alarms blaring at her to shut her mouth, avoid bringing up Will's sister, who'd been one of her favorite targets, always hit a second too late.

"Yeah." His lips tightened. "She might have her own ax to grind with me, too." He slid down in his chair. "But that won't impact her decision on the shelter. You'll be wading through your own trouble there."

She pursed her lips. "That's not all that comforting."

"Right. That's my point."

Neither of them smiled but some of the tension evaporated and Sarah was reminded of the connection she'd felt to Will while they sat on the couch in her cramped office.

"Okay. I'm going to go hunt up a computer."

He hesitated and then nodded. "And I'm going to try to find a temp to answer the phone. I'll let you know when to be ready. Think you can do this?"

Sarah straightened her shoulders. "I've done harder things in the past few months. This will be fun."

There. That's the parting line I needed.

She added a jaunty wave. "Thanks for all your help."

Will didn't wave back. Which was good.

It was a strange thing to do in the first place. Her arm felt out of whack when she dropped it, but she spun on one heel and marched right into his lobby.

With Chloe wrapped up in some game on the computer, headphones covering her ears while she jerked and twisted along with the knight on the screen, there was no audience for her clumsy victory dance, which was filled with more pure happiness than rhythm. It was absolutely nothing like the dancing she'd done in clubs with strangers or her so-called friends. This was not seduction. It was celebration.

She braced a hand against the desk to catch her breath.

And had an idea.

CHAPTER SIX

"CHLOE? ARE YOU up for heading to the diner?" He clicked through to the next email and waited for Chloe to answer his yell. "I need to visit some clients and you can't stay here by yourself."

"Um, so…"

Will jerked in his chair. Sarah was hovering in the doorway. "Chloe has headphones on," she said. "I don't think she heard you."

He cleared his throat. "Thought you'd left."

Sarah took a deep breath, the light pink in her cheeks making her even more beautiful than she'd been back in high school.

That was unfortunate.

"So, I was thinking…" Sarah shifted from one foot to the other, her fingers tangled in front of her.

He wasn't going to like this. The creeping sense of dread was difficult to ignore.

"There's this empty desk. It has a computer."

Sarah motioned over her shoulder. "You know? And I need a computer."

He could see where she was going, but he was powerless to stop her. The part of him that still felt like a high school kid enjoyed watching Sarah Hillman stutter and fidget.

"I could answer the phone in exchange for using it." Sarah raised a finger. "I did that at Hillman Luxury Autos three days a week."

Her pleading eyes would give Bub a run for his money.

And Will did need some help.

How badly could she mess up answering the phone?

If she flaked on the second day, he would be no worse off than he was right now.

Like a sign, the phone rang and she darted off to answer it. He could hear her pleasant tone, even if he couldn't make out the words. Was she going to transfer the call?

"Wrong number." Sarah was back in the doorway. "I'm pleasant. Professional. I can follow directions."

This is a terrible idea.

But he was going to do it, anyway.

"Make me a list of the biggest accounts in town." Will took a deep breath. "All you do is take messages. You do not give any information or ask for details, just name and phone number. I have to follow a pretty strict procedure. If you can't make that work, you'll have to…go."

Her victory dance was adorable and terrible at the same time, as if she'd mixed up gymnastics and martial arts and had never heard of rhythm. But she looked good doing it.

She might be exactly what he needed until the ad brought in actual candidates.

"I can't have you working here without paying you." If she did any actual work, he'd know Sarah Hillman had changed since she'd tricked him into helping with her algebra homework.

When she froze, the expression on her face one of delight and terror, he sighed. "Nine bucks an hour." He hoped she'd storm out. Her dancing resumed and the confirmation that he'd be spending more time with Sarah wasn't as horrifying as he would have expected. "And it's only temporary. Until I can find a suitable replacement, like two weeks max. More like one. A few days." If he kept going, a fifteen-minute coffee break would be his final decision.

"I'll do it. You won't be sorry." She disappeared around the door frame and then stuck her head back in. "Chloe can stay here with me while you run your errands, but I have to leave early today. There are dogs and cats and Shelly can't handle everything on her own and I promised…"

"That's fine. Part-time's even better." Then he realized Sarah was still watching him. "Let me know what time you need to leave. We'll go from there."

She gave him a thumbs-up.

"And make me a list before you get started on the proposal for Paws for Love. I'll head out to call on clients and prospects."

"Great. Chloe and I'll…hang out." Sarah held up both hands. "Or Chloe will kill trolls and I'll answer the phone."

"Chloe will head to the diner. She and my stepmother have a routine already worked out."

He wasn't about to leave Chloe with Sarah. She seemed nicer now, better because she cared about something, but he didn't want any lingering queen of mean attitude to rub off on his daughter.

His ex was not going to be happy when she heard about Chloe's unpaid labor at the diner. He'd sold this extended visit as a way to reconnect with his daughter. And they were, but he had to work.

Besides, Brenda needed some time with Chloe, too. His stepmom and Jen were family.

Sarah waved a hand. "Of course. But if she ever needs to hang out here, I'm happy to help."

Will almost explained again how short-lived this reception job would be, but Sarah was gone.

"I definitely need to get a grip." Will made sure he had plenty of his new business cards as he lectured himself on drawing a line with Sarah. So far, he'd helped her more than either of them had expected. That was enough. "No more."

"Here. Twenty names. I starred the ones who went to school with us. I don't know if that helps or hurts, but you might appreciate the heads-up." Sarah slid a piece of paper across the desk. "Can you read it?"

Will picked up the paper. "Almost all of

it." He shook his head. "Did you skip second grade or something? I've never seen writing this bad."

Sarah reached over to snatch the list out of his hands. "I thought you wanted it quickly. I'll type it up for you."

"Next time. Do you need me to show you how to work that computer?"

"My handwriting's bad. That doesn't mean I'm dumb." She rolled her eyes and marched out of his office.

Caught off guard, Will froze half out of his chair and replayed their exchange in his head.

"Nope. Still don't follow." Did he care why she'd jumped to the wrong conclusion? Considering the many and varied insults she'd heaped on him when they were kids, he should let her hold on to it.

Her ego could withstand a poke or two.

When he caught himself peeking at her around the door frame, he knew something had to be done.

Get out of this office before you lose what common sense you have left.

"Chloe, you up for a walk?" He eased around Sarah, who turned away to stare out the window, and tapped Chloe's shoulder. When she reluctantly removed the headphones, he said, "Let's go see Brenda."

Chloe immediately turned back with a disgusted huff, saved her game and closed the window showing a knight standing on a castle wall. "I'm not a baby. I can stay here by myself."

He had a feeling this was the whole issue with Chloe, currently manifesting itself as bright pink hair. She wasn't a baby anymore, but he still had a hard time letting her go anywhere by herself.

"Sure, but Brenda will need the help with the morning rush." Sometimes that worked, explaining it was about someone else needing help instead of babysitting.

Chloe narrowed her eyes at him, glanced over at Sarah and stood. "Some vacation this is."

She was out on the sidewalk before he could tell her to wait. Chloe pointed at the concrete and stepped to a spot framed by the window where he could keep an eye on her.

Sarah moved quickly to take the seat behind the desk. "Phone rings. I take a message. Otherwise, I'll work on the request for Rebecca. Good luck with...everything."

Will wanted to ask if she meant his clients or his daughter.

Then he realized it was clear which relationship he needed more luck with. But Sarah would not be the person he turned to for advice on how to deal with Chloe. "Okay. It's got a password. You can use *admin* and that will get you access to whatever you might need."

Her shoulders drooped. "Oh, okay. Thanks."

Determined not to ask a hundred questions to make sure Sarah Hillman was going to be all right, Will reached behind her and pulled out the big binder.

"You'll find notes on answering the phone and greeting people who come in without appointments in here." He flipped the binder open to the first section.

Sarah still avoided his gaze when she turned to scan the short outlines. "Wow. Thorough."

Since his last, short-lived assistant had called it something less flattering, he had an idea what she really meant. The heat washing his cheeks annoyed him.

"We're dealing with people's money. There are laws. I want to make sure I can document every single communication. That's all." The binder was overkill. He didn't care. This was his career.

He wasn't going to apologize.

"I get it." She shook her head. "Making sure every person who works with you is on the same page is important." Finally, she peeked up at him. "Whether you're running an animal shelter with a bunch of volunteers who come and go as they please or dealing with…a temporary employee manning the phones. We've got a binder at Paws for Love, too. Not like this, but that's on my list of things to do. I'm pretty good with checklists and procedures, Will. I get it."

And she wasn't going to make fun of him because of it.

Sarah Hillman…a checklist fan?

That was enough to make his head hurt if he thought about it for too long.

Sarah turned away to enter the password and the computer dinged in response. She bit her fingernail while the machine whirred, and when the screen lit up with a nearly blank desktop, she relaxed against the chair. "Now, then. Everything is set. No worries."

"Okay. I'll see you later." He waved the

list and stepped out onto the sidewalk. The day was bright with warm sunshine and blue skies. A perfect Texas morning.

And instead of staring at it from the fortieth floor of a Dallas skyscraper, he was… holding up sidewalk traffic in the sleepy downtown of Holly Heights.

Life could take some unexpected turns.

But the air was fresher here, even if the woman he'd stepped out in front of huffed in disgust on her way around him.

"What's the holdup?" Chloe fidgeted with her ponytail, removing the long pink hank she'd clipped in that morning to shove it in her purse. "I could go for some breakfast."

She thought about her stomach a lot. It was one of the qualities that made it clear they were related. Watching her march toward the diner reminded him of how he'd carefully followed behind her across the living room floor when she took her first steps.

Then the toe of her sneaker caught on a raised edge in the sidewalk. She tripped but regained her balance quickly. Was it a sign that she was catching up to her growth spurt, the ability to avoid a tough fall?

And now, while he was strolling down

memory lane, she was standing with one hand on the diner's door, a frown wrinkling her brow. "Are you *dawdling*?" Her reflexes were improving. So was her vocabulary.

"Dawdling?" Will caught up. "Yes, I believe I was. Could you define that word for me?"

Chloe snorted. "Dragging your feet. Brenda uses it to say she's got another job for me when I spend too much time at the video game. *You* use it to warn me about stranger danger on the sidewalk. I pick things up, you know?"

He'd probably gotten it from Brenda, too. She was a solid believer in being busy. *Everyone* should be busy.

"Good one." Will shook his head and spotted a guy who seemed to be following them. When he looked directly at the guy, who was dressed in a button-down and dark pants, the man cut across the street to head into the shop on the corner.

But Will was pretty sure he'd been somewhere in the background when he'd stepped out of his office.

Weird.

Holly Heights was a small town, where everyone knew everyone else.

In Dallas, he never would have noticed the guy.

Paranoia. With one last check over his shoulder, Will followed his daughter into the diner.

His mother would have launched into a cool dance of guilt and pleasure at seeing him.

Brenda had no time for anything other than honest emotion. She wrapped one arm around his neck and juggled the coffeepot in the other.

"I wondered when you'd slow down enough for a hot breakfast," she said as she hugged him. "Always such a go-getter. You haven't changed a bit, and your daughter? She's a chip off the old block, winning at the video game, clearing tables and earning tips. She's a Barnes through and through. Come in. Sit down."

Brenda steered him to a spot at the long counter, grabbed a cup and poured more blessed coffee inside, then jotted down an order and shoved it through the window. "Order up. Make it good. This is family."

Any other place, he might have worried that he'd given her no order.

But he trusted Brenda.

"Tell me how it's going. Chloe here says you work twenty-four hours a day." Brenda rested a hip against the counter. "Wouldn't expect anything less."

Uncomfortable with the cold, hard truth, Will slanted his eyes at Chloe, who immediately headed for the line of old-school video game machines along the wall.

When he noticed the same guy outside the window, this time staring down at his phone, Will pointed over his shoulder. "Do you recognize that guy, Brenda?"

She craned her neck to study the man on the sidewalk. "Nope. Probably looking for one of the businesses down on the corner. Some people have trouble with the address, the whole North Main versus South Main thing." Brenda waved a hand. "If he comes in, I'll give directions. Do it at least once a day. Now dish, Will."

Ignoring the man was his best move for now. "Well, thanks to the town's lottery winners, I've got some projects to work on. Rebecca insists on giving all of her winnings away, but Stephanie and Jen are as determined that nobody takes advantage of her or her good nature. And for my sake, I want to use the money to make more money." He smiled at Brenda. "Job security."

At the tinny rattle of a bell, Brenda turned to grab two plates and slid them onto the counter. Chloe abandoned her video game and settled next to him without a word. She wasn't one to waste time on social convention when the food hit the table. Brenda pointed at Chloe's bent head and mouthed, "Reminds me of you."

Will loved hearing that. Every single time.

"You always were a smart cookie. I told Jenny she needed to call you, take you on these shopping sprees she insists on. But if you've always been smart, she's always been stubborn." Brenda sighed. "So, now she's determined to buy a Toyota *new*—" Brenda whispered as if it was a dirty word "—and she's looking at houses. You should talk some sense into her. That money's nice but it won't last forever, not at this rate."

Will thought about disappointing Brenda by telling her that he'd bought all of his own trucks new, mainly because he worked hard and he wanted something new, and if Jen had the same philosophy, who could blame her? Or he could explain that if she'd wanted to waste money, there were better choices than a reliable Toyota.

Instead, he scooped up a forkful of eggs and shook his head consolingly as he chewed.

When he'd cleared all the bacon and most of the eggs, he washed it all down with hot coffee and realized the diner had emptied while he was in a breakfast haze. And Brenda was watching him with a small smile. "Guess you were hungry."

Will realized he was hunched over the plate as if someone was going to take it from him and straightened as he folded his napkin. Chloe had started bussing tables. Every tip was carefully deposited in the big jar on the counter.

"I've gotten tired of my own cooking. Frozen pizza. Microwave dinner. Alternate until you can't remember what real food tastes like." As a kid, he'd done pretty well at fending for himself, but as soon as he'd started making real money, he'd paid other people to cook for him through a variety of nice restaurants.

The selection here in Holly Heights was severely limited.

"Come to dinner. You can tell Jen why she needs to be more careful with this windfall. I'm sure she'll appreciate your advice." Brenda folded her towel and then blinked at him innocently. "Chloe needs real food, not frozen dinners."

Guilt. So much guilt. He appreciated Brenda's confidence in his judgment. But praising him at Jen's expense was not good. How could he tell Brenda to back off without disappointing her?

She'd been his strongest family connection for years, even after she divorced his father and he moved to Dallas.

Being a guilt-free stepson was hard. Being a guilt-free parent was impossible.

Will rested his elbows on the counter and propped his chin on his hands. Stirring up old history wouldn't accomplish much.

"Are you avoiding dinner because of Jenny?" Brenda shook her head. "You kids need to bury the hatchet. You're family."

They weren't, not really. His father had married her mother and for five years they'd been thrown together, first during awkward summers and then in the same small house until he'd graduated. After the divorce, there wasn't much holding them together.

The jutting chin he'd often seen on Chloe's face now showed on Brenda's. "She hired you. Now take that inch and turn it into a mile. Isn't that what you do? Talk to her. You're the smartest person I know."

"With money, maybe. Not women who've never liked me." When Brenda found out he was helping Sarah Hillman, surely even his biggest fan would change her mind about his wisdom.

Brenda picked up the plate and slid it under the counter. "Wish I knew how to smooth things over. You've never done anything but try to help."

Will appreciated Brenda's support. At some point, he'd probably have to track Jen down and make her explain the problem. Even when they were kids, her preferred method of dealing with him had been ducking him. She was fast, too.

Now he had even less leverage. No one was dumping her backpack in the trash can during lunch. The Sarah Hillmans of the world had stopped screeching names like Raggedy

Jen and Spots when she walked by. He'd once earned her nearly three weeks of blessed peace by helping Sarah's group with a science fair project his junior year.

Not that Jen had ever thanked him.

Her normal response had been drop-dead glares. At this point, he'd be lucky if she stuck to ignoring his calls. She could actually afford a hit man now.

"Come to dinner. When I invite you, show up. Jen will be there. You'll wear her down with your charm and success. It's that simple." Brenda raised one eyebrow in her best gunslinger stare. "Besides, Chloe's your ace. Jen never fails to mention a new photo on Chloe's Facebook page."

After a quick glance to see that Chloe had returned to punching buttons on the video game in the corner, Brenda leaned forward to whisper, "When she saw the pink hair, I thought she was going to go for a matching stripe. I had to convince her pink and red would clash." Brenda pursed her lips. "Of course, if any redhead could pull that off, it's my girl. Never seen style like hers." The pride in Brenda's eyes was unmistakable.

Will nodded. "Fine. I'll do it. Name the

time and Chloe and I are there. If you'll let me take you out somewhere nice in exchange."

Brenda rolled her eyes. "You and Jenny. Both of you are determined to treat me like an old woman. I like to work, a fact I remind Jenny of loudly whenever the suggestion of quitting, living on her winnings, comes up, which is almost every time we talk. It does my soul good to have my kids seated at a table, eating what I've fixed. Why would you rob me of that?" She clasped both hands over her chest and blinked mournfully.

"We want to take care of you." An apology burned on the tip of his tongue…for not doing more while he'd been charging at high rollers in a big city hours away. But first, there had been his mother. Loyalty suggested he should put her first. Then Jen's dislike was powerful. And he was lazy. Getting to Austin took time. So many excuses.

He could definitely show up for an awkward dinner.

Brenda sniffed. "Wash the dishes after dinner, same rules as always." Then she arched an eyebrow. "But if you really want to make me happy, you could try inviting a nice girl, too." Her singsong tone would have been cute if he had something to say in response.

He watched Chloe scoot closer, as if she couldn't quite hear the conversation. But he remembered what it was like dealing with new stepparents and siblings and how the holidays got so complicated. Adding a girl-friend into the mix would be a high-stress maneuver. He already had more women in his life than he knew what to do with. Rebecca, Stephanie and Jen were keeping him busy.

And then there was Sarah.

Who was beautiful.

But a mess.

Being reminded of her made him wonder about Brenda's opinion on the Bobby Hill-man situation.

And whether or not the diner ever made donations to area organizations like Paws for Love.

Which he was definitely not fund-raising for. At all.

Nope, he was doing dumbly heroic things like making electricity payments and call-ing in favors.

"What do you know about Bobby Hillman?

His embezzlement." Will sipped his coffee and then held the cup out for a refill.

"That's quite a left fielder. What makes you ask?" Brenda filled his cup and returned the coffeepot to the warmer.

"Uh, well, his daughter, Sarah, has asked me for some help with a charity. I was surprised a Hillman would need to ask for help with anything."

Brenda crossed her arms over her chest. "Half the town's convinced she's in on the plan, whatever it is. Can't imagine a man like Bobby—who doted on his kid—abandoning her, especially if she was involved. I know she's hanging in there. Some ladies scour the resale shop for her things, and they can name where Sarah wore or carried almost every item." Brenda sighed. "She never did work harder than she had to, but she was a beautiful little girl. Wish she'd had better direction growing up."

Brenda shook her head sadly. She'd always been able to find the good in everyone, even the girl who'd sent her daughter home in tears at least once a week for all of tenth grade.

"Heard much about the shelter? Good or bad?"

Brenda started to say something but changed her mind. Then she bustled around the counter and gave him a hug. "The only thing I know for sure is that a lot of people are mad at the Hillmans. Some folks have good reason, but I feel sorry for her. You do your best to take care of those animals."

"But keep away from the girl?" Will frowned. What difference did the answer make? He was too smart to fall for her.

"Well," Brenda said slowly, "I'd say be careful with the girl. She's got some baggage you might not want to lug around, you know?"

That was pretty good advice. If he thought about what Sarah had convinced him to do in the few days she'd strutted back into his life, he knew she was dangerous.

"Thanks, Brenda," Will said as he dropped a bill on the counter large enough to include a sizable tip. She narrowed her eyes at him but didn't argue.

He pointed at Chloe and Brenda nodded. "We've got this down to a fine art, don't we, Chloe?"

His daughter dropped onto the stool. "Yes, ma'am. You want me to wrap some silverware?"

Brenda set a tray down. "Yes, ma'am. You want a share of my tips?"

Will thought about arguing, but Brenda waved him off.

As he stepped back onto the sidewalk, he could still see Brenda's grin as she watched Chloe line up neat rows of cutlery. A quick check of his watch convinced him he had time to walk to the medical clinic, in case someone was around to shoot the breeze.

But the sight of his shadow propped against the wall across the street stopped him in his tracks. Either he could pretend nothing was out of the ordinary and go about his business— and worry all night long about why anyone would be following him or, worse, Chloe—or he could walk up to the guy in broad daylight and ask if he needed help finding South Main.

A quick scan of the fairly deserted sidewalks almost convinced him to go with his first option. Only action heroes and people who knew the script would do something crazy like confront someone on the street. Will was neither. He was just a guy.

But having a daughter to protect could make even the average man braver.

He trotted across the street at the crosswalk and held out a hand as the guy straightened to walk away. "Just a second."

The man's lips tightened but he relaxed back against the brick wall and Will slowed down. He didn't want this to escalate.

"Are you lost? I can help." Will pointed. "South Main is that direction."

The guy reached into his jacket and pulled out a leather wallet to flash a badge. "Luke Hollister. Austin PD. Didn't mean to alarm you."

Will examined the badge.

"Okay. But what are you doing here?" Will handed the badge back.

Hollister studied him closely. "We're interested in Sarah Hillman. You've heard about her father? We'd like to track him down and she's our best link."

Will was nearly overwhelmed by a wave of disgust at how dumb he'd been. If he'd been thinking for two seconds about all the trouble she could bring instead of all the help she needed, telling Sarah no would've been easier. And he certainly would not have given her a job, temporary or not.

"She's not an employee. I'm doing her a favor. That's all." Did that sound better or worse than hiring her?

"She answered the phone when I called." Hollister's expression said, *Try again.*

"She's borrowing the computer. In exchange, she answers the phone. She's a socialite, not a real assistant." Will propped his hands on his hips, determined to make it clear that his behavior was aboveboard. "I'd never let her touch anything that mattered."

The detective raised an eyebrow. "She sounded pretty official on the phone." He winked. "But I get it. She's kind of flighty. Can't hold down a real job. If you see any sign that she and Bobby Hillman have had contact, let me know. Immediately." He held out a card. "The people who'd like to be paid for their hard work would appreciate it."

Will studied the card. "You think she can lead you to Bobby?" What if Hollister was right? Bobby might not have been an honest guy, but he did dote on his princess.

And Sarah was near the end of her rope. She'd run to daddy pretty quick if she knew where to find him.

"I have a feeling Bobby's close. Sarah's

sold most of her valuables. He doesn't have much time left to save the day. You see anything interesting, call me. Otherwise, I'll have to start visiting in a police car, park right in front of your door. Town this small, the gossip will spread fast and people will want to know why the police are interested in you." Hollister slowly straightened. "Keep a close eye on the finances for that shelter. If you see any strange gifts, things you can't account for, I'd like to know about that, too. Bobby knows Sarah's clock is running out."

Most loving fathers would have stayed to face the consequences.

Or not embezzled funds from people who worked for them at all.

Will turned the card over and over as he watched the guy slide into the driver's seat of an unmarked police car.

"This new beginning is off to a great start," he muttered as he crossed the street and headed back to the office. He needed to get rid of Sarah. Now.

But if Hollister was right, Sarah really was out of options.

Chloe's cheerful wave from behind the

diner's counter confirmed that she hadn't seen anything to worry her.

That was good. He wanted her to feel safe here.

That was his job as a father.

He paused at his own door and wondered what Big Bobby Hillman believed a father's most important job was. They probably weren't that different. Except Bobby had left Sarah on her own. With no money and no job in a town where no one would hire her.

And she was doing her best to save the shelter, anyway. Finding a job might have been a better goal.

But this wasn't his problem.

He straightened his shoulders, grabbed the doorknob and shoved the door open. However hard it might be to say no to a beautiful woman, it was better for him at this point.

His resolve lasted five seconds.

Then he stumbled to a halt in front of the desk where he'd left a confident Sarah.

At some point, that woman had been replaced by one with a pink nose and brilliantly wet eyes.

"What happened?" The cop had been in and scared her. That was the only explanation.

"N-n-nothing. I'm having a day." Sarah stood up quickly. "I should take a break, now that you're back. I can scoop poop or walk dogs, something even my feeble brain can g-grasp."

Will should have been happy with the sudden turn of events. He could explain to her that he needed the desk and her makeup would be no more ruined than it already was.

But he'd feel like the biggest jerk on the planet.

"You can't leave yet." Will sighed. "Tell me what's wrong. Maybe I can help."

CHAPTER SEVEN

NO TEARS. THAT HAD been her philosophy for
as long as she could define *philosophy*, and
this man had seen her break her own rules.
What was wrong with her?

Watching Will and Luke Hollister talk on
the corner had convinced her every bit of
progress she'd made toward saving the shelter had been wrecked.

She couldn't start over. This was it. Rock
bottom.

If Will canceled her meeting with Rebecca,
Stephanie and Jen, she had nowhere else to
go. No one to call.

Would giving Hollister the number her father was using convince him she was innocent?

No. Of course not. Not even cooperation
would prove that she had nothing to do with
the embezzlement.

And the idea that giving them the number
might lead to her father's arrest...

She couldn't do it. He had always been her hero.

In elementary school, she'd been the worst speller in her class, but her dad's sponsoring of the third-grade field day had smoothed over most of her teacher's concerns and she'd moved to fourth grade.

In middle school, it had been almost impossible to pass English, thanks to tests with long essay answers. Her father had convinced the principal that her advanced thinking required special arrangements. His money had bought her an expensive tutor and enough time to catch up.

By the time she'd made it to high school, she'd learned to work the teachers to get her own special arrangements and the other students had learned not to complain. Anyone who took on Sarah Hillman could expect her to retaliate.

College had been eye-opening. Without her father's shield, her first composition teacher had identified the problem immediately. Writing essays by hand was impossible. Typing them removed the challenge of getting the letter from her brain to her hand

and she could actually *think* about what she was writing.

Maybe school would have been different all along without Bobby Hillman's defense.

She would be different if she'd learned to work through her challenges instead of protecting herself with barbs.

But he'd loved her. That she never doubted.

Now her father needed *her.* She wouldn't let him down. Hollister could get the number on his own. Surely the Austin police were monitoring her phone—unless they did that only in movies.

She couldn't lose Will, either.

She hated the pity card, but she was running out of aces.

Feeling like a tightly knotted wet blanket of epic fail, Sarah said, "Never mind, Will. One more day will get it. I'll be back in tomorrow with a fresh brain."

Will scratched his temple. He had the universal expression of a man who knew something was needed to smooth things over, but the answer was completely escaping him.

"Oh, I almost forgot." Sarah stretched over to grab the two messages she'd taken. "You had three calls. One was a wrong number.

The other two are here. I made note of the time, the caller's name, phone number and any stated reason for calling underneath it, as your procedure outlines." She pointed at the bottom. "And you didn't request this, but I asked for a convenient time to return the call. I hope that's okay."

He flipped through the pieces of paper while he studied her handwriting. She'd done her best to keep it neat.

Had she made a mistake?

Instead of accusing her of manipulating him with tears or correcting her, Will said, "That's helpful, Sarah. Thanks."

The relief was hard to describe. Jumping off the high dive, uncertain that the pool was filled with water, and then enjoying the cool splash, that might come close.

She had another shot.

"I should add that to the phone call procedure," he said. Will's surprise wasn't flattering but it seemed to be distracting him from finding a sniffling woman sitting behind his front desk.

Then he checked his watch. "You haven't been here long. Are you sure you want to quit this early?" For some reason, he hesitated, then added, "I could take a look at what you've got. Make suggestions."

He was offering to help her. Again.

Her deflection was working.

She wasn't sure which of them was more surprised.

"I can't get anything to print and I can't make the numbers work today. Usually, it's just the writing, but right now everything's a jumble. If I walk away for a while, I can refocus." She held up a finger. "And just because I'm not as good at this as you are, that doesn't mean I'm dumb."

There. That sounds like me.

He studied her tightly folded arms and then waved both hands. "Every day you wait, that's one more day without the funds you need."

Sarah tried to shake loose some of the tension in her arms. "I'm sorry. If you'll help me print the jumble I've got, I'll take it home and work on it. Bub's pretty good with numbers." She tried a charming smile.

It worked. "I could tell that about him." Will grunted. "Soul of an accountant."

He leaned around her to rest one hand on the mouse, and Sarah was suddenly aware that Will Barnes had gotten taller, broader and more handsome since high school.

Back then, he'd been lanky and awkward when everyone else was settling in. But he didn't have that problem anymore.

Instead of being hyperaware of Will intruding in her space, she was relaxing. The more she'd worried about Hollister and her father and what she could do to make everything right, the tighter the muscles in her shoulders had gotten. But now the tension headache had dulled to a throb, and some of the fear faded.

"Oh, see, something's wrong with the printer." He pointed at the error message and turned away, giving her enough space to get her head back on.

At first, she was grateful. But her relief quickly faded. It was tempting to hand her problems over. First, she'd almost let Shelly create the proposal for her, and now she wanted to step back and let Will handle things.

But that wasn't her life. Not anymore. She followed him to the printer to watch him open it up, yank and bang around inside as if the expensive piece of equipment was made of wood and rock and pull out a tangled sheet of paper. "Maybe Chloe jammed it and didn't clear the feed mechanism." He was shaking his head as he balled the paper up, then shot it in a high arc to land with a rattle in the trash can.

After a few whirs and beeps, the printer started spitting out sheets of paper.

"Unless you stop it, we're going to have about ten copies of my rambling." She squinted at the buttons and hit the big red X.

Will rolled his eyes and scooted back to sit on the edge of the desk. "All right. That's it. What's the deal? Why are you so sure I'm about to insult your intelligence?"

"That would only be fair, wouldn't it? A tiny bit of payback." Sarah sat behind the desk to assemble the printouts she needed. The rest she stacked neatly. "You need a recycle bin."

"Nope. Everything goes in the shredder." He pointed under her desk. "Don't change the subject."

Irritated at his tone, Sarah slapped the stapler hard on the desk. The loud bang and crunch of the staple joining all her hard work was satisfying.

She was too tired to come up with an

answer that would preserve her dignity, so she said, "I should be able to figure out the basics like pushing Print."

"And you did." Will tapped the desk. "When I left, you were take-charge. When I got back, you were sniffing into your hankie. What happened? Did someone come in, upset you?"

Sarah wondered who he thought might walk into his office and hurt her feelings so bad she'd be crying about it.

Hollister was the logical option, but she didn't want to get into a discussion of the policeman who'd been dogging her steps.

So she'd try a different version of the truth, the one she'd been setting the stage to reveal.

This one might get her some sympathy.

"I have a learning challenge. Makes it hard to write when I'm under stress." She sighed. "Without stress, I do fine."

"Like dyslexia?" He picked up a sheet of paper to read what she had, but Sarah snatched it away.

"Dysgraphia. Trouble with writing and organizing words." She shrugged. "Once I made it out of high school, things got easier."

"Yeah, high school was pretty stressful

for a lot of kids." Will's lips turned up but the smile didn't reach his eyes. "Bullies and such."

Sarah wasn't sure how to answer that. Would an apology mean anything at this point?

At least Hollister was forgotten.

"Who knew bullies had their own issues?" Will eased off the desk. "And at least we don't have go back to high school ever again."

He was going to let her off the hook. Again. Sarah heaved a gusty sigh. "I'm sorry, okay? I mean it. I'm sorry. I just… I knew what it was like to be picked on and I didn't enjoy that. It was…survival."

Will stared out the window as he considered that. "Survival. I never would have guessed you understood that."

Their eyes met. The silence in the small room was charged. With a past like theirs, hurt feelings and the desire to get revenge could derail any partnership.

But he was willing to let that go.

If she'd let him.

All her life, she'd circled men who had the right jobs or account balances, but Will

Barnes convinced her she was smart enough and strong enough to keep trying.

Falling for a guy like that could mean a lifetime of...confidence *and* security.

How wonderful that could be.

"Let me know if you want some help with the budget." Will walked toward his office. "Otherwise, I'll see you tomorrow."

As she walked out of the office, she turned the problem of Will, his kindness and her own inability to repay any of it over and over in her head. She was still working on the problem when she pulled up in front of the shelter. Everything was quiet when Bub met her at the door. "Hey, Shelly, I'm back. Any emergencies?"

Shelly bustled around the corner, retired veterinarian Les close behind. "How did it go?" She waved crossed fingers, her cheeks flushed and her eyes bright. "It's hard to work with my fingers all tangled, I'll tell you."

"Will's going to set up a meeting. He also loaned me a computer." She put the stack of paper on the counter and covered her face. "I'm going to pull this off."

Again with the emotion. Sarah pressed her hands to her stinging eyes. Whether it was the stress of the situation, the hope or complete mental breakdown, she was losing her grip.

Sarah waved a hand desperately in front of her face while Shelly hovered beside her, her forehead wrinkling.

"Did you have any doubt?" Shelly raised her eyebrows and Sarah realized she'd gotten pretty good at bluffing. Shelly had never once imagined they might fail.

Surely that was a sign she could fool the rest of town when the time came.

And with Will in her corner, it wouldn't be bluffing so much as convincing.

And that felt good.

"Let me change and I'll help walk the dogs." Sarah turned to go, but not before Shelly shot a look at Les.

Then Shelly blushed and nodded. "Yes. I could use your help."

Les's shoulders drooped. "Well, if you don't need me, then I'll be on my way. See you both tomorrow?" His eyes were locked on Shelly's face. At her nod, he saluted and left. Shelly trailed behind him and waved through the open door.

Young love. So awkward and sweet at the same time.

Why did she suddenly feel a hundred years old?

Sarah's lips twitched as she picked up her papers and led Bub back into her office.

It was time to work out some of the stupid emotions of the day doing something she was good at. As soon as she'd put on her jeans and ragged T-shirt, she dropped onto the sofa next to Bub, hauled him into her lap and rested her chin on his head.

Bub overflowed her lap, had ever since the day they'd met.

But he never once argued. Instead, he curled his head to press it under her chin and let out a happy sigh.

"I missed you, too." Sarah ran a finger over his silky ear. "Everything is better with you right here." She imagined giving Bub to some stranger and the tip of her nose began to sting with a vengeance. Tears spilled over. And Sarah realized she had to get a grip.

On Bub. He was hers. These moments made everything bearable.

The woman who was going to save Paws for Love deserved a dog of her own.

Did he deserve more?

Her life was going to get better, so his would, too.

Shelly stuck her head around the door frame. "Have you ever heard the phrase *foster fail*, boss?"

Sarah smoothed her hand over Bub's brow as he blinked drowsily at her. "No, but I think I get it. I'm not sure I was really a foster, but what we have here is epic foster fail." She glanced up at Shelly. "I want him. Forever."

Shelly sighed. "I had a feeling this would happen. There's the fees, the paperwork... I mean, you need an address."

Sarah nodded. "Right. I'll get it. He's mine." Will's part-time temporary job would pay the adoption fee. Spending it on this was probably foolish.

But sometimes being foolish was the only way to be happy.

Bub sighed deeply.

As much as she hated to do it, she was going to have to get a job. A real job. One that would last longer than a week.

Would anyone in Holly Heights hire the daughter of the town's most hated man?

For her sake and Bub's, after her temporary job was up, she'd have to roll the dice, take a shot that someone other than Will Barnes would help her.

CHAPTER EIGHT

THE NEXT DAY, Sarah brewed the coffee as soon as Will arrived. Beating him to the office had become a matter of pride, even if it meant waiting for him to show up and unlock the door. Will had said nothing, but he did raise an eyebrow when he opened the door and motioned for her to step inside.

Even Shelly wasn't so surprised that Sarah had cleaned out the pens before she left for Will's office.

Sarah from six months ago would wonder what sort of work program she'd been sentenced to, but today, she enjoyed proving her dedication.

Before she sat down to test her wits against the computer, she filled Will's cup and slid it across his desk. This morning he was doodling on his own notepad, the chamber of commerce's annual report in front of him.

"Thanks." He picked up the cup and sipped

before he sighed. "No, really, thank you. This is good."

"I'm glad." Sarah dawdled in the doorway, another favor on the tip of her tongue. It was such a small thing, she wasn't sure where the hesitation came from.

Before she could ask, Will said, "I'm going to set up a meeting with Rebecca, Stephanie and Jen out at the shelter this Saturday. Can you be ready?"

Sarah was immediately hot and cold at the same time.

Whether she'd be ready or not, she'd do everything she could to make it happen. Hoping Will had missed her adrenaline rush, Sarah cleared her throat. "I have a few holes to plug, more estimates, but I'll be prepared." She nodded firmly. Convincing him would go a long way toward convincing herself. "And about that…"

He'd been writing on the pad, one hand rubbing his forehead, but when she trailed off, he looked up.

"The moving boxes. In the corner of the reception area." She pointed out the door in case he couldn't remember what she was talking off. "Can I have…some?"

"I was planning to take them to the recycling center, but..." Will motioned at the notepad.

She wondered how he'd meant to fill in the blank. He'd been too busy? He thought he might need them?

Will leaned back to study her face. "Are you planning to move?"

Caught off guard, Sarah shook her head. "No way. Besides, I don't have much to pack anymore." She pressed a hand to her forehead, tired all over again after a rough night on the lumpy couch. "No, what I'd like to do is box up some of the old files. The previous manager never threw a thing out—which is probably a good policy—but I'd like to be able to move around the office without starting a paper landslide. If—no, *when*—we resume adoptions, I'll need that space to fill out forms and take payments. And when animals are surrendered, the office is a good place to settle the cat or dog before moving them to isolation."

Will had seen the room for himself, so surely he'd understand.

Finally, he shrugged. "Take as many as you like. Do you need me to bring them by the shelter?" He glanced away. "In the truck. It's good for hauling...things like boxes."

She should never have tried a conversation like this before his second cup. He was talking like the connections in his brain were missing.

"No need to do that. I can break them down and shove them in the backseat. On a pretty day like today, it's nice to ride home with the top down." She clasped her hands in front of her, regretting mentioning her car. It must seem ridiculous to hold on to the convertible in the face of having to beg the electric company for one more month.

But she couldn't let it go. Not yet.

Not while she could clearly remember her father's grin and the huge red bow on top of the black convertible. He'd be unhappy if she sold it without him.

"Fine. Let me know when you leave." Will loosened his tie. "Or if you need help."

Then he returned to staring at the notepad and Sarah knew she was dismissed.

WHEN THE AIR shifted to tell him Sarah had stepped back into the small front office, Will took a deep breath and a comforting sip of what was pretty good coffee. He had to admit he'd been surprised to see her this morning. But he hadn't said anything, wanting to avoid a repeat of yesterday's tears.

He'd almost convinced himself she wouldn't be coming back.

But here she was.

The Austin police detective's card was safely filed in his top drawer. And Will was no closer to firing Sarah than he'd been yesterday.

Instead, he was pretending to be busy.

Like a coward.

He was about to march into the front office when he heard the front door open.

"Cece, hello." Sarah's voice was pleasant, without a drop of surprise.

Will hurried to the doorway to see a well-dressed blonde inside the reception area.

"Why, Sarah, here you are again," she said with a false laugh. "Like a bad penny."

"I do like to surprise people." Sarah's voice matched the blonde's in tone and brittleness.

Time to step in.

"Celia Ames, right?" Will offered her his hand. "Holly Heights High School. You might not remember me. Will Barnes."

He wouldn't forget Cece Ames. She'd been

Sarah's right hand, always close by whenever the hallways turned into gauntlets. She'd also been a brunette then, but her true colors were easy to see.

Maybe Cece had changed since high school. Even Sarah had matured. The work she was doing for Paws for Love was proof that everyone could change.

Celia Ames was also a solid prospect. Her parents owned the Shop-on-in, Holly Heights's popular variety store. Dinah Ames had still been behind the counter when Chloe dragged him inside a week ago.

"Please, call me Cece. And it's Grant now." Cece slipped her cool hand into his. "My husband, Doug, said you'd stopped by."

Doug Grant. Will went through his mental list of contacts.

"He's a lawyer, Will. Has an office over on Jefferson," Sarah said.

"Right. You guys are building a new house." He held out his hand to urge Cece into his office. The tension in his reception area was sucking the air out of the room. "Please, sit down. Doug mentioned his beautiful wife but I didn't make the connection."

When Cece stepped inside his office, he

stopped to glance at Sarah. She seemed to be wilting.

Weren't she and Cece old friends? What was going on?

"I don't want to take up too much of your time," Cece said as Will hurried around to sit behind his desk. "Doug wanted my opinion on whether we should schedule a time to meet with you."

And? What was the verdict?

"I think I could help you and Doug plan for a comfortable retirement." Will rested his elbows on his desk. "Doug and I talked about taking some of his business funds and investing with a view to expand his office in five years. Always nice to talk to a man with big plans."

Cece glanced over her shoulder. "Yes, that's Doug."

Will was not getting a good feeling from this meeting. Normally, clients got more confident the longer they talked. Cece was perched on the edge of her chair.

"What kinds of questions do you have? I'll be happy to answer them." Will opened a drawer to pull out a folder with all his promo material neatly organized. "Here's a little information you and Doug can discuss. I'd also be happy to show you a template of the contract. The lawyer might like to take a look."

Cece made no move to pick up the brochure or smile at his attempt at casual conversation.

"It's quite a shock to find Sarah Hillman sitting at your front desk, Mr. Barnes." She crossed her hands in her lap. "You know her father's a *criminal*."

Mr. Barnes, is it? Obviously, he had his work cut out with Cece Grant.

As long as Sarah was sitting behind his reception desk.

"He's a suspect, right?" Why was he making distinctions? "Sarah's doing me a favor, answering the phones until I can get someone hired permanently. We're working together on a project for the shelter, Paws for Love. You've heard of the shelter, I'm sure."

Bringing up her volunteer work... Was he actually *defending* Sarah?

"Yes. I've recently made a donation." Cece sniffed. "But I'm sure you see the difficulty in having someone with her connections here. My husband's a lawyer. He would never associate or send business to a place that employs criminals. How would that look?" She tilted her chin down. "You understand, don't you, Will?"

He straightened his notepad and pen while he considered the problem. "No, I guess I don't."

When she blinked at him, he shrugged. "It's not like she has keys to the vault where your money is stored. There's no vault. No keys. No way she can access your account or personal information." Picking this particular moment to stand his ground might be something he looked back on with profound regret.

But watching Cece purse her lips in disapproval was satisfying.

"Perhaps. But you can agree it reflects poorly on your judgment. You'll have to fire her, Will." Cece leaned forward, a sympathetic frown wrinkling her forehead.

"I thought you two were friends." Will tapped his finger to his lips. "Who was sitting next to Sarah in the cafeteria all those days I had to race past your table?"

"I have some regrets, but people change." Cece stood easily, despite her dangerously high heels. "Give Doug a call when you're ready. That's *after* you get rid of Sarah."

Will stood and watched Cece head for the

door. He shoved his hands in his pockets and trailed her slowly, curious to see what the goodbye might look like.

Then he wondered what would cause one friend to turn on the other when she obviously needed help.

Envy?

Cece was right. People did change.

And not always for the better.

"I haven't forgotten your invitation to see your little charity, Sarah," Cece said brightly as she made a straight line for the door. "We'll definitely catch up."

No mention of her attempt to get Sarah fired. That was pretty devious.

"Hey, Cece, before you go," Sarah said as she held out a hand, "do you know anything about the Paws for Love donation box at the Shop-on-in? Do I need to come by and empty it?" A bright smile flashed across her face. But it wasn't real.

If the donation boxes were significant sources of revenue, Sarah had been a fool to leave them unattended while the shelter was struggling.

Cece frowned. "We don't have a box."

Will watched Sarah, certain she was going

to call Cece out on…whatever might have happened to the box. He'd seen collection boxes for a variety of causes around town.

None of them had been for Paws for Love.

Had something happened to every donation box?

Had every business in Holly Heights trashed them to avoid an association with the Hillmans?

Sarah waved easily. "No problem. We'll be setting out new boxes in a month or so. Can I still count on your support?"

Cece shifted from one foot to the other. "Of course," she said. "I'm always happy to support a fund-raiser that benefits Holly Heights." The hard line of her shoulders softened. Put on the spot, she had to agree or appear to be a real animal hater.

Sarah picked up her pen and made a note on what appeared to be a grocery list.

"Thanks for stopping in." Will ushered Cece out the door and then pulled it shut behind her.

He watched to make sure Cece was long gone before he turned back to face Sarah. "She gave me a donation last week, along with enough false sympathy that I understood how much our positions had changed." Sarah propped her chin on her hand. "But trying to get me fired? That's next-level girl fight."

Will shook his head as he chuckled. Again, she was rolling with the punches.

"Why don't you fire me?" Sarah closed her eyes. "I bet Cece's not the first person to ask."

Was she talking about the cop?

Will paced around the reception area, the sunshine warming the fabric of his suit. He tried to find the words to answer her, but he didn't really understand himself. "Here's the thing. I believe in the shelter. And no matter what I think of you, I know you want the best for it. No one's going to bully me into making decisions I'm not comfortable with." He tilted his head from side to side. "Well, Bub might. We'll finish this project. We've already got an agreement. Don't make me regret it."

Sarah studied her hands. "Fine. Thank you."

When Will turned to go, Sarah said, "The boxes. I do need to update them. Most of them have probably disappeared."

Instead of drooping as she had earlier, Sarah sat tall. "I'll call a printer and get a quote to add to the list. I can't imagine any one business takes in big donations, but all together, I might pick up enough to cover one of the smaller bills."

Again, Sarah's logic surprised him. Instead of throwing a fit—those boxes had probably been part of Paws for Love's fund-raising efforts for years—she'd studied the situation, brushed off the emotion and focused on what happened next.

Sarah had almost zero experience making these types of business decisions, but her aptitude was there. With enough time and experience, she could direct Paws for Love.

And a little confidence.

Will sighed. Building Sarah Hillman's self-esteem was not his responsibility. But he found it impossible not to offer encouragement.

It was for the benefit of the shelter.

"The boxes are a good reminder that the shelter's there. Every day, while customers are checking out, they see the name, address and a cute face. And kids? They have so much influence in pet acquisition." Acquisition? Could he be any stodgier?

Sarah didn't call him on it. "Are you the voice of experience there?" They both glanced at Chloe, who was curled up in one of the reception chairs, her feet dangling over the edge as she played a cell phone game and nodded along to whatever was playing through her headphones. "After cleaning the kitchenette and restocking the bathroom, she was ready to start counting carpet threads, so I handed her my phone. Maybe she can improve my score at Turn the Tables."

This time Will withheld the question. He never would have imagined Sarah Hillman playing games on her phone.

"It's easy." She shrugged. "Number tiles. Sort of a mix of dominoes and math homework."

She was doing it again, making him wonder if the mean-girl persona protected a normal human being.

"Am I the voice of experience on all things kid related?" Will rubbed his forehead. "No, that's not me. But even I've had the please-can-we-get-a-puppy argument." He motioned at Chloe. "This one can beg like a true pro." That scared cat at the shelter had done him a huge favor. The way he felt now, off balance and desperate to pull her close, he'd have said yes.

"Good to know." Sarah smiled innocently at him when he narrowed his eyes.

"We've had this talk. Do not plot against me." Suspicious and amused at the same time, Will frowned, but he wasn't sure his words had any effect.

Sarah made another note. "Don't suppose you have any graphic arts or photography talents."

"No, I'm not very creative. You're on your own there." He watched her slowly turn a page in the binder.

When she flagged the page and wrote a note, he asked, "What are you doing?"

She straightened in her chair. "Reading your procedures. It helps with the spreadsheet if I take a break."

"So you're reading my step-by-step instructions on…" He stepped closer to read the heading. "How to file emails. You don't get emails."

"No, but I might find some good practices to put into place at the shelter." She tapped the pen on the paper. "I don't get email there, either, but that's something I'm going to have to change. With her daughter's help, Shelly does all our website photo updates and posting on adoption sites on her own time." Sarah sighed. "She needs some help. I added a laptop to the fund-raising request. I'm afraid I'm asking for too much. What if Rebecca, Stephanie and Jen reject my whole outline because the bottom line is way too big?"

He didn't have much experience in fielding donor requests, but he had a hunch her fear would be on target for most organizations. Everyone had limited funds. That was true for corporations, not-for-profits, wealthy individuals and working-class citizens.

But Rebecca, Stephanie and Jen were not regular philanthropists. In the face of a solid request, backed up by puppy dog eyes and curious cats, they wouldn't stand a chance. Sarah could ask for the moon and get it, as long as she made a solid case.

But she should think about what would happen *after* this influx of money. Sarah needed long-term fund-raising.

"Put the donation boxes in. Keep the computer." He leaned over her shoulder to study her spreadsheet. Her figures were solid. "Overall, printing thirty or forty donation boxes won't make a big difference to the bottom line."

"Forty?" She bit her lip. "Really? You think that many businesses would be willing to put the boxes on display?"

"Better to have them and not need them," he said.

"Okay." Her doubtful expression was cute. That was unfair.

"I'm headed to the medical practice on the corner. I'll stop at the printer next door, ask them to work up a bid." Will abruptly turned toward Chloe so Sarah wouldn't seem him clenching his teeth. "If I bring them some business, maybe they'll listen to my pitch."

He eased the headphones away from Chloe's ears to get her attention.

"I'm headed out. Want to come with me or head down to the diner?"

She tilted her head over the arm of the chair and held up Sarah's phone. "Okay if I stay here with you? Your score is impossible. This is going to take some work."

Will glanced over his shoulder at Sarah, who shrugged at him. "It's okay with me if it works for you. I promise not to warp her too much."

He didn't need to look back at Chloe to feel

those begging eyes of hers. They had levels. Right now, they were set to Stun.

"Please, Dad? I don't want to listen to a lot of *business talk*." She wasn't complaining yet, but if he forced her to drag herself out of the chair, surrender the phone and march down the sidewalk, that would change.

"Fine. I'll call to check in every half hour." He waited for Chloe's nod. When she put the headphones back on, he knew it was settled for her.

"We'll be fine. Chloe will still be in that chair when you get back. As long as my battery holds out."

Will pretended to check the time. He had to admit, Sarah hadn't once unleashed her powers of destruction since she'd walked into his office with Bub on a leash—not on him or Chloe or even Cece.

He glanced over to see her waiting patiently, the corner of her mouth twitching. She was amused. At least one of them was. Chloe's growing up was breaking his heart in tiny little cracks.

Will opened his mouth to give orders or…something, but Sarah held up one hand. "We'll be *fine*."

He had one foot out on the sidewalk before he knew how he felt about the newest development.

Leaving his daughter with Sarah was a small decision but it felt big.

This meeting on Saturday might not come soon enough.

CHAPTER NINE

SARAH KNEW SHE should leave. Cece Grant wouldn't be the only client to complain about Will's new secretary. But she was stuck. Leaving would mean finding a new job and losing the small check she'd already spent three times in her head.

Will was honoring their agreement.

But as soon as she had her meeting and a solid plan for the shelter, she'd free him from it.

And do what?

That was the scary question. If she had the answer, doing the right thing would be so much easier.

But Will and his daughter—curled up on the fancy couch, bopping her head to music only she could hear—depended on this business.

Finish the budget. In case you need to leave soon.

The weight across her shoulders made it

difficult to concentrate, but Sarah did her best to stay focused.

Every now and then, Chloe piped up to give her a status report. So far, Sarah's high score was in no danger of being replaced.

Sarah was pretty sure that not gloating about holding her own against a twelve-year-old had to be a sign of her recent growth.

For so long, she'd had to fight mean and hard so that no one knew she was the slowest kid in her English class. But math had been easy. Fun. Something she could be proud of.

And now she had something new to be proud of—Paws for Love.

"Almost time for the lunch rush," Chloe said as she slid Sarah's phone across the desk. "Brenda could use the help and your battery's dead." When Sarah raised both eyebrows, Chloe shoved her hands in her back pockets. "Sorry. I wanted to get a better score."

"But you didn't?" Sarah dropped her lifeless phone into her purse. The next time she came into work, she'd better remember the charger. The gleam in Chloe's eye suggested she'd be up for a rematch.

"Nope." Chloe stopped with one hand on

the door. "Thanks for loaning me your phone. I keep hoping Dad will replace my tablet."

"You could buy one with your part of the tip money." Sarah pursed her lips. "Eventually."

"Yeah, like *next* summer." Chloe snorted. "Did you see Jelly today?"

Sarah barely stopped herself from grinning. "Yep. She sits in the window and watches down the hallway for people to walk by. I wave good morning every day."

"Good." Chloe tapped her sneaker on the floor.

Instead of turning back to the report, Sarah waited.

"Is it expensive to adopt a cat?"

Sarah had to smother her victory dance. Jelly and Chloe might still make the perfect match. "Well, the adoption fee's not too bad, but you have to think about all the other stuff. Vaccinations. Food and treats. Toys. It can add up. Besides that, cats like Jelly need time. She wants to be with her person."

Chloe hummed. "Yeah. And I don't live here all the time." She rubbed her forehead and then sighed. "Want me to bring you something back from the diner?"

Sarah scooted around the desk to pad bare-foot over to the door. "Nah. No money."

The sidewalk was warm when she stepped out to watch Chloe trot down to the diner. Sarah never would've volunteered to hang out with a preteen, but Chloe was easy to get along with. And funny. Smart.

It was easy to see Will's influence in her. As soon as she reached the door of the diner, Chloe waved the peace sign and disappeared inside.

That was less Will Barnes. And the pink clip-in hair probably irritated his upscale sensibilities.

There was still no doubt Will loved Chloe, even if he must be confused by her often.

Sarah remembered being that age. She'd confused her father on a daily basis.

Sarah scooted her heels aside as she slid back into the comfortable desk chair.

Sitting here was a vacation compared to the shelter's dilapidated chair. She closed her eyes for a minute to enjoy it.

Maybe that was just life: kids started out like their parents but eventually took the pieces they liked and added new ones to become who they were meant to be.

And that's enough resting your eyes. Back to work. The clock is ticking.

She was getting close. If she could focus, she might finish the first draft today. The next time the door opened, Sarah glanced up with a smile that slowly faded when she saw the detective who'd been making little surprise visits. Here he was again, twice in two days.

Did that mean they were getting closer to finding her father? Or closer to giving up? Surely bigger, more important cases were springing up every day.

"Hollister, it hasn't been that long since the last time we spoke. I still don't know anything new." Sarah fidgeted with the pen and highlighter on top of the binder. When they were perfectly parallel, she forced herself to meet his gaze.

"No phone calls. No emails. No postcards that say, 'Wish you were here.' You've had zero contact with your father. He could be dead in a ditch somewhere." Hollister grimaced. "But you're telling me you aren't worried. You haven't tried to track him down through less…obvious means."

Did he know about the text? Should she tell him?

"There was no plan. I don't know where my father is. He's…somewhere, doing his thing, or he's dead in a ditch, but there's nothing I can do about it." Saying the words immediately triggered the knot in her stomach. Sarah rested her elbows on the desk and covered her face with both hands, so weary of having the same conversation every single time Hollister showed up.

Hollister was only trying to scare her.

But what if something *had* happened? What else could explain the length of her father's absence?

What if he was one of those John Does who turn up with amnesia? What if he hadn't come home because he couldn't?

But she had the text.

She wished she understood why her father had left her here to deal with the consequences alone. How could he expect her to fend for herself when neither one of them had done much to make sure she could?

Sarah reached for her phone, ready to give Hollister the unfamiliar number, and remembered it was dead.

The detective braced both hands on the polished surface of Will's fine desk. "Reconsider working in a place like this, Sarah. Barnes has all sorts of federal regulations to meet, not to mention the expectations of wealthy and powerful people who are going to frown on the daughter of an embezzler manning the phones. Do him a favor and leave."

Hearing this from Hollister instead of Will, the guy who'd talked his way out of either firing her or losing a client that same morning, was hard. Will had reason. Hollister was using her conscience and fear against her.

At least he assumed she still had a conscience. That might be progress.

When the arm of the chair creaked to protest her strangling grip, Sarah forced her fingers to uncurl.

"Go ahead. Tell us where your father is. If we find him soon, there might be something left after he pays back his victims. The longer this drags on, the less likely that is." Hollister stepped back from the desk and the air returned to her lungs. "You don't have much left to sell, do you, Sarah?"

She forced herself to meet his gaze, determined not to give him the satisfaction of looking away. This guy didn't deserve her help. Of the two of them, it was clear who was born without a conscience.

"Thank you for your warning, Hollister. I'll turn in my resignation, and I hope Will's business won't be damaged by my current problems. How's that? Get what you came for?" She never would have spoken to a policeman like this before. She'd never felt the need to.

"No, I didn't get what I came for, not yet. But I will. As soon as the money runs out, you'll find a way to get to Daddy. That's how you work, am I right?" He slid a card across the desk. "Call me before you do anything stupid."

She wadded up the card and tossed it in the trash. "Will do."

Sarah tilted her chin and waited for him to leave. As soon as the door shut, she curled up, both hands clutched to her aching stomach.

Every time Hollister appeared out of the blue, Sarah felt the same. First, the shock robbed her of breath, until outrage chased it away. Today, there was an added flavor of guilt and worry.

So far, her "job" had involved answering a

phone that wasn't ringing and making notes on the procedure manual to collect a paycheck she desperately needed for work she really hadn't done.

All of that together would justify some guilt.

And her father... An honest man wouldn't have disappeared as he had. Hollister might be terrible, but his persistence suggested the police knew something she didn't.

Her father never cared much what other people thought. Only real fear of consequences would have driven him from town. Now that her doubts about his innocence were impossible to ignore, finding him and getting out of town was more important than ever.

Her dad was a good man, her hero. Even good men could make mistakes. When she found him, everything would be okay.

Sarah was still doodling question marks all over the margins of her notepad when the door opened, spilling warm air into the office.

Steeling her nerve to chase Hollister off again, Sarah had to do a double take when Will's stepsister, Jen, marched in.

At least Jen was unprepared, too.

She smoothed her shiny bob back behind one ear, jammed her sunglasses on top of her head and said, "What are you doing here?"

In a town where most people pretended to be her friend, Jen had always made it clear that she was happy to be Sarah Hillman's number one enemy.

High school was a long time ago, but Jen could hold a grudge.

Knowing exactly where she stood was refreshing, but Sarah always tried to keep her distance. Too bad she was stuck behind this desk.

"I've been working," she said, "answering the phone." Sarah pointed awkwardly at the phone and willed it to ring in a demonstration of how important her work was. It didn't ring.

Jen tapped the toe of her expensive cowboy boots. And Sarah knew just how expensive they'd been. She'd had to ignore the pinch of sadness at handing them over to Arlene at the resale shop.

"And Will was nice enough to let me use the computer to work up a…report." Sarah had no idea whether Will had mentioned her connection to Paws for Love.

That was a good reason to avoid the subject today. With Rebecca and Stephanie around, neither of whom had drawn much of her fire in high school, her chances were better.

"You. Working on a report." Jen snorted. "Never mind. I don't want to know about some gossipy list of trash talk. I can get that on the internet any day. Where's my brother? I'd like to tell him why he needs to dump you out on your...ear."

Sarah squeezed her eyes shut for a second. "He's not in."

Jen strode back to the door. "Fine. I only stopped in because... Doesn't matter."

"Want to leave a message? He didn't say when he'd be back, but Chloe's down at the diner." Jen hadn't asked about her niece, but if Sarah was in the same spot, she'd want to get to know Chloe better. Sarah flipped open the procedure manual but there was no entry for personal visitors.

But Jen was also a client, so she read, "If you'd like to tell me the purpose of your visit and a number to reach you, I'll have him call you as soon as he returns." She tapped the page. "And a convenient time." Sarah picked up her pen to make a note.

Jen shook her head slowly. "You almost sounded like him. How are you doing that? Shouldn't you be out burning hundreds and having your picture taken at some ratty club in Austin? Daddy's defection has really cramped your style, I guess."

Sarah flopped back against the chair. "I've never burned a hundred-dollar bill." She'd wasted money, but if her father had ever caught her burning it, even he would have washed his hands of her. "And the ratty clubs..." Sarah sighed. "Not even those promoters want to hire the daughter of an embezzler. I'm too notorious for most jobs and not nearly notorious enough for those guys."

But if the shelter closed and she had no other choice, gaining notoriety would surely be the easiest way to collect a healthy paycheck.

"But my dad... He'll be back. You'll all see how you misjudged him." Sarah crossed her arms over her chest, drawing on the old bravado.

Her words sounded a little hollow, even to her own ears.

Until she was ready to cooperate with

Hollister, she'd insist her father was misunderstood.

He would have done the same for her.

Jen snorted. "There's always waitressing. You know, like my mom? She couldn't dress me in designer labels or rent boats on Lake Travis for my sixteenth birthday, but she managed to keep food on the table. And now she waits tables. At *her* age."

Sarah studied Jen's face. She was surprised that being excluded from her birthday blowout would still sting—even more than the numerous barbs she'd thrown her way.

"You must be loving this. How the tables have turned." Sarah took a deep breath and held it before she let it out. "Those are great boots. They used to be mine."

Jen clicked the heels together. "I know. And *I* have the style to pull them off." Jen looked away and shoved her hair behind her ear again.

Did she regret her dig? Sarah had experienced that instant remorse for saying something awful and the grim determination not to back down. And she couldn't even argue with Jen's insult. Sarah had always been more Fifth Avenue than Texas chic.

"Well, it looks like they were made for you." In reality, they'd been handcrafted for Sarah, but there was no way she was bringing that up. "And I deserved that, so...I apologize for treating you badly in high school, for not inviting you to my party and for a million other things. I'm sorry."

There. A nice apology.

Sarah was proud of herself.

Jen's eyebrows shot up. "Of course you apologize. You want something." She waved around the office. "That's pretty clear. You never did anything nice without wanting something. To cut in line, to take my seat in the bleachers, to get homework answers."

More truth.

Sarah wished she'd known how difficult the day would be. She never would've left Paws for Love. Dogs and cats don't list a person's shortcomings in black and white.

"You're right. Why didn't you tell me no?"

"Because I was afraid of you," Jen said, enunciating clearly. "You and that pack of vultures that circled you. One 'no' and the whole school would have been laughing at some clever nickname or witty remark about my dorky clothes." Jen waved her hands in the air. "Even saying yes was no guarantee. And all I wanted was to be left alone. It's hard to be one person facing off against this huge crowd."

Sarah sighed at the irony. If she didn't know before, she was learning just how difficult that could be.

"Why were you so awful?" Jen's narrowed eyes didn't hold much curiosity. "I've been dying to ask that for years. You have everything. Why tear other people down?"

There was no easy way to dodge Jen's questions. Normally, she could wiggle out of tight spots. But as she tried to come up with a flip answer, Sarah realized that Jen deserved the truth.

"Do you remember seventh-grade English? Miss Lamb's class?" Sarah waited for Jen's nod. "Me, trying to write on the board? And everyone laughing at how often she had to correct my spelling?" If Jen needed more details, Sarah could remember the dress she was wearing, which of her brand-new shoes she'd picked and the color of the gigantic bow in her hot-rollered curls.

"'I swear, Sarah Hillman, your daddy better buy you a dictionary for your birthday.'"

Sarah wrinkled her nose. "He did not, in case you were wondering."

Jen shifted her weight from her left boot to her right.

Sarah shrugged. "Eventually, it was easy to make sure everyone was laughing at someone else."

"So, what, I should feel sorry for you? Because you were bullied once as opposed to every single day," Jen muttered.

"No, I just... A friend recently told me to try honesty." Sarah hoped Jen didn't ask which friend.

Calling her stepbrother a "friend" would not go well.

"Will might think he's on his guard, but you're tricky, too smart...especially now that you're acting all mature." Jen narrowed her eyes. "He's blinded by long shiny hair. But I'm not that easy."

Sarah got a boost of energy at being called smart, even if Jen meant she was manipulative, and that made it easier to do the right thing. "I am sorry, Jen. And if anyone deserves to have hit the lottery, it's the three of you. Rebecca always was the sunniest person I knew. All three of you are lucky to have the kind of relationship that lasts, grows stronger when times are hard or good or when you hit the jackpot."

Sarah leaned forward as if she was about to whisper a secret. "I'm jealous."

Jen yanked her sunglasses off, studied them carefully and then looked at Sarah as if she was waiting for the other shoe to drop. "Sarah Hillman is jealous. You just made sophomore-me's day."

Sarah chuckled. "Good. I'm glad someone around here is having a good day. The phone's not ringing. The only visitors I've had were more interested in gossip than Will's services." She ruffled the pages on the desk in front of her. "These numbers give me indigestion. But I've *still* had worse days than this."

Jen tapped her sunglasses on her wrist. "So, there's not a steady parade of clients." She wrinkled her nose. "Will Barnes, my mother's poster child for getting your life together, is not taking Holly Heights by storm. Topsy-turvy world, all right."

So many questions trickled through Sarah's brain as she watched Jen's shoulders slump.

She didn't know much about Jen and her mother or Will's relationship with them.

Apparently, there was some history there.

"Some of that's my fault." Sarah paused as she tried to figure out exactly where she was going. "But he made himself pretty clear this morning. He's going to honor his word and let me work for him."

Jen snorted. "It would be wrong to celebrate his difficulty—the first time Mr. Perfect hasn't succeeded immediately." She tapped her boot in a quick rhythm. "Right? Definitely. It would be wrong."

"I'll never tell a soul." Sarah mimed turning the key in the lock over her lips.

"Great. When should I expect the blackmail to begin?" Jen didn't smile but something about her disgusted pucker relaxed.

So did the tension across Sarah's shoulders.

"I'm still forming my list of demands. Should I give you a call when it's complete?" Sarah tapped her pen on the pad in front of her.

"Let's don't get too crazy. Besides, Will would not be shocked that I was behaving badly. My mother, on the other hand… That blackmail might work. But don't call me."

Jen opened the door. "Reclusive millionaires have to be careful. Have your people call my people."

Unless Jen was talking about Shelly, Sarah was certain she was peopleless.

"I mean Will, Sarah. Have him call me." Jen shoved her sunglasses on before she left without saying goodbye.

Sarah wondered if Will knew how lucky he was to have Jen looking out for him. At a time like this, Sarah would've called in every family tie she could.

When she was growing up, she'd had an imaginary sister. Other kids had imaginary friends, but Sarah had dreamed up a twin who liked to dress the same way she did and who'd always take her place when she had to read in front of the class.

Of all the things she'd asked for growing up, a little brother or sister had never been delivered.

Was this a way to repay Will's kindness? What could she do to bring Jen and Will closer?

Neither one of them liked her or trusted her much.

And was this another sign of maturity, caring about other people's relationships?

She wasn't sure she liked it.

CHAPTER TEN

AFTER A LONG day spent as far from his office as he could manage, Will stumbled through the front door. Two days of covering the town on foot had worn him out. And he'd kept going through lunch, after Chloe had called to say she'd be helping Brenda with a special project at her house. His feet were angry about that decision, but he'd made three appointments for next week, so it was a good kind of tired.

And if walking the sprawling streets of downtown Holly Heights helped him avoid Sarah, so much the better. They had to make it through only one more day of working in his small office before her presentation to Rebecca, Stephanie and Jen.

Then he was certain Sarah Hillman would forget to report for work.

He picked up the stack of notes Sarah had left in the center of the desk. "John Garcia.

Sarah called to confirm his appointment on Friday."

Will pinched the bridge of his nose as he considered how handy it was to have an assistant who could think for herself. Confirming appointments wasn't in the procedure manual, but a reminder never hurt.

Reminders were good for him *and* the client.

"Smart. Proactive. A good receptionist." He shook his head as he wrote a reminder to thank Sarah. He should also add this step to the manual.

The second message was from a pediatrician in Waco he'd been working with for years. His client wanted to meet to discuss his daughter's college fund.

And the last two messages were identical except for the names. One from Brenda, the other from Jen. "Dinner tonight. Six. Be there."

He pulled out his phone to give Brenda a call. Chloe was supposed to let him know when she was ready to come home. Maybe she and Brenda were working together. There'd be no way to avoid dinner at this point.

"I told her we were coming," Chloe said.

"She took me to her house, showed me dessert. It looks amazing, Dad."

Will loved seeing Chloe so excited to spend time with Brenda and Jen, but his own nerves were back. If he couldn't smooth things over with his sister, what was he doing here? He would have been better off in Austin. For the business, anyway.

"Good thinking. What are we having?" Will squeezed Chloe so tight she giggled and then he carried her to his desk.

"It's a secret. You'll never know if you don't show up." Chloe held one finger over her lips and he had a flash of Brenda doing the same thing while teasing him about something or other.

He was sorry it was such a distant memory. No matter how long it had been since his last visit, Brenda always made sure her house felt like home.

He had faith she'd do it again.

"No voice mail," he said, turning to his computer to see a large photo of Jelly on the shelter's website. So, they weren't done with this. He should have known. He minimized the browser and pulled up his email. "No email. No more work today." In his previous life, in Dallas, Will would've given a lot to sit at his desk after a long day of meetings and find no pressing business. When Chloe left, this much spare time might be a problem.

Unless he had to take care of a cat.

"Sarah just left. I told her I'd be fine." Chloe rubbed at the scratches on her arm. "She made me promise to call you, but I got distracted." She glanced at the computer monitor and then tried a sunny smile.

It worked, mainly because he did not want to talk about cats.

"All of a sudden, I'm hungry," he said. "Let's head for Brenda's." He folded the edge of Jen's message and tried to imagine what his conversation with her might be like.

Had Rebecca told her who they were meeting with on Saturday?

Dinner might not last long if that information set her off. Brenda would be sorry.

If not, could he avoid spilling the beans long enough to make it to dessert?

The drive through Holly Heights took almost no time at all. Brenda's house was still the nicest, smallest one on the block, freshly painted and landscaped.

As Will and Chloe walked up the driveway,

he realized he wasn't surprised nothing had changed. Once Brenda had made a decision, she was difficult to persuade. Leaving the place she'd raised her daughter was something she refused to consider even when he was a kid and they could have all used an extra bathroom.

Brenda and his father had argued more than once about the need to move. She'd won every time.

As someone who'd never been sure what address to call home, he sort of admired Brenda's commitment even while he wished Jen could talk her into something bigger and newer. She deserved the best.

"Are you coming in?" Brenda asked from the small stoop out front. She had a dish towel in one hand and held the screen door open with the other. Chloe's exuberant hug around her waist forced her back a step. "Once you've made it this far, you might as well."

"I was admiring how good the place looks." Will trotted up the steps and relaxed a fraction as Brenda wrapped her arms around his neck. No matter how many times he went to see his mother in her condo with the waterfront view, her greetings had never felt like this.

"I told you, Mom. Now that I'm signing his checks, he'll be here." Jen ducked as Brenda tossed the dish towel at her head. "I was right."

Caught between the urge to return the volley and Brenda's pleading stare, Will folded his hands together. "I wouldn't miss dinner when roast is on the menu. Do you know how bad frozen pot roast dinners taste?" Will sniffed, more than willing to enjoy the smells tumbling out of Brenda's kitchen. "Did you make bread?"

Chloe was standing near the kitchen table, trading close studies of the floor with glances at her aunt Jen. Brenda had been a simple conquest. Apparently, he and his daughter both had their concerns about Jen.

"Well, I tried." Brenda grimaced. "*We* tried. I don't think Jenny's got the knack."

Uneasy with the turn in the conversation, Will held up both hands. "Me, neither."

"Between you and Rebecca, I don't need to learn how to cook. I should concentrate my creative energies elsewhere." Jen pointed at her mother. "Don't ask me where. I'm still figuring that out, but now I have plenty of money and time to do it."

"As long as it's something besides cockamamy plots to get me to quit my job, I'm all in favor." Brenda wrapped her hand around Will's wrist and began towing him to her spacious kitchen. "Come in and help. I saved the most important job for last. You can carve the meat."

Jen rolled her eyes and snatched up the stack of silverware she'd obviously been about to set the table with. And she'd made bread and who knows what else, but he could come in at the last minute to carve and be a hero.

Brenda was humming as she bustled around the kitchen, oblivious to the way she was torpedoing his plans to win over Jen.

"All of you kids should spend some time learning your way around the kitchen. Chloe's already proven herself to be a pretty good assistant," Brenda said.

Chloe brightened at the praise.

"Good job, short stuff. Grab the plates off the counter so we can finish this table." Jen guided Chloe over to the dishes.

Will sighed in relief before he picked up the meat fork and carved the roast. At least Jen wouldn't hold her mother's lopsided appreciation against his daughter.

And already he felt the familiar comfort of stepping into a real home. Absolutely nothing had changed in Brenda's kitchen since he'd scoured it for food, more food, always more food, as a teenager. The cabinets were dark wood; the linoleum was spotless, harvest gold and caught in a time warp.

"Sit." Brenda guided him to a chair and gestured at the chair across the table. "You, too, Chloe. It's time to eat." Brenda turned to grab the first serving dish off the counter.

"Let me help you," Jen said, and shot him a superior look. She made three trips, each one more exciting than the last as vegetables and bread landed on the table. Then Brenda set the meat platter in front of him.

He clasped both hands in front of him and waited as patiently as he could.

Chloe leaned over and whispered loudly, "Aren't you glad you didn't chicken out?"

Until Jen ducked her head to catch his stare, he didn't realize how he'd been studying the roast on the table. She was shaking her head as he rolled his shoulders to ease some of the tension there. "I know you aren't starving, even if business is slow." She grabbed the platter and served herself and Brenda before handing it to him. "You aren't, are you?"

Brenda was smiling as if that was the silliest suggestion in the world. Will thought about waving it off, but the honest truth was that without Jen boosting his business, things might be pretty tight.

Chloe was buttering her bread with a dollop the size of an apple, one ear carefully cocked to catch his answer, but almost anything he said would be forgotten in the haze of warm bread and real butter.

"I have plenty of time to make sure my lottery winners are set." He scooped a heap of mashed potatoes onto his plate before he handed her the dish.

Jen pursed her lips and pushed food around her plate.

"I can't believe you're letting Sarah Hillman hang out in your office. Don't you remember how awful she was?" When Brenda cleared her throat and glanced significantly at Chloe, Jen raised both hands. "What? She was. Even Will can agree to that."

"Oh, yeah. She was." He sipped the iced tea—a drink that had been a part of every single meal Brenda had ever served. Sweet. Cold. Perfect. "But she's different."

"Different how?" Jen demanded, and took an aggressive bite.

"Hard to say, but she's impressed me. She could do the same for you." He hoped, anyway. If Sarah didn't impress them all, Jen would skin him alive for throwing her in Rebecca's path.

"I double-checked on the car Brenda mentioned you're thinking of buying. Good choice."

Jen blinked slowly at him but didn't answer. Brenda patted his hand.

"And the Realtor you're working with sent over some comps for Holly Heights, so I know you're looking in the right price range. If you ever want to sell the house you buy, you have to make sure to get one priced well and in the right location. I'm assuming you're going pretty high-end, so location matters even more." Will shoveled a heavenly bite of roast beef into his mouth and chewed thoughtfully. "That goes for any improvements you make, as well. Real estate is always a smart investment but some people still make bad decisions."

Brenda tapped his hand again. "You won't

let Jenny do that, though. Always thinking ahead."

Jen dropped her fork, letting it clatter onto her plate, but she didn't relax the clenched muscles of her jaw to speak.

Chloe ducked her head closer to her plate and Will got the feeling that he'd already overshot his goal—he'd gone way past being a supportive big brother.

But he wasn't sure how to reverse course.

Brenda was humming happily again.

Jen was vibrating with irritation, if the color of her cheeks was a clue.

They quietly devoured everything Brenda had put on the table.

And Jen had finally processed everything she wanted to say. "Instead of lecturing me on the proper way to spend my money, you might ask me for help, Will." Jen tossed her napkin down. "And you could also remember that whatever math skills you have, I do, too. No, I don't have a finance degree, but I understand interest, payments and planning for the future." She raised her eyebrows at her mother. "I can handle this money all by myself."

Brenda cleared her throat. "But you wouldn't have to if you'd let your brother help."

Jen's beleaguered expression made Chloe giggle. Since she'd been almost silent for the whole meal, Will wrapped a hand around her nape and squeezed. "That's the look you usually give me," he said.

Chloe immediately re-created it, so well in fact that Jen gasped. Then Brenda's laughter made them all join in.

Will held up both hands. "You're right. I know you're right. But I will say that I'm happy to help. We both know that's all it is, an opinion you can ignore freely. And…if you have a chance to work my name into conversation with anyone in town, I'd appreciate it." He rested a hand on Chloe's shoulder. "My beautiful daughter and I would appreciate it."

"You always do this," Jen muttered as she stood to clear the table. "Ignore *my* brains and *my* plans and *my* desires to do what *you* think is right."

When Chloe immediately stood to help, he made a note to tell Olivia how impressed he was with Chloe's manners. His ex was doing a good job teaching Chloe how to navigate society.

"Always? What does that mean? How many other houses have you bought?" Will braced his elbows on the table. Pursuing this was a terrible idea. He much preferred to sweep it under a rug and pull the table over the top.

Jen set the dishes in the sink, started hot water running and propped one hand on her hip. "When Joe Niemeyer stole my backpack, I wanted to go to the principal. He had a habit of doing that to lots of freshmen. Instead, you made a big spectacle of confronting him at his locker and taking it back."

Will opened and closed his mouth, exactly like a fish out of water.

"You forced Kelly Morris to confess to bumping my fender in the parking lot, so she made my life difficult on the basketball court every day for a week in PE."

She was right. He'd done those things. To help her.

"You did Sarah's science project to buy us both a week free of ridicule in the hallway. Have you forgotten that?" She shut off the water and plunged both hands under the suds.

"No. I haven't forgotten." Will stood up to

take the first clean plate from her. He rinsed it and wiped it dry while he tried to follow the conversation. "I only wanted to protect you. That's all I want now. I thought that was a big brother's job."

Instead of answering immediately, Jen washed silently and handed over every plate, piece of silverware and serving dish. He wasn't sure she was ever going to speak to him again, but she let the water out of the sink, then snatched the towel from him and wiped her hands dry.

"It's hard to stay mad at you."

Will did his best to control his eyebrows and the urge to blurt, "Really? You make it look *so* easy."

"You're the only sister I have, Jen. I don't want this distance between us." He towed Chloe over and clasped her hand. "We need you." He glanced down at Chloe, and sure enough, his daughter could be counted on. Her pleading eyes were second to none.

Jen grimaced. "No fair. Using the most awesome niece in the world against me."

Chloe held her hand up for a high five that he returned. The smack echoed in the kitchen.

When he tried to get Jen to join in, she crossed both arms over her chest. "Just...back off until I ask for help. That's what the *best* big brothers do. I need to do some things for myself, like standing up to those bullies. What you failed to grasp was that, once you were gone, I was a target all over again. But I had to fight my own battles. I can do it."

She shrugged. "But you are the only brother I have. Control your overprotective impulses and we'll be okay."

As long as he didn't do anything to stir the tempest again. Like, say, make her attend a meeting with her least favorite person in the world.

He should enjoy the détente while he had it.

"How's the house hunt going?"

Jen turned on the water again so she could wipe the countertops, a chore he'd seen Brenda do every single day when he'd been lucky enough to live in Holly Heights.

"Not bad. My agent has a long list of houses for us to tour tomorrow, after this meeting you've set up. I wanted to get Stephanie's opinion." Jen rubbed her nose on her shoulder. "Stupid itch. Never fails. When my hands are wet, my nose itches. Rebecca will love everything as long as it has a nice oven and enough counter space to roll out battalions of gingerbread men."

Brenda moved in short bursts around her kitchen as she packed up the leftovers in plastic dishes. "What about you, Brenda? Want to register your opinion?"

Before Brenda could answer, Jen said, "She has to work. She's always working."

"Because I like to work." Brenda started clearing the stack of dishes Will had dried. "Why don't you get that? You haven't turned in your notice at the high school. How many millionaires teach summer school, I'd like to know."

"That's different." Jen studiously wiped down the spotless sink before moving to the kitchen table.

Jen stiffened when her mother stepped right into her path, forcing her to halt. "It's not. You like your job, the kids, the teaching, even the math club. You'd miss it if you quit."

Brenda had never been one to back down.

He should have seen the same quality in Jen before she'd had to hit him over the head with her side of things. Did Brenda ever regret raising her daughter to be as tough as she was?

"Maybe. That doesn't change the fact that I'd like to have you around more." Jen dropped the dish towel on the counter and walked away. "I have a text message."

Chloe trailed behind Jen into the living room. Will watched her go and wondered what he could do to get Chloe more time with Jen.

Brenda shrugged as their eyes met. "These are for you." She took out a bag and placed a plastic container inside. "No one whose face lights up when homemade vegetables hit the table should be forced to go home without leftovers."

Will wrapped his arm around Brenda's shoulders as she fussed with the care package. "She's tough," he said. "Like you. You should be proud."

Her snort sounded eerily like Jen's. "I am. I wish she could remember who is the chip and who is the old block. I did stubborn first and better."

Will chuckled. "As long as you two are at odds, I'm making progress. Jen and I have a truce…for now at least."

Brenda tapped his hand. "Better make hay, my boy. We spend a lot more time in cahoots than fighting." Then her smile slowly faded. "I'm part of the problem between you two, though. Why didn't I see that?"

"You love her." Will hugged her tightly. "And you love me. Together, if you guys are patient with me, we'll figure this out. I want that. For Chloe." He sighed. "But mostly, I want it for me."

That was hard to admit. All along, he'd told himself he was upending his life to improve his relationship with his daughter. But the Holly Heights, Brenda and Jen parts of the equation were mostly about him. Chloe would enjoy having more family, but he needed them.

He'd spent a lifetime dreaming of being part of a close-knit family.

Surely this fight meant they were going in the right direction.

"And we all know Will gets what he wants," Jen said from her spot in the doorway. This time, her tone was more "annoying little sister" than "angry woman with a pistol in her pocket," so he was certain they were making progress. "Since Mom's busy tomorrow, Chloe has graciously volunteered to add her opinion on the house hunt. I like her style."

Jen winked down at Chloe, who had pulled her bangs forward in a close approximation of Jen's fashionable haircut.

"If that's okay with you, Will." When he nodded with so much enthusiasm the muscles in his neck cramped, Jen clapped her hands. "What's for dessert?"

"I made your favorite—apple pie." Brenda waved at the pie with a flourish and Jen made fists in the air with both hands.

"All right. *My* favorite. I like how this is going." Then Jen tapped his chest. "She'll do your favorite next time. Because you aren't missing dinner again. Got it?"

Jen scooped a huge piece of pie onto a plate, pretended to offer it to him and then slipped right by. She took a big bite and watched Brenda bustle around to serve him dessert. Chloe had switched sides of the table. At that minute, she was mimicking Jen's slump in her chair.

He might need to address that before he sent her home to Olivia.

Will was nearly certain things couldn't get any better, but then Jen said, "I'll get your opinion on whatever property I pick. Resale value and investment potential can be tricky to guess."

Instead of jumping up and down, Will nodded sedately. "Sure. Another calculation, an unbiased review of the pros and cons for such a big purchase, makes sense."

Jen tilted her head. "Right. When you take along Stephanie and Rebecca, the best you get are questions about how things make you feel and wouldn't you rather have the more expensive option. Stephanie's taken to spending my money while she hoards all of hers for HealthyAmericas."

"Buying new cars, new houses," Brenda said with a sad shake of her head. "It's like I taught you nothing."

"Hmm… When you sit in the new recliner I bought for you today, you may change your mind about the luxury of new."

Brenda opened her mouth to fuss but closed it. "Fine. I like furniture. I'll give it a try."

When Jen's mouth dropped open, Will said, "Watching the frugal versus fabulous money-spending showdown is going to be fun."

"Don't let her spend it all, okay?" Brenda pointed at Jen. "And especially not on me."

Will laughed at Jen's groan and Chloe's giggles and decided that he'd made the right decision. Win or lose at Barnes Financial, spending time with Jen and Brenda had been exactly what he and his daughter needed.

CHAPTER ELEVEN

MIDNIGHT WAS NOT the best time to redecorate, but it was more exciting than staring up at the ceiling and listening to Bub snore. Her proposal was finished and she'd spent the morning answering Will's phone and greeting his visitor: a nice doctor from Waco.

It had been refreshing to meet someone who didn't know a thing about her except that she answered phones and brewed coffee.

Since she'd made it back to the shelter, she'd hustled to take care of the animals, but the worry about her meeting with Rebecca, Stephanie and Jen was always ticking in her brain, draining her energy.

Unfortunately, that also made it impossible to sleep.

"Let's do something about this office, then." Bub seemed to frown as she got off the couch and bumped him awake. "Sorry. Don't let me disturb you."

The boxes she'd taken from Will's office had only added to the clutter, but she made quick work of taping them back together. "Eight boxes. Let's see what we can do."

Figuring the most important papers would be near the top, Sarah eased between the two largest stacks of files, pulled two boxes closer and started digging. Adoption papers, bills, donor information—everything was piled together but followed a weird system mainly organized by time. "Like the rings of a tree. The bigger the stack, the older it is."

She added a third box and started separating the papers into groups. Instead of getting overwhelmed as she read, something she struggled with on any big project, Sarah broke it down to make the work fast and easy. Once the first boxes were filled, she moved them out into the lobby and resumed with her remaining boxes, until finally...

"The stacks. I did them all." Sarah stretched the hard kinks in her back as she glanced at the clock. "Whoa. Three hours. Tomorrow will definitely be a concealer kind of day." Every muscle complained as she moved the last boxes into the lobby. The labels written in fat black permanent marker were bold, clear and satisfying.

It wasn't a perfect system, but if she had to find a piece of paper that had been previously buried in a teetering tower of paperwork, at least now she'd have a clue where to start.

"Why didn't I do that weeks ago?" Sarah mumbled as she made another peanut butter sandwich. Without Bub's shadow, she might as well be the only person in the world that night. The shelter was quiet.

For the first time in too long, she felt confident. Not pretending to be certain, but satisfied she'd conquered a gnarly task.

Other people would have done it differently.

But they weren't here.

And that was okay.

Measuring herself against some other standard of performance, one that might exist only in her head, had kept her from doing what she could do.

Did she like paperwork? No. Was it needed? Probably. Was there any reason to be afraid of making a filing mistake? Nope.

Discovering she was a paperwork genius was encouraging, even in the early hours of Saturday morning.

And the meeting with Rebecca, Stephanie and Jen would go a different way if someone else was in charge, but she was here, she'd prepared and, whatever happened, she was sure doing *something* was a lot better than standing aside, letting Paws for Love fail because she was afraid.

As she walked back into the office, Bub lifted his head and sniffed the air, as if he could smell the bouquet of peanut butter. Sarah waved both empty hands and Bub stuck his nose back under his tail to resume his nap.

"All right." Sarah braced her hands on her hips as she surveyed the still-small but now-adequate office. "The suitcase stands out like a neon sign. And the papers scattered across the desk look even worse."

Now that she'd started, Sarah was determined to ignore how late it was. She sat down in the awful desk chair and created stacks following the same system. She made a note to clear the decrepit filing cabinet of everything but current business and the previous year's.

"Organize filing cabinet. Paint. New chair." She winced as a fold of tape poked her thigh. "I should have put that at the top."

Under that list, she started a new list. "Paint for the lobby. New bulletin boards." She stared up at the grimy window and added curtains to the list. Her first night in the office, she'd been worried about people looking in. Eventually, she decided it was too far off the ground for the casual Peeping Tom.

And that had to be good enough.

Looking out the window, she almost thought she could see light, as if a car or truck was out front. Bub, her crack security team, was snoozing comfortably, so it was easy enough to let go of her paranoia. Who would want to break in? It was clear the place had zero dollars on hand.

Besides that, the lights were on. A clever thief would wait until the place was empty before breaking in.

"It's late." Sarah refused to check the clock again as she flipped the light switch and ignored Bub's grumbles to stretch out beside him. "I'll start again in the morning."

Which came entirely too soon. At least having no window coverings meant she didn't need an alarm clock.

"Up and at 'em, Bub. We've got a big day." Sarah stretched and slipped into her work clothes before she let Bub outside. When the first group of dogs had raced out to the play yard and their pens were cleaned, water re-filled and the food distributed, Sarah ate her peanut butter sandwich and then scoured the place for a closet that could hold eight boxes of paperwork.

"Morning, boss. You beat me to the punch already. Got a late start," Shelly said cheer-fully as she wandered down the hallway. Then she said the magic words. "I brought coffee."

"Thank you, thank you, thank you, thank you. I needed this." Sarah raced down the hall to slide to a stop in the lobby. Shelly held out the cup. Sarah snagged it and drank deep.

She closed her eyes and waited for the caf-feine to ignite.

"All right." She blew out a breath. "I'm going to kill this day, Shelly. That was all that was missing."

Shelly pointed at the boxes. "Late night?"

"Yeah." She cradled her coffee.

"Me, too," Shelly whispered loudly, al-most vibrating with excitement. "You'll never guess what happened. Les and I, we went *dancing*. In *Austin*. On a *date*."

Shelly and Les, her two retired volunteers, had been out dancing while she stared up at the ceiling and worried about bills. What had the world come to?

Watching Shelly bounce up and down on her toes lightened Sarah's mood considerably. "Wow. And you're still dancing."

"I may never stop," Shelly answered in a singsong. "Man, it's just… You know how life makes you think all people do is let you down and then you meet the one who doesn't? You *have* to dance."

Sarah forced herself to set the coffee cup down before she spilled any. Then she surprised Shelly and herself by hugging her tightly and dancing around with her. Whether she knew the feeling Shelly described or not, she knew it was worth dancing over.

Will immediately came to mind and Sarah could picture the smile he'd give them if he were here.

The fact that she missed seeing it in person should frighten her, but Shelly's exuberance was impossible to shake. When they caught their breath, Sarah decided business would keep her on track. "I hope this is just the first celebration of the day." Shelly nodded and raised her coffee cup. "Unless I can find a place to put those boxes, they'll go right back into the office. Got any ideas?"

Shelly frowned and studied her coffee cup. "I don't know when I'll get over being surprised by you, Sarah." She picked at the plastic lid. "But you work so hard."

Sarah smoothed the wrinkles out of her shirt, a knit that had once been part of an amazing outfit she'd worn for lunch at the country club. Now it was covered in hair and had three small holes, thanks to a puppy named Zelda.

When she drank her coffee too fast and had to cough and sputter, Sarah muttered, "Thanks. If I don't choke myself to death with overexcited coffee drinking, I'll get back to work."

Shelly giggled and Sarah felt something loosen inside her chest. Ever since she'd been on her own, she'd wondered if she had what it took to make people like her. Not her money or what she could bring, but her. All by herself.

Making someone laugh confirmed that she had at least some of what it took. Her own chuckle was small, but sharing it with Shelly, who'd propped her up for so long, was sweet.

"I know where we can put those boxes," Shelly said before easing around the counter. "Follow me."

In the center of the storage room, Shelly said, "We can move all these bags into cans and store them in the hallway. That will make feeding the dogs easier." She tapped the big bags of dog food. "That's what we did before Marley took over."

"Think we have time to do that after the second group goes out?" Sarah grabbed her cell phone to check the time. Then she noticed a missed call from a number she didn't recognize. Was it a wrong number or had her father changed phones again?

Anyone could lose a phone. But this seemed like a clear indication he was changing them to avoid...something.

Shelly grunted as she tried lifting one of the large bags of dog food. Sarah hurried over to help. "I'd like to have the place in good shape for this tour. Hiding those boxes will help."

Shelly set her coffee cup down and brushed

her hands together. "The two of us? Yeah, we can do whatever it takes."

Just like that, Sarah's face hurt from grinning.

She was almost convinced Shelly was right.

"Dog food. Here we go." Sarah put her own coffee cup down and committed herself to Shelly's direction. By the time they'd cleaned the cans, emptied the food, moved the boxes, let the second group out into the play yard, cleaned their pens, restocked their food and water and fed all the cats, Sarah was aching from head to toe.

But there was no denying Paws for Love was ready for its audition.

They couldn't do a thing about the state of the roof or floors or yellowed paint, but every surface was clean, the animals were happy and her report was as ready as she could make it.

All that was missing was another cup of coffee.

"Hello, hello, hello!" Les called as he brought in a wave of warmth and sunshine. The smell of hamburgers drifted out of the paper bag he set on the counter. "I got here in time to miss all the hard work. I guess I have the knack." He froze in front of Shelly, one hand held out, until she shook it slowly. Then he held up a cardboard drink carrier and Sarah had to clasp her hands together to prevent grabby motions. "However, I did bring food. And drink."

All three of them gathered at the long counter in the lobby while Bub meandered in from the office. He settled hopefully on Sarah's foot.

"Burgers. Sodas." Les pointed. "I hope that's okay."

If rich Sarah Hillman had ever imagined that one day she'd view a hot hamburger as one of life's true delights, she would have been convinced the future was one of horror.

But this Sarah shifted her weight back and forth as Shelly handed out the food.

"You guys, I don't know what to say." Sarah clutched her hamburger. "I should be the one buying food and drinks for you. There's no way to repay what you've done for the shelter or for me, but this…" She waved the hamburger but didn't let it go. "This is kindness and generosity on top of hard work."

How easy it was to say "thank you" when she meant it so sincerely.

Lately, she was getting good practice.

"These aren't quite as good as the burgers from the little hole-in-the-wall place outside Austin, but they'll do. That's where we're heading tomorrow." Les winked at Shelly, who glanced at Sarah out of the corner of her eye.

Sarah took that as a warning not to make a big deal out of their second date. In a weirdly chipper voice, Sarah said, "These are from Sue Lynn's, so they'll hit the spot."

Shelly cleared her throat. "It's a burger, Sarah. We've all got to eat."

Les took a big bite and then said, "Gonna have a shadow, kid from the high school, for a month or so. Thought he'd get a handle on the day-to-day operations today. Then he can assist with any simple procedures. That okay?" Les chewed and tilted his head to the side.

Suddenly the fatigue caught up to Sarah. She eased back against the counter. Hot coffee, hot food, laughter and now a new volunteer. It was a lot to handle with ragged emotions, too little sleep and too much worry.

She blinked rapidly and tried to sniff quietly.

Then Les put down his burger and took two steps back, his hands raised in alarm. "Whoa."

Sarah wiped one finger under her eye. "Sorry." She swallowed hard. "That's just… awesome. See if you can find more. We'll have shadows running all over the place. Okay?"

Les rolled his shoulders and glanced at Shelly again.

"She was up all night, clearing out the office." She patted Sarah's hand and that comforting touch was enough to make the tears well up again.

"I should change." Sarah ran a hand down her ponytail. "Big investors mean big guns, right? Should I go with the heels?"

Shelly wrinkled her nose. "Only if you want them to think you don't do much around here." She winked at Les and he wrapped an arm around her shoulders. In a flash, Sarah went from overwhelmingly grateful to a little jealous. "No one could do real work in those shoes."

Facing off against Rebecca, Stephanie,

Jen and Will without her designer labels and killer footwear would be scary.

"I'll change and toss these clothes in the washer so they'll be ready for tomorrow," she said. Win or lose, maintaining the appearance of wealthy Sarah Hillman would keep her emotions under control.

Given the tears she'd already embarrassed herself with, control mattered.

But before she could skirt Shelly with her mildly disapproving grimace and Les, who would have been happy to be elbow-deep in anything other than emotions, the door to the shelter opened.

Will, dressed in a T-shirt and jeans instead of his oxford and shiny wing tips, stepped over the threshold. "I'm early," he said, checking and rechecking his watch. "Thought I'd see if you had any last-minute questions." Chloe followed him in, waved one hand and immediately headed for the cat room. Will shoved both hands in his pockets and surveyed the lobby as if it were brand-new. Was he nervous, too?

Shelly and Les followed Chloe down the hall, leaving the two of them alone.

"So, do you? Need help?" After all he'd

done for her already, he'd come early to offer his expertise. He really was too good. "Chloe's been up since dawn, watching the hands on the clock." He squeezed his eyes shut. "We should talk about adoption procedures. After."

Sarah had to clear her throat. "Really? What brought this on?"

"I thought she'd forget. Then this morning she showed me a blinged-out cat carrier and said I could take the money I'd spend on a tablet and get her a cat." He sighed. "She's been complaining of mistreatment all summer because she has no tablet. And now she wants a cat enough to give that up."

"Are you sure she won't go back to the tablet after she gets her cat?" The lump in her throat made it hard to talk. This guy was wrapped around his daughter's finger. Why did that make him even more attractive?

"With Chloe? I'd almost bet money that she will change her tune once the cat's moved in." He shrugged. "But it doesn't matter. I love her. I'm happy to give her both if I can."

Instead of shoving aside the loose ends of her emotions, she watched Will kneel to give Bub a hearty scratching. Her dog rolled over on his back, both hind legs twitching in ecstatic pleasure.

And the odd, strangled gasp that escaped her was the last straw. "I need a minute."

She skirted Bub, ignored Will's frown and stepped inside the office to rest her back against the door. "Nerves. That's all this is. Get a grip."

All her life, she'd pretended she was bulletproof. Now was not the day to show her soft underbelly. "Business. Keep it business, Sarah."

While she concentrated on breathing evenly, she tried to decipher the low voices outside the door. No doubt Shelly was explaining that fatigue was the issue again.

And it was.

Along with the bone-deep certainty that, if this didn't work, she had no more fight left in her.

"Let me in, Sarah." Will's voice startled her, and his solid thumps on the door indicated his patience was as thin as her control.

Sarah stiffened her shoulders and stepped away from the door. At this point, she had to go all in, leave nothing in her pocket. Either she'd run the table, get exactly what she needed, or she'd walk away with no regrets over playing it safe.

That would have to be good enough.

She closed her tired eyes and took a deep breath. Then she pulled the door open and made a grand gesture. "Please, come in. You won't recognize the place."

AFTER HE WALKED into the office, Will studied her face. Bub was a warm weight against his leg. If Sarah was crying, he was going to do something stupid.

Even *more* stupid than showing up early to make sure she had everything she needed and pick up a cat.

He wasn't sure what that would be.

But in three minutes or less, she'd managed to chase away the tears.

Impressive.

"We have some time, so I'll give you the adoption contract to look over. Now I even know where they are." Sarah yanked open a creaky drawer, walked her fingers over the files and pulled out a sheet of paper.

Will couldn't help thinking she fit perfectly in the run-down shelter. As if she'd always been there or she was an extension of the place.

Except she was bright and shiny, like her vision of the future of Paws for Love. He wanted to squeeze her tight, tell her she'd done an awesome job and eliminate whatever it was that had kept her up too late. Sarah Hillman was beautiful, even fresh-faced and doing hard work, but more important, she was strong.

"Did you work all night long?" To fight the urge to touch her, smooth her ponytail back over her shoulder, he propped his hands on his hips and turned slowly to see how much bigger the office appeared without the file stacks creating a fire hazard. Her fancy suitcase seemed like modern art because everything in the room was old, worn down, held together by tape and dust, but she'd done the best she could with what she had.

For the rest, she'd need some cash, a bucket of paint and an office furniture budget.

"Almost all night, but it was worth it." She rubbed her eyes and then shook her head. "I should at least put on makeup. I always look like a ghost without mascara."

Will almost argued.

Without mascara and bright red lips, Sarah Hillman was girl-next-door sweetheart material. If one knocked men out of their shoes with sex appeal, the other brought out the urge to tease and flirt and go for old-fashioned chivalry.

Neither one was safe.

Eyes on the contract, Barnes.

Will picked up the piece of paper and studied the short list of terms he'd have to agree to for adoption. "Are you at all worried that neither Chloe nor I have ever had a cat? We might need some training."

"Cats like Jelly are pretty easy. Food, water, litter box, attention." Sarah shifted her shoulders tiredly. "She'll take care of the rest. We'll send you home with a few days' worth of dry food and a list of the vaccinations she's had and when she's due for boosters. You can even borrow a carrier."

Will took out his checkbook, scribbled out a check and slid it across the cleared desktop. "I had a bad feeling the first day I walked in. I should have been less worried about you and more worried about losing my home to a cat."

Sarah pinched the check and waved it in the air. "True. Very, very true. They get you when you least expect it. I've already promised all the money you're going to pay me to free Bub from these circumstances." She sighed. "Last thing I needed was a big, hairy dog riding shotgun in the convertible." She leaned across the desk and offered him her hand. "But I still think it will be the most satisfying check I've ever written. I hope you can say the same."

Will wrapped his hand around hers, braced for the immediate warmth that spread from her to him or vice versa. He wasn't sure which way the heat was flowing, but it was there.

And it could be a problem.

"We'll settle up after this meeting." Will reluctantly let go of her hand. "Then we'll all be ready to celebrate." If Rebecca, Stephanie and Jen were able to say no to Sarah Hillman, he'd have his doubts he knew them at all. She loved this place and she was giving Bub a real home. What monster would be able to deny her anything?

Obviously, not him.

Will realized that Big Bobby Hillman had likely felt the same—Sarah's father never said no to his only daughter—and a brief shot of sympathy flashed through him. Then he considered his own daughter and her influence.

Someday, Chloe would be as powerful as Sarah Hillman.

He really needed to make sure she used that power for good instead of evil.

Sarah tugged the sleeves of her shirt. "I was thinking about changing into something more impressive in honor of my guests, but—"

"But we're already here and none of us are impressed by haute couture, Hillman." Jen stood in front of Rebecca and Stephanie. Whatever she planned to say next was muffled.

By Rebecca's hand.

Chloe giggled from her spot behind Jen.

"What she means to say is we know you have a lot of work to do, so it's fine with us if you want to go as you are." Stephanie smiled at Will over his sister's shoulder. "Worked like a charm. We told her we were going out for lunch first, then we gave her directions here."

"You let her drive?" Will shook his head. If she had her own keys, Jen would be a flight risk.

"She insisted. She loves that new car." Rebecca sighed. "I told her to go for something smaller, but the sedan became an SUV. Used. Can you even believe it?"

Jen's eyes met his and they both nodded. "Knowing her mother, yes. Brenda always says used cars are the best. The SUV should hold its value, too."

"Now the only problem is that we promised her pie." Stephanie sighed. "She's going to be unruly without pie."

Rebecca guided Jen into the office and pushed her down on the couch. "I will make you all the pie you want. Just be good."

"I like pie, too." Chloe eased down beside Jen and peeked up at her.

"Of course you do. Pie rules." Jen gave her a fist bump. Will watched his daughter light up and knew that Jen, even if she was tough, would have lots of students who loved her. Kids would work hard to earn her respect.

Bub climbed up on the couch and sat on the armrest, two feet braced against Jen's leg. Before Will could shoo Bub down or Sarah could...do whatever she'd started across the room to do, Jen wrapped her arm around Bub's neck. "You're a good dog, aren't you?

You'd never trick me with promises of sweet dessert. You're my only real friend…"

She glanced at Sarah and raised her eyebrow.

"Bub. His name is Bub." Sarah pointed at the chairs crammed in opposite her desk. "If you'd like, you can all have a seat. I'll ask Shelly to let Bub outside to make room."

"Nope. My biggest ally is staying." Jen wrapped two fingers around Bub's collar and tugged him down across her lap. "There. We're comfortable now. Let's get this started."

She made small motions with her hands and Bub rolled over to offer her his stomach.

Will would have laughed at Sarah's dumbfounded expression, but she'd already had a long day. They should get the meeting moving.

"Rebecca, Stephanie, have a seat." Will motioned to the chairs in front of the desk. Sarah handed out a slim report that Will recognized…because he'd searched through the trash to get a sneak peek. He'd had his doubts she'd stick around, and he'd never even imagined that she'd put together such a concise but well-researched plan.

"I'm not sure where to start. It would be best to talk about what's critical instead of what's just...needed." Sarah's words stumbled to a halt and she licked her lips. "As you can see, I've broken this up into three groups. Now, next and eventually."

Will watched Rebecca and Stephanie trade confused looks. Jen shook her head slightly as she ran a finger down the columns.

"Let me start over." Sarah pressed both hands on the desk. "I'm blowing this. Nerves."

The urge to take over was nearly impossible to stifle. He could sum up this request in five minutes.

But his sister's speaking glance helped him to fall back. Jen had said she needed to do some things for herself.

Will relaxed against the wall. Sarah could do this.

She had insisted on this opportunity. Sarah needed to make it on her own.

The only real question was why Jen wasn't shouting from her seat on the couch about Sarah wasting their time. One glance made it clear why. The paper report was discarded and Jen was staring deeply into Bub's eyes.

Bub. The secret weapon. Sarah might do better to shut up and wait for her dog to conquer the entire room.

"You know, I've decided that when I have a lot of things tumbling through my head, I sometimes think better on my feet." Stephanie stood up. "Let's take a tour first. Then we'll understand these numbers better."

Sarah jumped up from her ragged chair, a smile on her face.

And Will wished he'd thought of that.

"Great idea. You guys come with me." Sarah was out the door before Rebecca and Chloe followed.

Jen seemed a little disgruntled at having to get up.

"Are you coming?" He offered her his hand and then yanked it back as Bub ran a large pink tongue over the back.

"I guess."

Will almost asked her how often her students used the same disgusted tone, but he wasn't sure he'd built up enough goodwill yet.

"Is that a suitcase in the corner?" Chloe pointed and then stepped closer to the desk.

"Yes, I think Sarah's sleeping here."

Jen slowly turned to scan the office. "Weird. No way I would've ever guessed that." Then she smoothed her hair. "You could've given me fair warning Horrible Hillman was going to hit me up for an investment. That's low, Will. And now I don't even have any pie."

"She deserves a fair shot," he said. "Take a look at what she's managed. Then do what you want."

Jen spun on one heel and marched out of the room to rejoin the others.

Will trailed behind the group as Sarah did her best sales routine in an impossibly perky volume that in no way matched her earlier fatigue or teary eyes.

Everyone had a mask. Hers was nearly flawless.

The only problem was that the longer the tour and the quieter her audience, the more brittle Sarah became. One wrong word could break the whole situation into dangerous shards.

"Why don't you introduce us to the volunteers." Will interrupted her spiel about how much food the shelter went through in a year and pointed at a man and woman who were removing stitches in the exam room.

Sarah stepped into the room as the dog jumped up, newly stitch free, and sat perfectly while he waited for his treat. "Uh, sure. I can do that. Les is a retired vet who provides a great deal of medical support on a day-to-day basis. He'll be bringing students through on a mentorship program. I'm hoping some may convert to volunteers after the shadowing is over. We also work with the clinic in town for spaying, neutering and treatment. Shelly here is…" Sarah had to clear her throat. "She keeps the doors open. Has since before I started spending time here."

Shelly blushed and waved her hand as if Sarah was exaggerating.

He was happy to see that, whether or not she had much experience in running a business, Sarah knew enough to give recognition of solid contribution.

"And this is Meatloaf." Shelly ran her hand over the dog's head and dodged his kisses. "He was surrendered after his family moved away. He's desperate for another human to love." Shelly bent to press a kiss on Meatloaf's head. "Also, he might like a new name but that's for his family to decide."

Immediately, the tension in the room eased. Sarah relaxed and the tour resumed. Chloe had disappeared earlier but when they visited the cat room, she waved, a black cat perched on her shoulder. They inspected the play yard, the outside kennels—used for holding new dogs for observation—and ended up in the large, scrupulously organized storage room.

"Is that a knife sticking out of the washing machine?" Jen asked.

Sarah shrugged awkwardly. "Sometimes unusual engineering is required, but we'll use that washing machine until the door falls off."

Jen crossed her arms over her chest and turned away to study the stack of boxes that explained what had happened to the office.

Stephanie and Rebecca exchanged a look. Will wasn't sure what they were saying, but he expected they were communicating about which way they wanted to go with the fundraising request.

Sarah must have caught that, too. "Let's go back to my office."

The group was quiet until everyone was settled. Then Rebecca glanced at Will, and he wasn't sure which way this was going to land.

Jen was trying to make herself as small as possible in the corner.

"That shadowing program?" Rebecca tapped her chest. "That's mine. I started it with the help of the administrator at Holly Heights Hospital."

Stephanie reached across the desk to pat

Sarah's hand. "And nobody can say you're not doing the best you can with what you have."

They both turned to Jen, who sighed loudly. "I don't like you. I don't want to help you." She pressed both hands over her face. "But I can't walk out of here while Meatloaf is galumphing happily around, clueless at how close he is to losing this home, too."

Rebecca and Stephanie wore identical expressions—a smug twist of the lips—and Will wondered if they'd also suspected Jen wouldn't be able to say no in person.

"We're going to write you a check for the 'now' part of your funding. And that's it. We'll talk again when you're ready to tackle the next piece." Jen held her hand out toward Rebecca. "And there's no way we're going to let her *have* that much money. What if she needs a plane ticket and she's out of here with the rest? I mean, what if she follows her daddy?"

"You think you can be insulting now that you have a lot of money?" Sarah eased up from her desk.

"Coming from you, that's hilarious." Jen squared off against her.

Will bit his lip, determined not to charge in to defend either Jen or Sarah.

"Save the drama, both of you. Nobody wants it." Stephanie waved her hands in the air. "You don't have to like each other, but put away the weapons."

Jen eased back. "Fine, but I expect close oversight because this is a lot of money."

Rebecca glanced at Will over her shoulder, her bright blue eyes as innocent as could be, but Will was nearly certain she was working her own plan.

"We'll create a board of directors. You'll all serve on it. Sign off on expenditures." Sarah sat back down. "I was about to suggest that." Her lips tightened at Jen's disbelieving snort. "Honestly."

"Great idea. Since Stephanie won't be here for much longer, thanks to my brother's insistence that she's needed in Peru, and no one trusts me to make the proper financial decisions—" Rebecca nodded toward Jen "—she needs to serve."

Will might have laughed as he glanced from Sarah to Jen and back. Neither one liked that suggestion. At all.

"I'd be happy to help." He rested an elbow on the filing cabinet. "Not that I don't trust Jen, but it might be nice to have an unbiased member."

Sarah and Jen both snorted at that.

"She was answering your phone yesterday. We all know why." Jen crossed her arms over her chest.

Sarah lurched out of the chair again. "Oh, yeah? Why?" She pressed one hand on the desk. "Because he's a nice guy. He's keeping his promise by letting me work for him but he'll always put family first."

Rebecca whistled quietly and turned to him. "Hard to say who you'd choose in this epic battle, Will. Glad I'm not in your spot."

Will clenched his jaw and bit back the retort that she was the one who'd put him in the crosshairs. He wasn't sure who would shoot first, but he had no doubt he'd be the target.

"You're both right. I have a bias." He tapped his chest. "And it's all for me. I'll make decisions based on what makes the client happy."

"That means your sister." Sarah shook her head. "Which is fine. We've worked together so far. I trust you."

Sarah eased around the desk, her hand held out to Jen. "You, Will, Rebecca, Stephanie and maybe…I don't know, someone else, a board of five. To watch over me, make sure I don't waste your investment or…worse. And you'll have my eternal gratitude and as many dog kisses as you can stand."

Jen's frown deepened as she considered Sarah's offer and Will wondered if she was regretting her decision already or if she was trying to wrap her head around the changes in Sarah.

In high school, that hand would have been a trick, some way to hurt or embarrass Jen.

But now, Sarah's hand was shaking. She wanted this. She needed their help.

And she was smart enough to understand that Jen was the one she had to convince.

Reluctantly, Jen shook her hand. "Fine. But you see that we'll always have control, don't you? We'll have four votes."

Rebecca cleared her throat. "Assuming that we'll always agree is a pretty big leap, Jen. You know that."

Stephanie was grinning. "I didn't want to say it, but I'm glad you did."

"I'm the one who got us these millions, don't you forget it," Jen muttered, and stepped over to the couch to rub Bub's ears.

Stephanie sighed. "You'll never *let* us forget it."

When Will's eyes locked with Sarah's, his lips were twitching. The three of them might as well have been sisters. They bickered and teased, but they'd managed to stick together for a long time.

"Maybe you can be the fifth," Rebecca murmured as she tapped her chin. "After we hire a new shelter manager. You can go back to doing what you're good at—working the crowd, emptying pockets. Let someone else handle the day-to-day operations. We should try to find someone who has grant-writing skills or a proven track record with another shelter."

Sarah wilted at the suggestion that someone else would be taking over. It made perfect business sense to hire someone with experience and a shot at turning the shelter around.

But Sarah had been eating, breathing and sleeping Paws for Love. How easy would it be to give that up?

"We'll get someone with real qualifica-tions. Relevant work experience, a solid busi-ness education and a reputation that's still... smear free." Jen brushed imaginary lint from her jeans. "And I guess I see how you'd want to serve on the board. If you have to."

"She has to." Will wasn't sure his opin-ion bore any weight, but if they couldn't see how the conversation had leveled Sarah, he'd have to step in.

Then he remembered that she needed to speak up for herself. She'd done a good job of keeping the doors open. If that wasn't "rele-vant experience," he had no idea what would qualify.

"We've got time to iron that out," Rebecca said.

Sarah didn't argue. And judging by the fa-tigue in her eyes, she'd pretty much reached her limit.

"You'll have the funds on Monday." He patted her back awkwardly, aware of his au-dience. "And all those plans for your fund-raising open house, you better get them rolling."

Instead of responding with a business-like affirmative, she stood and wrapped her arms around his neck. Ignoring the rest of the world and interested onlookers was easy with her pressed against him.

"Thank you for giving me a chance," she whispered before she stepped back.

He almost pulled her close again. Will wasn't quite ready to surrender her, but Stephanie's and Rebecca's expressions were the perfect mix of shock and amusement. Jen's had an added touch of disgust but she didn't say a word. That had to be progress.

He needed to clear out his clients while the getting was good and before Sarah folded in exhaustion. Adrenaline would get her only so far.

"Everyone congratulate me. I'm about to become a cat owner. I'm sure Chloe is dying to make the introductions." Will ushered them out of the office, but Jen's feet were glued to the floor.

"A cat? Really?" She blinked. "Did I fall and hit my head? I'm in cahoots with Sarah Hillman, of all people, and you're adopting a cat."

"Once you meet her, you'll understand," he said, and guided Jen over the threshold. "We need a minute."

Jen tilted her chin down. "For what?"

"To talk. About things." She narrowed her eyes but reluctantly took slow steps toward the lobby.

CHAPTER TWELVE

FOR SOME REASON, watching Will herd his much smaller, much more stubborn sister out of the office didn't worry her a bit. In fact, she wanted to laugh and laugh and laugh.

Hysteria or happiness, sometimes it was a fine line.

The shrill ring of the phone in the lobby added tension to her relief.

Despite the celebration going on inside Sarah's head, her emotions and the sleepless night were about to overwhelm her. Then Shelly stuck her head around the door frame. "Boss, I'm truly sorry to interrupt but the sheriff's office called. They've had a complaint of animal neglect. Deputies are on the way, but they'd like us to be on hand if the dog has to be removed."

Sarah's first instinct was to tell Shelly to… handle it. She'd certainly never answered a rescue call and had zero desire to start with one of neglect.

But Will and Shelly had both turned to her.

As if she would know what to do first.

Apparently, a nap—or exhaustion coma—was out of the question.

So she'd make it up as she went along. "Grab the surrender forms. Is Les still here?"

"Yes, he's got his bag, ready to go." Shelly pointed over her shoulder. "But the van's out of commission, remember?"

"Right." Sarah tapped her lip as she tried to come up with a reasonable suggestion. Shelly's smart car wouldn't haul a Chihuahua. Given her luck, this would be a Great Dane they were talking about. "And Les's station wagon…"

"Would have to be unloaded. He doesn't haul animals around anymore." Shelly grimaced and Sarah could see the apology about to spill over.

"No problem. Here's what we'll do. You and I ride over in my car, Les follows." Sarah turned to Will. "You guys understand I have to go. Go ahead and take Jelly. I'll bring food over later."

He was about to argue, so she added, "I'll

be in early Monday. I'll start the coffee and we can talk money then. You've been such a big help." *But you have to go now.*

She hoped he could read her attempt at polite dismissal. The temptation to take the easy way out, to let someone else handle the hard calls, would be impossible to avoid unless Will left now.

"Boss, to clarify…" Shelly held up one hand. "You want to close the shelter? Saturday's a good day for walk-in adoptions."

"There's no other option. Put up a sign that says we'll be back soon, in case anybody comes by." Sarah pulled her purse out from under her desk and slung it over her shoulder. "This dog needs us now."

Stephanie, Jen and Rebecca appeared in the doorway—when had they come back?

"Wait. I have an idea." Will propped both hands on his hips and studied the water spots on the ceiling. Whatever he was about to say, he was having a hard time believing it himself. "My truck's outside. If you have a carrier, I'll help. And Shelly can stay here, keep the shelter open while you're gone."

Jen did a double take and even Stephanie and Rebecca traded wide-eyed looks.

"Can I go, Dad?" Chloe elbowed her way into the office and folded her hands under her chin. "Please? I want to help."

Will immediately shook his head and Sarah was relieved. There was no telling what they might be walking into.

"No, you go on with Aunt Jen, take the house tours. I'll catch up with you as soon as I can." He put a hand on Chloe's head. Instead of arguing or wheedling, she glanced over her shoulder at Jen and then sighed.

Will's plan made sense. And she wanted his help. So badly. She was afraid. Even with the sheriff's deputies on hand, the situation could be dangerous. The owner might not be happy with losing his or her animal. But Sarah needed Shelly's direction, too.

Sarah wanted to stay here and celebrate her winning proposal.

But this was a part of the job.

It might even be the most important part.

And it was *her* job. Not Will's. Not Shelly's. *She* was in charge.

"The sign on the door will be fine, Will. Thanks so much for the offer. But the van needs to move up on the list of priorities, doesn't it?" She straightened her shoulders.

Everyone eased out of the office ahead of her, but Will turned back in the doorway to block her. He bent his head down. "Have you ever done this before? Won't it be dangerous?"

Instead of annoyance or even anger, Sarah could hear concern in his voice. Whatever courage she'd been building wilted under his warm regard.

But she wanted Will's respect. Doing this would prove she was serious about Paws for Love.

"Nah, the sheriff's deputy will be there and Les will have a sedative if we need to treat the dog."

Will didn't budge at her breezy tone. If he was learning to read between the lines already, she was going to have a difficult time working with him. His broad shoulders were right there, ready to be leaned on. If he didn't step away, she was going to fold.

"I've never done it before." She held a hand over her heart. "But Shelly and Les are pros. We've got it."

Competent. As if she knew what had to be done and was prepared to do it.

Will murmured, "I admire your bravery, Sarah. Please don't get yourself hurt." Before she could step closer to press her forehead against his chest, he stepped back.

Everyone had gathered at the doorway. Shelly had a sign in one hand, the paperwork they'd need in the other.

Jen smacked both hands on the counter. "First order of the board's business is to overrule this plan. You need help. Will's offering it. Take it. You two will go in his truck. Les and Shelly will follow. Chloe and I will keep the shelter open. We will reschedule the house tour for later this afternoon. Any proper candidate who comes in that door will not leave until they've picked out a dog or cat and you've filled out the forms and collected the money. I swear it."

Jen's determined nod was seconded by Chloe's crossed arms. She'd back Jen up with the force of her personality alone.

"You guard the back door. I'll get the front," Stephanie muttered to Rebecca, who elbowed her in the side.

"This is a serious situation," Rebecca said.

"You can't overrule me anytime you like. This has nothing to do with money." Sarah held the door open. "And we don't have time to waste."

"Then grab the carrier and let's go. We can iron out all the particulars later, after the dog is back here, safe and sound." Will's eyes convinced Sarah she could accept help this time.

The fact that it was Will helping again bothered her, but not as much as the idea of some poor dog needing them while she argued out of pride. "Fine." She navigated the crowd to pick up the largest carrier they had and shook her head sternly when Will tried to take it from her. "I've got it. Let's go."

Sarah and Will waited for Les to pull out ahead of them. She wasn't sure what to say. This imbalance between them was growing larger instead of stabilizing. At first, guilt had made it awkward between them, but now the overwhelming gratitude made her feel even less worthy of his help. He kept giving.

And she was taking. Again.

Her phone rang. She checked the display to see the same strange phone number. The urge to answer was powerful, but there was no way to take that call with Will listening. "Wrong number."

Maybe a text. Her fingers hovered over the keyboard but the right message escaped her.

Will didn't answer as she dropped her phone back in her purse.

"We could have handled this, but I do appreciate your help." Sarah stared out the window.

"Sure you could. You've handled everything else." Will turned off the highway onto a dirt road that grew wilder and narrower as they went.

His answer eased something inside her. Sarah felt a warm glow in her chest that didn't disappear even as Les pulled over behind two sheriff's deputies and Will braked behind him. The yard didn't inspire a lot of confidence. Trash, rusted metal, broken-down machinery littered the place and there, in the hot afternoon sun, stood a pit bull mix chained to a pole. She'd wrapped herself so tightly that her cheek was pressed against the pole with no room for movement.

And still, when they walked up, her tail was wagging.

"Collar's embedded in the skin," Les muttered. "No water. No food I can see."

The rest of them stood back with the deputies while he eased closer to run a hand over the dog's back. Her ribs were easy to see.

"Is the owner around?" Sarah asked. She wasn't sure what she'd do if the answer was yes, but she wanted to see the person who'd treated the dog this way.

"No one answers the door." The deputy motioned toward the back. "We did a check but there's no sign anyone's home."

Sarah shifted back and forth, afraid of what that meant for the dog, but Shelly pulled out her paperwork. "We'll leave a copy of the surrender form in the mailbox." Her lips were grim. "If they want their dog back, they'll come talk to us. We'll hold her for one week, waiting for the owner to make a claim, but then she's ours."

The deputy nodded. "Yes, ma'am. We'll leave a number, as well. The owners are welcome to ask for an explanation. We'll give it." He ran a hand over his face. "I hate these calls. I'd be more than content to explain to anyone why we don't treat animals like this."

Relieved that this dog's life was immediately going to get better, Sarah moved over to help Les. "The carrier's big enough. Here's the leash." She bent down next to the dirty dog, who cowered away. When Sarah didn't move, the dog's ears shifted forward and all Sarah could see was hope in her eyes.

"This day," she muttered as the tears welled over. "I cannot catch a break with this day." Stupid emotions. They were going to be the death of her.

"This is why what you're doing matters," Les murmured, and took the leash. "I'll have to remove the collar with anesthesia. It's not coming out any other way. She's had puppies, so we need to take another look, make sure we can't find more dogs." After he clipped the leash to the dog's collar, he handed her the looped end. "Let's get her out of here." His warm hand wrapped over her shoulder and Sarah's gratitude was overwhelming. Life was hard. Some people were so, so good in spite of that.

Sarah stood slowly and urged the dog away from the pole. The way the pit bull eased down on her belly to crawl across the grass was enough to break Sarah's heart in two all over again. "It's okay, girl. We'll take it easy."

By the time they'd made it to the truck, Will and everyone else was working their way through the yard, checking for more dogs. Sarah lowered the tailgate and sat while she watched the dog stare wildly around and shake.

"Scared to death. I know what that feels like." Sarah eased down to sit next to her on the ground. "You need a name." The dog lowered herself on her belly and rested her chin on Sarah's knee. "That's adorable. Keep that up, okay?" She ran her hand over the dog's head and bony back, the embedded prongs of the collar making her stomach twist. When the dog blinked up at her, Sarah whispered, "Hope. That's your name, girl."

"Fits her." Will had rested both forearms on the truck. She didn't know how long he'd been there or if she cared that he could watch her meltdown. If anything deserved a puddle of tears, this dog did.

"No more dogs?" Sarah asked, and took even breaths in case she could get control.

"No. I guess that's a good thing." Will moved around the truck and the dog immediately cowered next to Sarah. "I was going to lift her, but..." They both watched the dog try to move behind Sarah. "Think you can do it?"

She'd asked herself that question so many times.

Here, there was no other option.

And as she'd proven more than once, when there was no other option, she could totally do it.

"Open the door for me?" Sarah stood and watched the dog cower. With easy motions, she reached under Hope and lifted her, ignoring the way the muscles in her back protested, even after weeks of hard work at the shelter.

Hope was frozen in terror when Sarah managed to ease her inside the carrier, but Sarah was covered in sweat. Adrenaline, anger at the way people treated animals and her own fears had shot Sarah's blood pressure through the roof. She needed to lie down somewhere cool and quiet for hours.

"Paperwork's done, boss." Shelly and Les were on the other side of the truck. "Meet you at the shelter?"

"Yeah," Will said, "we'll meet you there." Neither of them moved as Shelly studied Sarah's face for a second and then got in Les's car. "You okay?" He wrapped both hands around her shoulders and guided her around the truck to the passenger's side. "You did it. All of it."

Where was the pride she deserved to feel?

Burned away in fear and anger, emotions she couldn't control.

Adrenaline was powerful, but she could feel the crash rolling in.

"So pale," Will murmured as he ran his hands down her arms.

Don't lean against him. Just a little bit longer and you'll be okay. You can do this.

Sarah tried to straighten her back, but Will wrapped his arms around her, pulled her against his chest and stood there, strong, silent, steady in a crazy world.

"Just for a minute. Stop." His voice next to her ear sent a shiver through her, along with a surge of restless energy.

Sarah closed her eyes, determined to enjoy every second of that minute. It had been so long since she could do this, relax and know that someone else was watching over her. His hands rubbed circles on her back that erased the tension and replaced it with something else.

"Thank you." Sarah leaned away and felt the separation like a tear. The concerned frown as he studied her face, the way he held her carefully, it was too much for her.

The kiss was unavoidable. When a woman met a prince like Will, kissing was expected.

If that woman was brave enough.

Sarah pressed her lips lightly against his, prepared for his rejection. Instead, Will sighed and pulled her closer before exploring her lips. The world disappeared. So did her exhaustion. Only Will's kiss and his hands and his solid presence mattered.

Until he stepped back. Then it was too hot and too bright and she could barely hold her head up again. His silence could mean anything, but when he helped her up to her seat and quietly closed the door he didn't seem like a man thrilled with a kiss.

Which was good. She'd done it. He hadn't felt the same desire. And now, she'd go and die somewhere and everyone would believe it was because she'd worked so hard.

Sarah shook out her tingling fingers. "Don't forget the tailgate." With her last bit of energy, she turned to watch him close the tailgate carefully, quietly.

He started the truck and navigated the bumpy road. His concentration made it easy to convince herself no conversation was needed. Will turned the air conditioner up as high as it would go, pointed all the vents in her direction and eased onto the highway. Sarah watched the pet carrier in the back, but it stayed in place. She realized the trip back to the shelter was taking at least twice as long as the trip over. Will was driving slowly.

As if he knew his cargo was important.

When he pulled into a small gas station about a mile from Paws for Love, she said, "Why are we stopping?"

"Wait here," Will muttered as he hopped out of the running truck and jogged inside.

Sarah alternated between watching Hope's carrier and the glass door. Will ran back out so quickly, a bag in hand, that she couldn't imagine what he might have accomplished.

He thrust the bag at her as he shut the truck door. "Ice-cold Coke. Good for what ails you."

Clumsy in her haste to get the bag open, Sarah almost dropped it, but by the time he pulled into the Paws for Love gravel lot, she had the can open. One long, satisfying swallow was all it took to see that Will knew exactly what he was talking about.

"Thank you." Sarah didn't turn to look at him. "I might live."

He nodded. "Think she'll be okay?"

"Yes." Hope would be better than okay. Sarah would do whatever she could to make it happen. "All she needs is some good food and love, and she's going to be fine."

Sarah had to believe that. If she didn't, why keep battling to save the shelter?

"I believe you."

Sarah glanced at Will as he parked the truck. "I don't know how this happened," he said, "but if there's one thing I know about you—aside from our history, who you were, what you want to do—it's that you'll make sure that dog is okay."

Sarah couldn't stop herself from gasping. "Why? Why would you believe that?" For so long, she'd been sure she was going to let everyone down. This man, who had every reason to know how she could fail, seemed pretty convinced she had Hope's future under control.

He shook his head. "Good question."

Will slid out of the truck and Sarah had to wonder how she felt about that answer. Given the circumstances, she respected the truth. He was still giving her the truth.

Asking about the kiss? That might be too much honesty.

By the time she made it to the back of the truck, Will had the tailgate down, the carrier open, and he'd stepped way back to allow Shelly to approach with the leash.

Sarah wanted to tell Shelly to back off. The words were on the tip of her tongue, but there was no way she was better prepared to handle this situation than Shelly.

"C'mon, girl. You're doing beautifully," Shelly murmured as Hope slid out on her stomach, her large brown eyes searching their faces anxiously. Instead of seizing her immediately, Shelly held her fingers up for Hope to sniff. When Hope's tail wagged, Shelly ran a hand over her silky ears. "You're gonna make it, aren't you, girl?"

Shelly lifted her down and the somber parade followed the dog as she took wobbly steps at first and then started to explore.

"Let's get her inside. We'll weigh her, check for heartworms, ehrlichia. Then we'll tackle that collar." Les shook his head. "This one's going to be banged up for a while, but the right person could turn her into a beauty."

Will held the door open and they all filed past. Jen had both hands propped on her hips while her shadow, Chloe, cradled Jelly. Rebecca was in the middle of the floor, both arms wrapped around Bub. "How did it go? No visitors here."

As soon as Jen stepped around the counter, Hope glanced up. Jen slid to her knees in front of the wobbly dog.

"What did they do to you?" Jen whispered, her fingers hovering over the metal prongs of the collar.

Hope inched forward on her belly until she was close enough to rest her chin on Jen's knee.

Sarah wiped her eyes and glanced around the room. At least she wasn't the only one gulping away tears.

"A weakness. Jen Neil has a soft under-belly just like the rest of us," Sarah murmured over her shoulder to Will. "And now you have something else in common. You're both owned by pets."

He shrugged. "Sure, but she's a dog person and I'm totally pro-cat."

"I'm still house hunting," Jen said softly, "but I'll have a big fenced yard." She traced delicate fingers over the white stripe down Hope's nose. The dog sighed happily. "This is my dog."

"We've got to give the owner time to protest and claim her," Shelly said, nodding firmly in response to Jen's madly shaking head. "Yes. If the owner shows up, he or she will have a chance to answer charges of neglect. Then Hope is ours. Otherwise, we wait a week, usually extra around here. And she's not going anywhere until she's been spayed." Shelly turned to Sarah. "I mean, those are the rules. Right?"

Jen opened her mouth to argue, but Sarah held up both hands in defense. "Yes, those are the rules. No one's saying you can't spend every single day here in the meantime. She's going to need some socialization." The dog sighed happily and licked her lips as Jen ran a hand over her back. "Or that's a good theory, anyway. It seems like she socializes like she falls in love. Instantly."

Will and Les shifted at the same time, and Hope immediately crawled closer to Jen, a quiet whimper punctuating her distress.

"Want to help with the tests? She's calm with you around." Les held out a hand to Jen.

"Definitely." Jen stood slowly and Hope followed behind her, head down and tail tucked between her legs.

"Rebecca, Stephanie, thank you for staying." Sarah leaned heavily against the counter. "This is kind of the way it goes with me. I ask for one thing. You say yes, and then watch out. One favor after another."

Rebecca bumped her shoulder. "Admit it. You found Jen's soul mate as the ace in the hole."

For a second, Sarah had a hard time following Rebecca's train of thought.

"No way she's saying no to any of your requests. Not now." Stephanie crossed her arms over her chest. "I wish Hope hadn't needed to be rescued, but if you wanted to convert your biggest critic, that match is foolproof."

"You guys, don't give Sarah false expectations." Will placed his hands on her shoulders and squeezed. Immediately, Sarah realized her shoulders had been up around her ears and her muscles were so tense that her neck hurt. "The thing about Jen is that she can continue to give you grief, even if she likes you."

Rebecca and Stephanie both nodded sheepishly.

"You guys want a ride home?" Will asked. "Sarah needs to…unwind."

Unbend, unwind, come apart, fall to pieces.

Something like that. But he was right. She wanted to celebrate winning the funding, and she needed to process her grief and joy over Hope's rescue and the way she and Jen had found each other. Sarah couldn't help worrying that Jen would change her mind and Hope would lose that connection.

"Ah, sure, we'll tell Jen we're leaving." Rebecca motioned over her shoulder, Stephanie hurried to join her and the two of them turned to go.

"Chloe, could you go ask Shelly for a carrier?" Will smiled down at his daughter.

"We're still taking Jelly home?" Chloe wrapped her arms around Will's waist. "Thanks, Dad." Jelly, being the confident cat that she was, yawned. She was ready for her nap. "Back in a flash. We'll need to stop and get her some toys and treats, but this is going to be so much fun."

"And more expensive than a new tablet before it's all over," Will muttered.

When they were alone again, Sarah realized Will's hands were still on her shoulders.

And she wanted to keep them there.

But he stepped back and frowned. "Uh, big day."

Sarah bit her lip and nodded, not quite sure what to say and what to never, ever admit aloud.

She'd thanked him already.

And if she explained what his steady support had meant, even though she'd blackmailed him into it, everything would get even…weirder between them.

They worked together. His sister might disown him if he lost his mind and took it any further.

But right there, in that run-down shelter, after a day of highs and lows, Sarah wanted another kiss.

Will Barnes must have been reading her mind again, because he pulled her closer. "One second. That's all." He wrapped his arms around her and Sarah closed her eyes to savor this connection.

When she would have stepped away and stuttered out an incoherent explanation for her lapse in judgment, Will covered her mouth with his. His lips were warm and Sarah got an immediate boost of energy. He kissed as if he was certain, without a doubt, that this was the right thing to do.

That was why Will was dangerous. She trusted him to do the right thing. Always.

The sound of chuckles from the exam room reminded them both that the world hadn't stopped turning.

Even if they might wish it could.

"Oh, man, Will. You missed..." Stephanie stumbled to a stop. "Well, I guess..."

She shot Rebecca an awkward look, and Rebecca chimed in with, "Hope stole the bag of dog treats while Jen was distracted."

"Her appetite and coordination are solid," Stephanie said with a grin. "Hope's. Your sister is way too slow. That dog's gonna weigh three hundred pounds if Jen doesn't get quicker."

Sarah and Will both laughed. She refused to gawk at him like some kid who'd gotten her first kiss outside the Holly Heights Country Club.

"Let's go." Will's voice was rough and Sarah nodded. "See you Monday. We'll talk money."

CHAPTER THIRTEEN

THE TENSION INSIDE his truck had easily passed could-cut-it-with-a-knife stage. Rebecca and Stephanie hadn't said a thing...yet. Maybe he'd get lucky and Chloe's presence would dampen any grief they might wish to give him.

He didn't know whether they had seen the kiss. And if they had, what would they think about it? There was no need to guess what Jen would say. Fraternizing with the enemy. Forgetting where they'd come from. Disappointing his stepmother.

"Nice weather we're having," Stephanie said from the backseat. "Lovely day to spend a fortune."

Rebecca pursed her lips. "Honestly, there hasn't been a day that wasn't perfect for that, rain or shine."

Will tightened his hands on the steering wheel and decided his contribution wasn't needed. He stopped in front of Rebecca's house.

"Thanks for the ride."

He nodded.

Neither one of the women slid out of the truck.

"Your plan worked flawlessly. Jen had no clue until we turned off." Rebecca shook her head. "Although she was driving. She should *not* operate heavy machinery on an empty stomach."

Will stared harder out the windshield.

"You did good, Will Barnes. This was what I had in mind, although I was nearly sure you wouldn't be able to pull it off." Rebecca leaned forward to get his attention. "Without Jen's approval, we all would have been heartbroken."

"Yep, all for one and one for all. That's the way it's always been, and to be honest, your sister has been the wrench in the works more than once since we met that day on the bus ride to school," Stephanie murmured. "But I always suspected she wasn't as tough as she pretends."

"Hardly anybody is." Will clenched his jaw, determined not to bring up all the ways

Sarah had proved to be different from how she'd once seemed.

"Hmm," Rebecca said. "Clever observation."

"That Sarah. She's sure surprising." Stephanie's game-show-host tone suggested she was reading a script.

Will wished he'd gotten a copy of it. He glanced back at Chloe and saw that her eyes were wide, but she had zero plans to interrupt this conversation. She wanted to know where the whole thing was going.

"Not as surprising as the guy who *kissed* her." Rebecca blinked her eyes and Will reminded himself that, while all three of them were dangerous, she might be the most dangerous, mainly because it was easy to forget how clever she was with her wide blue eyes and golden curls.

Chloe clapped both hands over her mouth, but he couldn't tell if there was anything other than surprise going on. Also, he was going to have to murder his clients.

The circus would get an extra ring if they found out it was actually their *second* kiss.

"Do we know anybody who'd be that brave? To steal a kiss from the meanest girl in town?"

Stephanie was still using her tell-him-what-he's-won voice.

Will closed his eyes. "Don't share that with Jen."

The silence was heavy until their chuckles filled it. "Right. We can't make that promise."

Stephanie held up her phone. "I was thinking of texting Jen as soon as we slide out of this truck. I mean, I'm amazed we made it this far."

"You need to figure out why you'd ask us that." Rebecca sighed. "She'll come around."

"Sarah doesn't need to come around. We work together." Will shook his head. "Don't worry. I haven't forgotten to keep my distance." Though distance had been the furthest thing from his mind during the kisses. Closer had been his focus.

"I was talking about Jen," Rebecca said. "Sarah's all on you."

She and Stephanie shared another meaningful look and Will turned to stare out the side window.

"How's business?" Rebecca asked. "Lots of new clients?"

He nodded firmly. "Next week, I want to

talk to you guys about a new investment opportunity, one with solid return-on-investment potential. Now that we're spending money."

"Okay." Rebecca nodded. "We're in. And we'll have a nice check. For you."

"Fine," Will said.

Stephanie gave Will a thumbs-up and she and Rebecca slid out of the truck. He took a deep breath.

Kissing Sarah Hillman—in full view of his clients—hadn't been his best move. He'd made Rebecca, Stephanie and Jen happy and they'd all helped a worthy cause. But right now, Will couldn't enjoy the day's successes because panic, of the what-did-I-do variety, was clanging in his brain.

"Not *what* did I do?" Will muttered as he backed out of Rebecca's driveway. "*Why* did I do it?"

Chloe rolled her eyes in a flawless impersonation of her aunt. "K-I-S-S-I-N-G."

He shot her a look, bumped against a curb and decided he'd better watch where he was going. "Sorry about that."

She sighed. "Yeah, it's weird, but you should see the way Mom and Charles kiss."

Her gag would have been cute if they'd been talking about anything else.

He'd been so careful not to drag Chloe into one relationship after another. He remembered the awful feeling of being an outsider after every single one of his father's marriages. "What do you think about Charles and the wedding?"

Chloe studied him before saying anything. Whatever the answer was, it would be a doozy. "I'm in favor. He's nice enough and I'll have a brother or sister soon. I'm ready." Then she straightened her ponytail. "But he'll never be the guy who gave me Jelly, Dad. Once you settle down, find yourself a nice girl, everything will be back on track." Will's mouth dropped open. He could hear Brenda's words in his daughter's voice.

At least she hadn't mentioned Sarah. Her reputation in Holly Heights, his job, Jen's high school resentments—all were solid reasons that the "nice girl" wouldn't be Sarah. Stopping this attraction before it got too painful to end was the only option.

As he drove home, Will was afraid that his simple solution was going to take some real work.

PRESSING HER FOREHEAD to the desk was not exactly professional.

But her relief at having the cool wood against her heated cheeks made it impossible to care.

Sarah closed her eyes and enjoyed the silence. As soon as Jen left, she'd tell Shelly and Les she needed a break, close the door, turn out the lights and unscramble her brain.

Then she'd make a to-do list for Monday.

And in ten seconds, she'd straighten up and go help with Hope.

But for nine seconds, she was going to remember the most successful meeting ever, the most satisfying rescue and the sweetest kisses in the history of kissing.

Nine seconds of celebration.

Two seconds in, her cell rang. She debated declining the call, but then she realized it was the same number her father had used to text. "Daddy, is that you?"

"Be ready, sweet Sarah. Talk soon."

That was it. Nothing more. The phone beeped and the call had ended.

Sarah put her head back down on the desk and wondered why, after all the emotion of the day, the near-certainty that the hero she'd been waiting for was guilty of stealing money from friends and neighbors only left her numb.

The crashing realization that she'd never be going back to her old life really deserved a tear.

But she'd cry tomorrow. At this point, she was all cried out.

"This is no time for a nap, princess. Les wants to wait on the collar. Says he can cut out the prongs at the same time he spays Hope. That's five days away." Jen braced both hands on the desk. "Are you okay with that?"

The jut of her chin indicated she wasn't. Jen wanted immediate action.

Sarah swiped her fingers under her eyelids to wipe away stray mascara and remembered she hadn't put any on. Facing a worn-out ghost woman didn't put any hesitation in Jen's step.

"I trust Les. He's got decades of experience." Sarah scooted back in her ragged chair. "Sorry. I know how you feel."

Jen raised an eyebrow. "About Hope? I might believe that."

"It's hard to be patient when animals are hurt. We want to do everything all at once for every animal that comes in the door." Sarah had started to learn patience. That was going to be a lifetime lesson, though. "Les makes sure we don't harm them while we try to help them, you know?"

Jen gripped the arms of her chair and exhaled noisily. "Right. Good."

"You could stay, help us get her settled in her new home." Sarah opened her soon-to-be-organized desk drawer and pulled out the file for adoption paperwork. "And if you're serious about taking Hope, you could read this. I can't let you adopt her until the waiting period is over, and you can't take her until she's been spayed. But…" Sarah shrugged. "I know you want to do something."

"You aren't going to give me grief?" Jen pinched pleats in her jeans. "You could. I deserve it. A dog was the last thing on my mind before I was tricked into driving over here today."

"The same way adopting a cat had to be the loose crumb stuck under the last thing in Will's brain." Sarah sighed. "If you're caught, you're caught. I don't know how it works, but these furry babies, they have some magic."

She tilted her head sadly. "For the right people, I guess. Not everyone feels that way."

"Some people are wrong. There's no way around that." Jen pressed her lips together and stopped there. Why? Not out of consideration for Sarah's feelings or even polite rules of behavior.

"I don't know anything about having a dog," Jen said. "But I'm about to buy a house. And I'll take a class or something. There's no reason not to give her to me."

Sarah held up both hands. "Hey, when I tumbled for Bub, I didn't have *that* much. No job. No yard." Her lips were twitching. "You have all the right stuff. Money really can buy happiness sometimes."

"But I still have to wait." Jen's eyebrows formed an ominous V. "Even with all that money to throw around."

Sarah wondered if she was going to have to call in reinforcements. Rules were rules, and the adoption guidelines applied to rich people just the same. "Yes. Every rule is in place to protect the animals. A little time and she's all yours. That's it."

Then Jen ran a hand through her hair. "Long as I get what I want, I can live with it. There's a lot to learn about being the rich jerk, you know?"

Sarah pursed her lips. "Some of us have natural skills, but I see real progress in you. You'll make it."

Jen's lip curled up. "Insulting so well that the person doesn't know whether to be mad or gratified. Another rich-guy talent. You could teach classes."

"I might need to." She couldn't put off finding a real, permanent job anymore.

Sarah pushed aside her suitcase to reach the small, cramped bookshelf. "Here. This will help."

"I'm not much of a reader." Jen held the book out at arm's length. *"Raising Puppy, The First Year."* As she glanced at Sarah, her doubts were easy to see. "Hope's not a puppy. And is this book for kids?"

"Buy another one, then. Since I decided Bub's mine, I've felt a little like you. I never had a dog, but I want to do things right. And I think unwanted chewing and peeing can last long past the puppy years." Sarah folded the adoption forms into a neat package. "Hope might have some of the same issues. Anyway, it's quick, gives you some basics. And I'll send you home with the food we use, paperwork that tells you about her next shots, any medicine. After that, all you have to do is love her." Sarah pressed both hands to the desk. "And house-train her. That's important. Make that pretty high on your priority list."

Jen turned the book over and over in her hands. "Okay. I'll read it."

Sarah nodded. "And after the hold is up, we'll fill out paperwork. And you'll write me a check."

Jen stood slowly. She held up two fingers. "Fine. But first, this doesn't make us friends. And second, leave my brother alone. He's got enough to handle right now without adding a needy, rich girlfriend to the mix."

Had Jen actually seen the kiss? Or was Sarah's guilty conscience transmitting a signal?

"Needy? Okay. I can't argue with that." Sarah waved a hand to indicate her clothing. "Rich? Not hardly." And *girlfriend* she couldn't even repeat.

"Rich is a smell that sticks with you, Horrible Hillman." Even though Jen had used the old nickname, her tone didn't have the usual sting. "And a third thing, you can't live here."

She pointed at the suitcase. "I know you need a space, but now that the funds will start again…" Jen shrugged. "You need to come up with a new solution. Surely there's a legal something or other to rule this out."

Rubbing the crease on her forehead didn't do much to ease her tension, but Sarah would do whatever she could to chase the inevitable wrinkle away. "It will be hard to give up all this luxury and space, but I'll see what I can do. Bub's ready to go home."

Jen laughed. "Sarcasm. I speak the same language."

"I'm not as fluent, but it's a beautiful dialect." Neither one of them was happy, but something had changed between her and Jen. Sarah was almost certain that whatever Jen still hated about her, at least now she could see some redeeming qualities.

That was all anyone could ask for after the world's longest day.

"Next week, I'll figure out the rest. And I'll definitely be out of here by the open house." Sarah sighed. "In case there is a legal something or other I don't know about."

"And we wouldn't want all your friends to

see how far you've fallen." The trace of sympathy was gone from Jen's face.

"Oh, don't worry. They know. You don't have to spread the word. I've already begged for every favor I could. They're about as fond of the Hillman name as you are." Sarah studied the hole in her knit shirt to avoid Jen's stare.

"Except they enjoyed the connection while they could." Jen tsked. "Then ignored you when you needed help. You were awful, don't get me wrong, but being dropped by hypocrites who'd fawn all over you while you were buying drinks is no fair. Not even for you."

Sarah tightened her lips. There wasn't much to say to that. Defending them would make her seem out of touch. Weak. And agreeing... Well, she might still seem out of touch and weak but for a slightly different reason.

In the beginning, she honestly hadn't understood the rejections. Now she got it.

"This time around, I'm going to make a better class of friend. Even if they can't write me a big check, they can help me when I need some support. That's the kind of friend I want." The sting of tears for the horrifying millionth time that day was too much.

Jen nodded, although her eyebrows were a disapproving line. "Absolutely. Of course you do." She didn't say, "Duh, you idiot," but it was close enough that Sarah had to chuckle.

"Go see Hope. And know that if you come back tomorrow, you'll be scooping poop. It's inevitable." A sudden bolt of inspiration had Sarah straightening in her chair. "Bring in some volunteers, students who need… volunteer hours or extra credit or college recommendation letters or…something, but if we have more volunteers, everyone's job gets easier. More time to cuddle Hope, see?"

Jen grunted. "School hasn't started yet, genius." She shoved her hands in her pockets. "My last summer-school class is this week." Then the frown disappeared. "But I see where you're going with this. Clever." She shrugged. "And I'll be back to do whatever I can. Make sure we get an invitation to the open house. You've never seen anyone work a room of donors like Rebecca and Stephanie. Seriously. In the middle of a glitzy ballroom, I watched the head of Austin's biggest tech firm empty all the change out of his fancy suit pockets because he was concerned the four-zeros check he wrote for Healthy-

Americas wasn't big enough." Jen shook her head at that and left Sarah's office.

After that, Sarah didn't care who was still here, who needed her, what crisis was coming. As soon as she found Bub, she led him back to the office and closed the door. Sarah sat with her sixty-pound dog sprawled across her lap, shut her eyes and pressed her nose into his neck.

CHAPTER FOURTEEN

HALF AN HOUR late and rattled over the changes his new cat had made to the morning routine, Will struggled to find the right words to apologize for the delay. Sarah was outside the office in her usual spot, and the effects of the emotional Saturday had been erased by cool clothes, a smooth updo and bright red lipstick.

Sarah did not look like a person who'd spent entirely too much time thinking about a kiss that should never have been.

Since she'd started the whole thing, that seemed unfair.

After he'd unlocked the door and held it open for Chloe to march through, Sarah said, "Let me take this...castle?"

But he was too slow to stop her from struggling to fit the monstrosity through the doorway. Will shook his head. "I should have handed you the cat instead."

"I can't believe you brought Jelly in after your look of horror when I invaded with Bub." Sarah dumped the castle on the lobby rug and reached to take Jelly's carrier.

"You should have warned me I'd completely lose my mind if I adopted a cat. Chloe was worried about leaving her home alone and that made me worry, so we're going to give this a try." Will motioned at Jelly's carrier on the empty receptionist's desk. "As much as I've already invested in the finest food and toys, I'm afraid someone will break in to steal my luxury cat."

Chloe was already clicking away on the keyboard, so he pulled his cell phone out and slid it across to her. "Sarah needs to work, Chloe."

His daughter studied his phone, and for half a second it looked as if she was going to make some comment about how all teenagers deserved their own phones, especially if they didn't have tablets.

She'd come up with that one on Sunday evening. After he'd explained that just-turned-twelve was not a teenager and that saying something dramatically didn't make it true, she'd resumed brushing Jelly.

He was still convinced that wasn't the end of the conversation.

"I'm going to check on Brenda," Chloe said. "See what the tip jar looks like."

Will nodded and held the door open for her, then watched her skip down the sidewalk to the diner. "Guess I'll have to add 'must like cats' to my help-wanted ad."

But Sarah was already gone. He could hear the unmistakable and welcome sounds of coffee being made.

Get to work, Barnes. Burning daylight here.

Sarah didn't say two words to him as she bustled into his office to slide a cup across his desk and walked right back out. Jelly? Oh, Jelly had gotten quite a cheerful one-sided conversation before she'd drifted into his office and hopped up on his desk.

He knew because he was listening intently, hoping to be prepared for...whatever conversation Sarah might want to have.

Listening had turned to brooding, one hand scratching his cat behind the ears while he studied his inbox. "Lots to do today, Jelly." And he needed both hands to do it. Will shifted the cat castle closer to his desk and set Jelly inside the highest turret.

Head in the game.

Two clients wanted to increase their retirement investments, three of the doctors he'd met last week had asked for one-on-one consultations and Doug Grant was ready to discuss the boilerplate contract.

Apparently, Cece had dropped her demands or her husband was prepared to move forward, anyway.

Business was picking up.

And the résumés were coming in. He had four from the newspaper ads and the employment agency had emailed two promising candidates.

The days of carefully navigating his relationship with Sarah were coming to a close.

At least, here in his office.

"And that's a good thing." Jelly's gentle meow made it seem as if she agreed. "Although we'll still have to weed out the noncat lovers."

Otherwise, his next secretary would quit because he talked to Jelly as if she would answer back.

Only animal people would get that.

"It would be nice if every animal hater

came with a warning." Sarah leaned against the door frame.

Will sipped his coffee. "Well, some people would be mistaken about not liking pets. They just haven't found the right one to fall in love with yet." Love. Had he lost every single brain cell over the weekend? "I bet you'd like some money."

"Well, I wouldn't say no, that's for sure." Sarah sat down across from him. "I've already scheduled the fence guy and the roofing company. Both are certain they'll finish before the open house."

Will nodded as he opened the locked drawer where he was storing the check signed by Rebecca.

"Should I have waited until after the open house?" Sarah shifted in her seat. "People might understand how much help the shelter needs with the leaky roof and falling-down fence."

Will tapped his finger on the check.

"Seems like…" He weighed the options. "Having donors already on board—people who are committed to the continued success of Paws for Love—will make it easier to find more donations." He shrugged. "I honestly don't know. I've never been the charitable sort. With my money, for sure."

"You've been generous with me." Sarah nodded once. "But you might be right. Besides, I couldn't wait. I want the best for those animals."

They both nodded and definitely did not look at each other.

"Shelly and I are going to get the battery replaced in the van tomorrow. With Les's help. Today I'm getting the ball rolling for the open house, so I'll leave around noon." Sarah clasped both hands over her knee. "And I think…"

"At this point, you need to concentrate on the shelter instead of staring at the phone." She did. That was a relief and a disappointment at the same time. He reached back into the locked drawer and pulled out his own ledger to cut her a check for her hours at the front desk. "I've gotten a couple good candidates to interview. I won't be running the place by myself for long."

He ripped the check from the ledger and slid both of the checks across the desk, one with Sarah's name on it and the other made out to Paws for Love. "I appreciate your help."

"I wish I could do the right thing here and

turn down your check. You and I both know you were a bigger help to me than I was to you." Sarah tapped the check against her hand. "But I can't. Your sister, acting board of director–ish, informed me that I have to come up with a living arrangement fast. Camping out in the office doesn't send the right message." Then she wrinkled her nose. "Find a place. Find more money for Bub's adoption fee. Budgets are complicated."

Will met her stare. "They are. Stay here for the second week, like we talked about."

"As long as I can keep my lips to myself?" Sarah asked.

An impossible question to answer. The right response? Say yes. Laugh about it. Move on.

Take the easy way out.

He couldn't do it.

This time, Sarah was strong enough to do the right thing for them both.

"It's time to come up with a plan, something that can get me through more than just a week. I've been fooling myself that someday… Well, it's hard to let go of my old life, but I need to face the truth."

Had her father contacted her? Told her he wasn't coming back?

Or had she really believed he was innocent all along? Until now.

She shouldn't have to deal with a burden like that alone, but he had to let her make her own decisions.

Right?

Sarah nodded sharply as she stood. "If you hear of any cheap housing that loves big brown dogs, could you let me know? That may be the biggest challenge of my life."

Will didn't answer and he didn't step back outside his office until he heard Sarah call goodbye.

Then he picked up the phone, scheduled four interviews for the next day and wrote up three investment options for Rebecca, Stephanie and Jen. Right now he had plenty of work.

He also had a cat. His daughter was happily bussing tables at the diner. And tensions were easing between him and Jen. That was enough to concentrate on at the moment.

ALTHOUGH AN IRRITATED curse rattled around in her head, Sarah didn't make any sound when she parked the shelter's van next to the roofing company's work truck. Of course Jen was already here, waiting on her. She wanted to see Hope. The ominously tapping cowboy boot suggested she might have a secondary motive, as well.

"Sorry to keep you from visiting Hope. She's doing pretty well. We let her out in the play yard this morning. At first, she was timid, but Shelly said by the end of the hour, she'd loosened up. That's a good sign."

Sarah shoved the key into the lock and opened the front door to the shelter. "Our normal afternoon hours are three to six, but I'm late because the repairs on the van took a bit longer. Still, I'm happy to cross one thing off the to-do list. Next up, figure out the invitations, order them and then decide how to make peanut butter cookies in Shelly's oven. That should take care of Wednesday and Thursday or the rest of my life."

Her chatter was out of control. Jen's single raised eyebrow communicated, "Are you done?" louder than the actual words would have.

"Yes, I'll stop now." Sarah checked for any phone messages. No blinking light equaled no escape from this awkward conversation. "If you want to take Hope outside, I'll wait fifteen minutes or so to let the first group of dogs out. That might give her time to get comfortable." And when the second yard opened up, things would be so much easier. All the dogs would have more time running free. They could even open up more pens.

But Jen knew that. It had all been a part of the shaky presentation.

"Got you a volunteer. His name's Desi. He'll be here on Saturday. Needs volunteer hours for his college application." Jen walked behind the counter. "You're welcome."

Sarah wrote a note that no one would be able to read. "That's great news."

"And keep your lips off my brother." Jen's disgust was clear. It would have been sort of cute except Sarah knew she meant every word.

Sarah hung the van keys on the inside of the counter door and closed it. "A new place to live is on my list. His place is not. You don't have to worry."

"I'm *not* worried. He's smart. Don't tell him I said that." Jen rolled her eyes. "And you're not dumb and horrible, but that doesn't mean I want to sit next to you at dinner."

"Good to know." Sarah saluted her and

waved to Shelly and Les, who had followed her from the repair shop. "All right. Open house, you will be mine."

Eventually, Jen left. Shelly and Les closed the place down, cleaning pens and feeding the animals after the walk-in hours were up, and Sarah vaguely remembered calling goodbye to them before the lights outside her office went out.

Bub's snores were comforting background noise as she worked out the wording for the open house's invitation. She reviewed her list of donor contacts—the people who'd been solid supporters for Paws for Love before the shelter manager disappeared—and her own former friends.

"As soon as the invitations are printed, we're set." Sarah sighed as she crossed her legs. "Less than two weeks. I'll go to the printer tomorrow, get these in the mail Saturday and then…" Sarah closed her eyes. For every single item she crossed off the list, two more replaced it. But she was on track to make up lots of ground.

If she could keep up the pace.

"Peanut butter. I missed my dinner, Bub." At the word *dinner*, her companion flowed off the couch to stretch his front legs and his back while his mouth yawned wide enough for her to count every single pearly white tooth. "You could go for some dinner, huh?"

He walked over to the door, his tail lazily wagging as if he didn't have anywhere to be but he'd wait right there for her.

"So patient with me." She ran her hand over Bub's head and fought with the office door until it opened. "Handyman. Moving right up the list."

After making her sandwich and giving Bub the treat he deserved for being her late-night comfort, Sarah took a quiet turn through the cat room and the dog pens, where not a creature was stirring. Not even Hope, the nervous pit bull. Instead, she was rolled up into an impossibly small ball, the tip of her tail twitching as she dreamed.

Sarah rested her forehead against the glass pane in the door to the play yard. Now that she could worry about work instead of money, it was hard to sit still. Sleeping hadn't gotten much easier, either.

"Could be because you're such a couch hog." Bub settled more securely on top of her bare foot.

If she was going to find a place to stay by the open house, she had to do something quickly. With Will's check and the last of her consignment money, she could get a small place. Her measly stipend wouldn't be enough for rent, so she'd have to get a job, a real one, with a boss who'd expect her to work set hours doing...something.

Which meant she'd have to step back from the shelter.

She glanced over her shoulder at Hope.

A job would mean she'd miss out on so much.

Experience answering a phone and years of volunteer "work" were what she had to recommend her.

In a town where her last name was mud.

Homelessness was a true, scary possibility.

Angry that she'd given up before she'd even started, Sarah grimaced at her pale re-flection. She could give it a shot at least. As a waitress, she might have shifts that would leave her free to work at the shelter in the mornings.

Or retail. That could be a better choice. Her lousy handwriting and her family name might make waiting tables a high-conflict, low-tip proposition.

If she'd learned one thing while finding donors for Paws for Love, it was that she couldn't be afraid. She needed a job. She'd do whatever it took to find one.

And if she was lucky, she'd find someone as open-minded and generous as Will Barnes to help her along the way.

Bub slumped against her leg, clearly in need of his beauty rest, so Sarah decided she could spend another hour staring up at the ceiling.

When Bub was settled comfortably on the couch and she was contorted around him, Sarah said, "Tomorrow, we're going computer shopping, too. Then I can make this insomnia work."

As her eyelids were growing heavy, lights reflected across the ceiling.

Bub raised his head, both ears forward.

This time, there was no convincing herself she was imagining things. Someone was in the parking lot. In the middle of the night.

Sarah stretched to grab her phone off the floor. Who could she call? The sheriff's office would respond, but how ridiculous would she feel if it was some delivery driver or high school kid turning around?

She eased up and listened as hard as she could for doors opening or any other noises.

Half a second before Sarah pressed the emergency button on her phone, she wondered again who would want to break into the shelter.

Unless it was Hope's owner.

Could someone be mad enough about losing his or her dog to break in and take Hope back?

But the first time she'd seen the lights had been before Hope's rescue.

Sarah stood slowly and walked over to the shelter's front door. With her ear pressed against it, she thought she might hear an engine running, but nothing else.

After an eternal minute, she eased back from the door. Being afraid had never gotten her anything but bad decisions and enemies. Sarah stepped over to the window and shifted the blinds.

The parking lot was empty.

Her heart pounding with adrenaline and fear and relief, Sarah double-checked the locks before she went to sit down next to Bub.

When he climbed into her lap, Sarah realized she was *his* guard dog. And that was fine.

"It's nothing. Maybe I imagined the whole thing. Fatigue will do that." Sarah forced herself to put the phone down.

No matter what, she had to find a place soon. Being surrounded by people would make it harder to panic over every single passing car.

Instead of falling asleep, she reorganized her to-do list. Stopping in to see Will rose to the top.

Checking what brand and model of computer he had made perfect sense.

And if she managed to work the late-night visitor into the conversation to hear his thoughts… Five minutes, tops. There was no reason to feel guilty about a drop-in visit when it was that short.

Even if she'd meant to keep her distance.

Why his opinion was the first one she wanted regarding either electronics or potential problems…

That wasn't quite as simple.

"Yes, Doug, I got the signed contract. Everything looks great." Will clicked on his email as a reminder popped up. His first interview should be arriving shortly. "I've already set up your account with the mix of short-term and long-term targets. I usually send monthly updates, but I'm going to send you a link with a username and password so you and Cece can check your balances anytime you like. And I'm always here for questions. We'll reevaluate in six months unless something changes."

"Thanks for all your help," Doug said. "This thing with Sarah Hillman, I'm glad it's resolved. Cece can move on to something else now." Doug Grant cleared his throat. "Old grudges are the worst, but I know firing's never easy."

Will rubbed one eyebrow to smooth away his frown. This again. He should let it go. What difference did it make what Cece, her husband or the rest of Holly Heights believed about Sarah's temporary assignment? None. He'd do a good job and eventually people would forget.

But Sarah was still dealing with the stares and whispers.

This was one bit of gossip he could try to set straight, even if he knew it was a waste of breath.

"Sarah was only helping short-term. She's pretty busy at the shelter, and I've got some interviews today with experienced assistants. It was temporary for us both, and actually, I'm sorry she couldn't work this week, too."

Will missed Sarah's coffee, and more than that, he missed her sunny morning greeting.

He needed to stop thinking about Sarah and focus on the job.

Just as he had before Sarah Hillman came back into his life.

But even Jelly had had trouble keeping up her end of the conversation. Chloe had skipped her two-hour battle with wizards to head directly to the diner. Either he was boring her, or his mood was so dark it infiltrated headphones and role-playing games. He should straighten it out before he hired an assistant who had to read his mind.

He was half a second from taking his grim mood out on poor Doug Grant, a man who already had to live with Cece.

"Sure, sure," Doug said. "I understand the official line."

"How did you know she's not working in the office anymore?"

"She stopped at the Shop-on-in to ask Cece's

mom if she was hiring part-time help." Doug whistled. "Brave. Or crazy."

Will frowned as he wondered why it had never occurred to him that Sarah would be making the rounds, talking to the same people he'd been trying to secure as clients. Somehow, even with all the changes he'd accepted in Sarah Hillman, he'd never quite adjusted to the fact that she wasn't rolling in cash anymore.

"Flexible hours would be good for her. She'd have plenty of time to keep up the work she's doing at Paws for Love."

"Right, but Cece's mother will die there, behind the counter at the Shop-on-in. Not sure who's hiring now." And the distraction in Doug's voice suggested he didn't really care, either. "You don't sound like a man talking about a temp, Barnes. Maybe instead of gossiping about Sarah's work life, Cece should have been focused on her personal life. You two have a thing? That makes a whole lot more sense than hiring a criminal out of the goodness of your heart."

An immediate surge of anger at Doug Grant's sleazy insinuation made Will's head throb. Counting to ten to regain his equilibrium would have been a good idea.

Will had no time for that.

"Let's get a few things straight, Doug," Will snapped. "Sarah Hillman is no criminal. This town has tried and convicted Bobby Hillman, but Sarah didn't run. She's still here, doing her best to save some animals and help this town while she ignores insults like yours. Instead of building all these conspiracy theories, maybe take a look at how her friends, the good people of Holly Heights, are treating her and ask yourself if it's fair."

He'd done his best to charm Cece into forgetting that she'd demanded he fire Sarah, but he wasn't going to back down on gossip like this.

Sarah worked hard. She deserved respect.

Was he ready to lose a client to stand up for her?

"Come on, Barnes. Sarah Hillman's no angel. Never has been. Just be glad you're done with her. You'll see. Once the buzzing at the club stops, your business will benefit." Grant lowered his voice to add, "And if you aren't exactly done with her, keep it hush-hush."

Slamming the phone down would be so satisfying, but anger made it hard to think. Defending his honor and Sarah's could lose not just the Grants as clients but the rest of the sharks they traveled with.

The blessed door chime gave Will the perfect excuse to get off the phone. "Check out all the information on the website and let me know if you have any questions."

"Will do." Doug wasn't happy with their conversation, either.

Before Will could respond, he heard the dial tone.

Will carefully hung up, his hand shaking. He should have told Doug Grant where to go and asked him to take his two-faced wife and all their money with him.

The Grants would not make or break Barnes Financial. If the business failed in Holly Heights, he'd move to Austin.

Why had he hesitated?

Why was gossip he would have secretly enjoyed—before he'd worked with Sarah—making him so angry?

Success mattered.

But so did Sarah.

He was still shaking his head as he paused

in the doorway. Sarah was studying the computer on the front desk. Her hair was neatly rolled up in a bun and she was wearing the nice suit he'd realized was her only business attire. "Did you forget? You don't work here anymore."

Nice. It's always good to start a conversation as if you're a jerk with no social skills.

"I meant to say good morning." *And why did you quit if you still need the work? How can I help? Do you know what people are saying about you? How can you stand to live here?*

Sarah was smiling as she straightened. "I wanted to make a note of the kind of computer you have. Today's the day I choose one for the shelter and I'm not sure where to begin."

She pulled a list out of her purse. "I need to post an ad for the manager position, get some résumés for the board to review. Then I'm on my way to pick up invitations for the open house, along with the new donation boxes. Shelly took some great photos so the graphic artist will have lots of cute faces to work with." She smoothed a stray hair behind her ear. "And I'm boring you."

She studied his face. He had a feeling his expression was not boredom. Seething anger would probably show in the set of his jaw.

Time to get a grip.

Will crossed his arms over his chest. "I thought you were my first interview of the day." He checked his watch. "Fifteen minutes. I expected her to be here by now."

"Is she late because she's not early?" Sarah's lips quirked up.

"Well, my last assistant beat me to work every day." He held both hands out. "I have high expectations."

Sarah blinked and he wondered if she realized he was referring to her.

"Got a job interview yourself?" He watched her shift from side to side. The heels were nice, but he'd gotten used to seeing her in jeans and dog hair.

"Making the rounds. I'm not qualified for the suit jobs, but it's the only other option." She tapped her pen on the note she'd made. "Jen will expect some progress, so I better see what I can do."

Sarah would work hard at whatever job she landed. She deserved a shot at the one she wanted.

Will nodded. "After you get your computer you could draft a résumé and throw your hat in the ring—apply to become the new manager of the shelter."

"What about business experience? I don't have it." She held up her hand to tick off points. "Previous shelter work, professional grant writing or organized fund-raising experience. Nope. And if the board was going to make allowances for any candidates, I would be at the bottom of a lengthy list." Her jaw tensed. "It's the same list I'll face for every job in Holly Heights, but someone will hire me. Maybe I'll threaten them with my howling dog. I *know* that works."

"Maybe you should try somewhere else, a town closer to Austin." Will leaned against the desk. That would be best for her, breathing room from this town and her former friends.

"If I have to, I will." She waved her note. "But I realized last night, in the middle of the night, that Paws for Love has made all the difference in my life. Fighting for it proved to me that I can do hard things. And even if I have to face off against petty thieves or angry owners, I will. Those animals depend on me. I'll find a job here because I can't lose the thing that's going to make me who I want to be."

In the early-morning sunlight, she was fierce and determined.

And so beautiful it was nearly impossible not to step closer, to pull her nearer.

This was what had been missing from his day.

Then he noticed the dark shadows under her eyes and her words clicked. "Thieves? Angry owners? Did someone try to break in last night? Why didn't you call me?"

She opened her mouth and then closed it as if she was changing her mind about what she wanted to say.

"Maybe someone tried. Or I'm crazy. There was a car in the parking lot. I couldn't sleep, making lists in my head and trying to ignore Bub's snoring and the way his feet press into my calves." She waved her hand. "Never mind about that. I don't think anyone got out of the car. By the time I got brave enough to check, the parking lot was empty."

Will wasn't sure what he planned to say but the door opened and a professionally dressed, petite woman stepped in. She was startled to be walking into a conversation, so she glanced over her shoulder as if she intended to wait on the sidewalk.

"You must be Alice. I'm Will Barnes. If you'll go on into my office and have a seat, I'll be right there." He and Sarah stood there, hands clasped awkwardly in front of them, until the woman disappeared inside his office.

He turned back to Sarah, but a violent sneeze coming from his office caused him to pause.

Sarah wrinkled her nose. "Do you have more interviews scheduled today?"

Alice's second sneeze followed a minute later. Unless she wanted to invest in allergy medication and a lot of it, she wasn't the right match.

The urge to make a funny face just to hear Sarah laugh was hard to fight. They both needed a laugh.

"Yeah. But listen," Will said as he walked over to hold the door for Sarah, "if you see lights in the parking lot, don't wait. Call the sheriff. And if you won't do that, call me. I'm close." Or Les or Shelly. He should definitely add them to the list of options, but he didn't. "And don't open the door."

"I appreciate the concern." She smoothed the wrinkles out of his tie and he couldn't keep his eyes off her hand. This time, she wasn't trying to distract him. She wanted to touch him. He understood the urge even as he glanced through the window to make sure no one was watching. "And I'll call you if it happens again." Sarah stepped out into the sunshine. "Good luck with the interviews."

She waved and let the door close. Will scrubbed his hands over his face.

Sarah didn't need him to ride to the rescue late at night. The police could do that. She didn't *really* need advice on the right computer or the right job. So why was he giving it?

Because she'd asked.

This time, instead of taking over or interceding, he'd answered.

Almost as if they were friends.

Or more than friends.

Except one of them was a brave woman doing her best in a difficult situation and the other was dodging gossip like a coward.

Was he falling for Horrible Hillman?

At this point, could he stop the fall?

The violent sneeze from his office was a

welcome prod. If he didn't get through his first interview quickly, Alice's eyes would be swollen shut before she made it out of there. At least it wouldn't take long. If she was no friend of Jelly's, she was not the right person for the job.

CHAPTER FIFTEEN

"THOUGHT I MIGHT catch you here," Luke Hollister said with a wink. He was leaning against the brick wall under the awning of the business next door. "I was going to check in with Will Barnes, make sure you weren't a chip off the old block."

It had been a while, but Sarah pulled off a credible sneer. Sometimes being a mean girl was a good thing. Even though Hollister couldn't touch her—she hadn't done anything wrong—he never tired of the threats. She surveyed the deserted sidewalk. "Hollister."

He towered over her, but the ice in her stare was effective. "I stopped in to get some advice from Will. I don't work for him anymore. Now that I've raised funding for Paws for Love, I'm full-speed ahead on getting the shelter back up and running." She quirked one corner of her lips. "If you have a donation, I'll happily write you a receipt."

For some reason, she was fearless in pressing for money. Should she come back on Saturday with a folding chair and a donation box?

Or…an adorable dog available for adoption. She studied the businesses on either side of the street to try to assess weekend traffic. Monthly pet adoption days in the right place could do a lot to increase adoptions and drive traffic to the shelter.

Her lack of attention didn't sit well with Hollister. His ugly frown indicated he'd said something she missed. "You were saying…"

This was her cue to cross her arms and tap one perfectly manicured fingernail on her fine suit sleeve.

But her manicure was long gone. Tapping her finger would only call attention to that fact.

"Heard anything from your father lately?" Hollister pulled a card out of his wallet.

Sarah snatched it from his fingers and balled it up. "Harassing me at my condo, then the place I'm working, now in the middle of the sidewalk. I guess it's not much of a stretch to lurk outside the shelter in the middle of the night, is it?" If it was him with the headlights, she could be twice as angry the next time it happened and half as afraid.

"Middle of the night? Don't get ahead of yourself, princess. I drove down from Austin this morning." He jangled the change in one pocket. "Got a lot of traffic out there?"

As much as she hated Hollister, she believed he was telling the truth. What if her father was closer than she thought?

"Not enough to concern you." Sarah dropped his card on the sidewalk. Panicking in front of the detective would be terrible.

"Finding your daddy is at the top of my to-do list." Hollister pointed at her. "You hear from him, you call." He took two slow steps back toward his car and Sarah had a split second to decide what she was going to do with the wrong number.

It seemed as if the police were the only ones who could bring her father back.

If she believed Bobby Hillman was innocent, she might try for patience.

But her certainty had faded along with the idea that leaving Holly Heights would be worth any trouble, even hiding from the police with her father. Right now, all she wanted was to know her father was all right. She needed some breathing room from Hollister and the people of Holly Heights.

So she pulled out her cell. "I have had a couple of wrong numbers. No message. It's a number I don't recognize." She rattled off the phone number and tried to gauge Hollister's reaction. Did he already have the information because he was monitoring her phone or was he surprised at her cooperation? No expression showed on his face. "You're welcome." He was still watching her when she sighed and marched away.

Fatigue weighed her down immediately. None of her problems had solutions. Hollister wouldn't go away until he found her father. No one in town would hire her until Hollister found her father. Probably. Maybe.

"Do what you can right now. Put the rest away until later." Sarah rolled her shoulders. Giving up was impossible. "Attractive, but impossible."

And Brenda Barnes was staring at her through the diner window. Of course.

Sue Lynn's was on her list of possible employers, so her dilemma was even tougher.

"You can do this." Sarah smoothed the loose hank of hair behind her ear and walked quickly to the door.

The cheerful jangle of bells ratcheted her nerves up a notch.

"Table, booth or counter." Brenda's expressionless face spoke loud and clear.

"None. I was, uh, hoping..." Sarah turned slowly to see the place was nearly empty. "Is Sue Lynn around?"

Brenda slapped the menus she was holding onto the hostess station. "Nope. Could I take a message?"

"I could wait?" The question in her voice irritated Sarah. She wanted to be confident.

"Table, booth or counter?" Brenda asked slowly.

"Counter. Could I get some coffee, please?" She almost asked for a glass of water. That would be less expensive than coffee, but it would also be pretty transparent. She *was* too broke to buy a real meal. Coffee was a compromise.

Without a word, Brenda put a cup and saucer in front of her and poured. Then she slid the creamer and sugar closer. Marching as far away as she could get, she picked up her dish towel and started to scrub the shiny counter.

Sarah sipped her coffee and wondered what family dinners between Jen and Brenda must be like. Were all the meat loaves shaped like her head with a bloody ooze of ketchup for effect?

Her stomach growled in response and Sarah did a quick tally of how long it had been since she'd had actual meat of any shape, form or fashion. Then she remembered the hamburger Les had brought. It had been lost in the excitement of a big day.

Vegetarian by accident. How sad.

"Can I get you some eggs?" Brenda held her notepad in front of her like a shield.

"Not unless you have a get-one-free, get-one-free special today." Sarah rolled her eyes. "Not in the budget."

Brenda whistled loud and long. "A Hillman. Using that word. And not like a curse. All the years I served your father his two eggs, sunny-side up, he was a big spender. Terrible tipper, though." Brenda nodded. "Everybody knows you can tell a lot about a person by the tip he leaves."

"It's pretty easy to pinch pennies when you have no other choice." Sarah pulled out her wallet. "I should have checked to make sure I have coffee money before I even ordered that."

Having to borrow money from Will to pay her tab to his stepmother would be a serious embarrassment. Sarah had no doubt he'd loan her the cash, which said a lot about his generosity.

Or her lack of shame where he was involved.

One or the other.

"But I have it. Not to worry." Brenda had turned away to put an order in the window. Clearly, she wasn't worried. At all. Sending the sheriff after Sarah if she decided to drink and dash would be the easiest thing in the world.

When Brenda turned around with eggs and toast and slid the plate in front of her, Sarah raised both hands. "I don't have that much cash."

"It's on me." Brenda leaned a hip against the counter and waited. As if this was a test and she was curious to see whether Sarah would pass.

She reluctantly picked up a fork and scooped up the first bite.

Then all bets were off.

When Brenda raised her eyebrows at how quickly she was eating, Sarah decided to concentrate on the food. Any judgment Brenda might make would dim the joy.

Her stomach grumbled happily when she finally set her fork down on the empty plate. "So good. Real food. Someday, that's all I'm going to eat. No peanut butter. Ever."

"Good plan." Brenda swiped the plate and dumped it under the counter. "Don't want you to scrape all the white off the china."

Since absolutely nothing could be as embarrassing as burying her face in scrambled eggs like Bub with his dog food, Sarah asked, "Is Sue Lynn hiring? I need a part-time job."

"Seriously? It's like that?" Brenda's doubt was loud and clear.

"Yeah. It's like that. I've sold everything I can and now I've got to find rent money fast." Sarah sighed. "Not a lot of opportunity for a girl with an art degree and no practical experience outside working for the most hated man in town."

Brenda twisted the towel in both hands. "You should have heard the way Jenny talked about that dog, the shelter, everything she was going to do to make sure it runs like clockwork."

Sarah didn't know what to say to the change in subject. Her relief that Jen had been impressed with Paws for Love was a nice boost.

"And the houses she's looking at? She's lost sight of the number of bathrooms in the quest for a safe, fenced yard." Brenda chuckled. "Dog crazy. She always had a touch of it. Sort of makes me wonder how many dogs she'll end up with, you know? Then there's Will, covered in cat hair. You must be some kind of magician, coaxing out these hidden dreams people have forgotten they had."

"I hope so. There are so many animals in this world that deserve to find their people." Sarah tipped her chin up. "I'll come back in an hour." That should be long enough to get to the printer and back, even with a stop or two to ask about any job openings.

Brenda reached under the counter. "The only time there's a rush is lunch hour, and few people want to work three or four hours a day, right in the middle. Sue Lynn and I usually end up splitting the shifts, but..." She slid an application across the counter. "Go ahead, fill this out. I'll make sure she gets it."

Sarah sat down and concentrated so hard on legible writing that she could feel the crease forming between her eyebrows.

"Don't try to set the thing on fire with your mind." Brenda poured her another cup of coffee. "Put down the years you went to school. All that creative work experience won't fool Sue Lynn."

Instead of explaining that she was only trying to do her best, Sarah nodded and added a note across the section for previous work experience. A shift from eleven to three would be perfect, and if Brenda was right, that might be exactly what Sue Lynn needed.

"Thanks for the help, Brenda." She slid the application back across the counter and watched Brenda pick it up.

"I haven't done anything. Not really." Brenda pursed her lips and then shook her head. "But I've been preaching second chances to Jen for long enough that I have to take some of my own advice. She and her stepbrother are making good on this do-over. You could, too."

"Next meal's on me, Brenda. It's the least I can do." Sarah picked up her phone and walked slowly out of the diner. Then she realized it wasn't all she could do.

She stuck her head back in and Brenda turned away from the office door.

"Thank you. For the meal, the application, listening to what I had to say." Sarah bit her lip. "I'm sorry I wasn't better to Jen and Will when I was a kid, but you should know that they're both pretty awesome." Sarah waved awkwardly. "That's it. You should be proud of the people they've become. Generous. Smart…" Then, before Brenda could say a thing, she turned on her heel and made a quick getaway. All the emotions that had been blindsiding her lately were so annoying. For years, she'd shown people what they expected to see. Now her ooey-gooey center was oozing through the cracks in her armor.

If her father had somehow appeared right in front of her on the sidewalk, she'd give him a piece of her mind. All this mess he'd left behind, and still the good people of Holly

Heights were picking her up. They deserved better from him. They always had.

If she ever had a chance, she'd return all this kindness to the people of Holly Heights. First, she had to put a roof over her head.

CHAPTER SIXTEEN

SARAH WAS ALREADY five minutes late for her third shift at Sue Lynn's when she locked the front door of Paws for Love. "Starting a new job four days before the open house that will change everything? Worst planning ever." She immediately dropped her key ring and cursed under her breath as she searched for it in the predawn light. "My regular shift will be better. Lunch will be better. Lunch will be better." She'd been repeating that for days, ever since she'd bungled her way through her first breakfast shift with Brenda.

Something shifted under her new, cheap running shoe, making her curse again.

"What is…" She bent down to snatch up her keys and then tried to tug the envelope out from under her foot. It finally slipped free and Sarah ran to the car, tossed everything inside and sped through the deserted streets to make up two of her five minutes.

"Sorry I'm late," she said as Brenda let her into the brightly lit diner. "Car trouble." Little white lies had always been her first line of defense. When Brenda made the "continue" hand motion, waiting for the truth, Sarah sighed. "My car can't break the sound barrier yet, so it was entirely too slow to make up the five minutes I was late before I left the shelter."

Brenda handed her a tub of silverware. "Wrap quickly."

Sarah saluted and got started. Focusing on work made it easier to ignore the worry that she'd been working day and night to throw a party that might not bring in a single donor.

By the time she'd finished mailing out invitations, she might as well have sent one to every house in Holly Heights.

"Ready?" Brenda was standing by the door, her hand resting on the lock. From her spot at the counter, Sarah could see the line of regulars on the sidewalk. If she'd ever wondered how Sue Lynn stayed in business, now she knew that "regular" meant…regular, like every single day, breakfast or lunch. This was her last morning training shift, but Sarah could already name the usual orders for almost every person who'd come in that morning.

Luckily, that made it easier for everyone to decipher her writing.

Sarah set the tray of wrapped silverware under the hostess station and nodded. "Ready as I'll ever be."

If someone had told her at sixteen that she'd be wearing discount store shoes and worrying about losing a job waiting tables, she would have destroyed them. Or her father would have, because she would've cried to her daddy.

There were brief moments she wished she could still do that. They were mixed up with flashes of pride that she was pulling it off. All of it. Saving the shelter, getting a job, keeping the job.

For the next three hours, she served delivery guys, a group of nurses from the hospital, shop owners who had previously lived to cater to her and almost half of her graduating class, most of whom had filled office spots or started their own businesses to stay in Holly Heights.

And instead of insults and grief, she got polite requests and respectable tips.

Because people were good. They were treating her better than she would have.

When Dinah Ames, Cece's mother, slid onto a seat at the counter, Sarah poured her a coffee to sip while she waited and thanked whatever lucky star had saved her from a job at the Shop-on-in. Dinah seemed nice enough but Sarah was certain every single mistake she made flowed directly back to Cece for her enjoyment.

"Your usual to-go order?" She had the special written down before Dinah nodded and immediately turned away to put the order up. While she was congratulating herself on efficiency and surviving another day without breaking plates or melting down over some stupid mistake, Dinah doctored her coffee.

"Got your invitation to the open house," Dinah said, then paused to sip the hot brew carefully. Sarah knew she was staring too hard while she waited for more, but if no one showed up to see the revived Paws for Love, all her plans would be wasted.

Not even Rebecca, Stephanie and Jen would permanently bankroll the place if the town didn't get behind it.

"Gonna have refreshments?" Dinah raised

her eyebrows. "If I shut the shop down, I'm going to need to eat my lunch or…something while I'm there."

"To-go, order up."

Sarah waved thanks at the cook, grabbed a paper bag and snapped it open before she slid Dinah's container in, along with a stack of napkins, plastic fork and two grape jellies. She was getting the hang of it.

"Strawberry, not grape." Dinah shook her head slowly. "So close."

Sarah squeezed her eyes closed and said, "Almost had it today," as she changed out the jelly.

She carefully folded the top down and slid it across to Dinah. "I'll make you a deal. If you close the shop down and come out to the shelter, I'll send you home with all the cookies you can carry."

"An offer I can't refuse. You had me at *cookie*." Dinah slid money across the counter, perfect change down to the penny.

Except today there was one dollar extra.

Things were looking up. Dinah had left her a tip.

Sarah couldn't stop a chuckle and she waved at Dinah as she left. "A tip and an

RSVP from Dinah. At least I can count on one person showing up," Sarah murmured as she wiped down the counter.

"Two. I'll be there," Brenda said. She reached around Sarah to grab the coffeepot. "Can't deny I'm curious about this place Jen disappears to every day."

Sarah could vouch for Jen's perfect attendance. Ever since Hope had come in, Jen visited in the afternoon. While she was there, she helped. She was the kind of volunteer Sarah wished they could order out of a catalog. She asked for jobs, carefully paid attention to instructions and then went and did exactly as she was asked. Nothing more, nothing less. She cared about the animals so she always did a good job.

"I'm going to miss her help when Hope goes home." Sarah riffled through her notepad to count her tickets.

"When school starts, she'll be busy, but if you listen to the way she talks about that place, you'll understand she's not going to disappear that easily." Brenda shook her head sadly. "The house she picked is normal enough, but the lot is huge. Out in the country, perfect for a pet shelter annex. I'm guessing she'll have as many dogs as she has fingers before this whole phase is done."

"From zero to ten. How long do you expect that to take?" Sarah asked as she pulled out her tips to count them.

"She's making up for lost time. I'm not sure how she made it to this age with none." Brenda held out her hand for the money Sarah owed to the kitchen's tip jar and slipped her own stack of cash in. "I never thought we had enough space or time. And Billy, Will's dad, he wouldn't stand for animals in the house. Seeing how she lights up when she talks about this ragged pit bull, I realize I should have pushed harder. And Will... That boy, he's even worse. At least now they have something in common. They both love their pets more than most people. And it looks good on them."

Sarah smiled despite the reminder that she hadn't seen Will in days. She'd almost wished to see the headlights across the ceiling again for a legitimate reason to call him, but the preparation for this open house in addition to her new job and regular duties at the shelter meant she barely got her legs folded up around Bub before she was asleep at night.

Missing Will like this was crazy. They barely knew each other.

But she valued his opinion more than anyone else's. And his confidence in her made it easier to take scary steps.

She hadn't stopped thinking about his lips on hers, the weight of his hands against her skin or the restless anticipation that made it difficult to sit still when he was around.

And his goofy, totally in love grin when he set Jelly in her castle... That had become the expression she hoped to see on a man's face across a crowded room.

Will could seduce her with his lips, but that mix of love and joy marked the difference between for now and forever.

Measuring her future happiness against Will's love for his cat was sad.

Obviously, she was tired. Thinking crazy thoughts. Envying a *cat* should mean bed rest, at the very least.

Brenda bumped Sarah's shoulder. "I know you're swamped. Get out of here. I'll bring your check tomorrow when I come, okay?"

"I don't want to leave you shorthanded." Now that she'd lived her life shorthanded, she'd be the last person to walk out on someone else. "Besides, I've got everything under control. Don't tell Jen, but she's washing cats this afternoon."

Brenda blinked slowly. "Will your delicate relationship handle that?"

Sarah laughed. "I like to push the boundaries."

Brenda held up both hands. "My daughter is not one to take her boundaries lightly. Still, if anyone can get her bathing cats, it might be you."

"Really?" Sarah untied her apron and folded it. "That's the weirdest compliment I've ever heard, but it still makes me feel like a superhero. Jen gets her way with words from you."

When Brenda brushed her shoulders off as if it was all in a day's work, Sarah's confidence ticked up another notch. Before working the first shift with Brenda, Sarah had fortified her nerves with extra coffee. And like almost every other person to cross her path lately, Brenda had surprised her with kindness, generosity and patience.

Shelly had started the coworker-to-friend trend by hanging tough at the shelter through some serious challenges.

Then Rebecca and Stephanie and even Jen had gone above and beyond the description of *donor* to help her.

And then there was Will.

"All I'm saying is that you jumped in to work faster than other people I've vouched for." Brenda shook her head. "Don't know exactly where you got the work ethic but it's nice to see. And picking up the usuals as fast as you did shows a sharp mind." She grinned. "Too bad you've been hiding it behind shiny hair and expensive clothes all these years."

Instead of apologizing again or explaining all the reasons she'd thought she had to be who she was, Sarah surprised them both by wrapping her arms around Brenda. "Thank you. If you only knew what these weird, slightly insulting but mostly encouraging comments mean to me, you'd know how badly I needed them."

Brenda squeezed her and then stepped back. "Go on. I'll hold down the order pad until Sue Lynn comes in. She sure is going to be happy when you switch to the lunch shift. I might miss you."

Sarah wrinkled her nose. "Stick around. I still owe you a meal. You could do lunch next week, right? Then, if I need you to save my bacon, you'll be close by."

"You can save your own bacon, but I'll take the lunch invitation. Be nice to sit in one of the booths and ask you for a clean utensil every three minutes." Brenda sighed. "Like the woman of wealth and leisure my daughter wishes I would aspire to be."

Sarah almost groaned when she checked the clock. Any advantage she might have had in leaving early had evaporated and she was late. Again. What a day.

"Gotta run. Meeting with my board of directors." Sarah peered down her nose haughtily, hoping for a laugh. When she got it, she waved and trotted out to the car.

Sarah raced back through town and squealed into the parking lot of Paws for Love on two wheels, happy to see that she was the first to arrive. Shelly would take care of the afternoon feeding. Already three steps ahead of herself, Sarah raced to the door and fumbled her key ring.

She bent, picked it up and turned back to the car to grab the envelope she'd just remembered.

It was thick, as if it held paperwork, but had only the shelter's address on the front.

No return address. No stamp. "Weird. I'll figure you out later."

Today, she'd get approval on the next round of spending, including a series of adoption events. She also planned to discuss the employment ad for the new, improved shelter manager with Rebecca, Jen, Stephanie and Will. But mainly Jen. She was the only real obstacle keeping Sarah from officially taking over the shelter and fund-raising.

First, she had to wash the smell of hash browns out of her hair and change into her clean pair of jeans. It had been a good week at the diner. She might even be able to keep working there if she got the chance to take over full-time operations of the shelter. It was a job that took way more than forty hours a week, but there was no reason they had to fall from eleven to three.

If she could keep both jobs, she would. Coming this close to homelessness had made it clear that just getting by could be dangerous. She'd love to have a chance to get a little ahead.

She hadn't met Jen's deadline, not quite, but she'd shove her suitcase in the car before the open house, and next week, she'd move into her own tiny apartment.

She wouldn't have a stick of furniture, but she and Bub would have plenty of room to spread out.

And she'd sleep through the night without staring up at the ceiling, watching for head-lights.

She jumped into the cramped shower in the employee bathroom, washed and dried her hair and then got dressed. On her way back to the office, she started a load of laundry, gave her shadow, Bub, a treat and eased into her ugly chair.

She checked for new email. None. The shelter's website had been updated with new hours and a large, splashy graphic. She and Shelly had spent two days coming up with the announcement for the shelter's open house and the image of Bub wearing a party hat. At this very moment, she was as ready as she could be.

Except the envelope was ruining the clean lines of the stacks on her desk.

She flipped the manila envelope over, but there was no address on the back. The clasp was the only thing holding the envelope closed, and as soon as she opened it, a stack of cash spread out across her desk.

She wanted to toss the bills in the air like a game show winner. How long had she been dodging bill collectors and worrying about rent? But she'd never have enough time to restore her office before Rebecca, Jen and Stephanie walked in.

Rolling around in cash would send the wrong impression.

Then she realized she had no reason to celebrate. This wasn't a windfall like the lottery. Only one person would have left this for her and he'd stolen it from the people who were helping her.

But she needed it so badly.

Sarah carefully counted as she restacked the money. "One thousand dollars." And a handwritten note inside the envelope. "Tampa. Monday."

Sarah had spent a lot of time studying handwriting growing up.

She wouldn't bet her first month's rent on it, but with a free roll, she'd gamble this was her father's handwriting.

And possibly her chance to get her old life back.

Temptation in an envelope.

"I did *not* need this today."

All she had to do was get up right this second, leave Bub and the shelter and everything else behind to head for the airport. This was more than enough cash to get her there and buy a nice hotel room for a few nights.

Except she'd be blowing off everything that had come to mean so much and the people who'd helped her.

To join her father, the man who'd stolen from his employees and run away.

Sarah rubbed the hard knot in the center of her chest and realized she was struggling to breathe.

There was no way to deny it now, not even to herself. Her father had no intention of coming back to Holly Heights with some breezy explanation.

Her father was a thief, one who'd left her here. All alone.

He was also the man who'd make sure she didn't have to worry about rent money, who'd stood up to her teachers and faced down her critics, and he was the only family she had left.

If only he'd knocked instead of leaving the envelope in the middle of the night.

Like a coward.

With Hollister watching so closely, maybe that had been her father's only choice.

Aside from doing the right thing: confessing, turning himself in to face the fallout.

And it seemed as if her father wasn't sure which way Sarah would go.

If he'd knocked on the door and come inside Paws for Love, would she have left with him or called the cops?

Her uncertainty rattled her.

Sarah shoved the money back inside the envelope and pressed her forehead against the cool surface of her desk. Such a headache. After all the late hours and hard work, any reminder of Bobby Hillman could make a headache bloom right between her eyes.

"Hey, boss, good day at the diner?"

Sarah jerked up to see a smiling Shelly. "Sure. And after this afternoon, we're going to know which direction to go next. It's a great day."

Shelly gave her a thumbs-up. "I'm headed for sudsville, population me and every animal in this place. Call if you need me. Les will come by with food." She wrinkled her nose. "He says he can't stand to miss a meal with me." Shelly whistled as she strutted away, but the tune was loud, a little off-key and entirely too happy.

No one should be that cheerful about giving dogs and cats baths.

"Wait for Les, and leave some of the cats for Jen. She wants to help," Sarah called out before Shelly disappeared. Then Sarah straightened in her chair as Will appeared in her doorway.

Sarah shuffled the envelope under a stack of file folders, then stood and smoothed her hands down her jeans. "Come in, everyone."

"How's Hope?" Jen glanced around the room, challenging anyone to give her a hard time over her affection for her soon-to-be dog.

"Great. Les is going to remove the stitches today. All of them. They'll wait on you." Sarah waved the adoption contract she'd placed on top of the most important stack of papers on her desk. "When you're ready, we'll do some paperwork."

"I'll go help with the cats, okay, Dad?" Chloe started to inch away, but not before Will tugged the pink stripe in her ponytail.

"Be careful. Cats are smart. They might gang up on you."

Chloe glanced at Sarah and rolled her eyes before she trotted off to the cat room.

"Are you ready for us?" Will asked, and Sarah realized she'd been staring at him, cataloging any differences she could see after their time apart. Was his hair longer or mussed from the cool breeze? There was no way he was actually taller. Was there?

Sarah shook her head to clear it. At this point, there was no option but to execute her plan A. The envelope was a problem for later.

"Uh, yes, I'm ready. As you all know, the open house is on target, so I wanted to take a few minutes to discuss the next phase." She handed out the list of proposed events, all of which had dollar estimates.

Then she threaded her fingers together in a tight knot and rested her hands on the desk, determined not to hurt her chances by talking too much. The second part of this meeting depended on convincing everyone she could be cool, calm and collected as needed.

"You've done a good job with the budget so far." Stephanie put her copy of the proposal down. "You're almost ten percent under."

"The roofer, the general contractor and even the printer were happy to give me a discount for displaying their signs at the open house." Sarah twisted her pen in circles. "But you can't count on that."

The way Will's eyes crinkled at the corners might have been better than a full-blown grin. Sarah couldn't sit still thanks to the warm glow in her chest, so she twisted back and forth while she waited for Rebecca.

"We should wait until after the open house," Jen said slowly as she inched the paper across the desk. "We said in the beginning we'd wait to see whether Paws for Love could build community support."

Rebecca wrinkled her nose. "Doesn't the fact that you've been here past closing hours every day for a week indicate that it can? New volunteers. Two new students anxious to shadow Les. Discounts from local suppliers. Paws for Love is starting to gain ground."

"And this budget—" Sarah picked up Jen's copy "—is all about building that support. Whatever glimmer you can see now, we can fan to a flame with the right kinds of events, publicity and the continued lucky streak."

Rebecca was nodding. Will's lips were

twitching. Stephanie glanced from Sarah to Jen and back like a tennis spectator. Only Jen narrowed her eyes in consideration.

"Fine. We'll start the next phase. But I want to do a short dog show tomorrow. We'll put three or four on leashes, add cute bandannas, walk them out among these donors. I've got two more kids who'll come and bring their families. Good for publicity and public opinion." Jen shrugged. "And I can't take them all home."

At this late stage, Sarah was certain she couldn't handle one more event.

But it was a great idea.

So she shook Jen's hand. "Done."

"And another idea I had…" Jen licked her lips and frowned at Rebecca, who blinked back at her, as if she'd never interrupt. "You should take family photos. When the dogs or cats are adopted, make a snapshot with the first names and the animal's name. Then we could make a billboard or some kind of wall display showing the people who support Paws for Love." She glanced down at the pleat she was pinching in her jeans. "Then, if someone comes in and they're on the fence about the shelter or rescue animals or whatever, they'll see somebody they know, and they can get a reference, a glowing endorsement."

Everyone was quiet as they considered her suggestion. Then they all turned to Sarah.

As if it was her decision.

"I love it. We'll need to add a digital camera and figure out printing the photos…" Sarah jotted a note that she hoped she'd be able to read later. "Or what if there was a scrolling display. The pictures might get ragged, but a digital slideshow that could be updated quickly…" She trailed off as she tapped her lips, considering the cost. Then she waved off that big dream. "For now, printing photos. Someday, we'll go high-tech."

Stephanie patted Jen on the back. Will offered her a closed fist. Watching them bump fists might have been the highlight of Sarah's day.

The blush on Jen's cheeks was truly satisfying. She was so intimidating, and it turned out that bluster was her own shield.

Finally, Jen cracked her knuckles. Rebecca winced at the sound. "I have other ideas. Those were the best two."

"The new managing director is going to love them," Rebecca murmured.

"Got an employment ad for us to review?" Jen straightened in her seat, ready to get the meeting back on track.

"Yes." Sarah handed out a second sheet of paper. "I hope I got everything you asked for. If not, let me know and I'll make adjustments. If we're going to advertise, I'd like to submit the ad this week."

Sarah tried to relax against the back of her chair as she watched the three of them study the advertisement. Will finished first. "Sounds like the ad for my secretary."

"Which worked wonderfully. That Alice is a pleasure to talk to." Rebecca waved a hand. "Kind of sniffly, but very business savvy."

"Yeah, she's got an allergy, but we're working our way through it." Will caught her stare. "It's not easy to find someone who appreciates well-documented procedures. Add that to an affinity for cats and the field around Holly Heights gets impossibly narrow. Alice was happy to get the job, and eventually the allergy meds will start working. I hope."

"Couldn't you leave the cat at home?" Rebecca asked as she made a note on the employment ad.

Will and Jen shot Rebecca identical outraged looks.

"Fine. I forgot who I was talking to. Pet-crazy-come-lately and his stepsister, Just-plain-crazy." Rebecca shot the paper back across the desk. "Nothing major, a tweak."

Sarah nodded and stacked Will's on top. "Jen? Stephanie? Anything to add?"

Stephanie tilted her head to the side. "I've never hired someone, but I have this feeling we'll know her when we see her."

Sarah waited for a second to see if there was anything helpful to follow that response and turned to Jen.

Jen's lips tightened into a flat line as she shook her head.

"All right, before you go, I was hoping you could review this résumé." She carefully placed the résumé she'd worked and reworked in front of them. Then she folded her hands. "It's mine. I'd like to be considered for the new full-time position of shelter managing director, complete with a seat on the board, the new combined salary I've already budgeted and an assistant manager who will work part-time and help to oversee the volunteers I plan to pack this place with."

"Art? You majored in *art*?" Jen grunted. "That says so much about you, none of which makes me want to hire you."

"I started and finished in four years," she said. "And I've got plenty of fund-raising experience. No one can say I haven't done good work here. Yes, I needed your help, but I've accomplished a great deal in a short time."

When no one spoke up in her defense, she stood to pace in a small circle. "Hard work. Good ideas. Commitment to the mission of the shelter. I have all those."

"A solid reputation. Goodwill in the community. The ability to influence the decision makers in Holly Heights." Rebecca sighed. "You don't have any of those. Not anymore."

That was impossible to refute. And the fact that Rebecca was the one bringing it up instead of her harshest critic was depressing.

"Fine. I'll run the ad. Promise me you'll give me one more interview before you fill the spot." Sarah wasn't sure what she could do, but one thing she'd learned with all the ups and downs lately was that time could change things.

Good or bad, in three months or six months, everything could be different.

"Would you keep your job at the diner?" Jen rubbed her forehead. "And take this on, too?"

Sarah weighed her options while she tried to guess which answer would be the most persuasive. Then she slapped one hand on her thigh. "I don't know. Honestly, to pay the bills, I need both jobs. The lunch shift would make it easy enough to help with the morning and afternoon feedings and playtime. If we hired a part-time volunteer coordinator," she said as she held up one finger, "something we've already talked about and budgeted for, he or she could make sure the volunteers have direction anytime I'm out."

Will gave her a small nod. "As one of Sarah's former employers, I have to say she's resourceful, determined and dependable. If you tell her to improve the visibility of Paws for Love, that's what she'll do. I have no doubt. My suggestion is to give her the job, subject to a six-month probationary period."

Sarah clenched both hands into tight fists. Mainly to keep from pumping them in the air. Having his support, even his presence firmly in her corner, made it easier to pretend she knew exactly how this would work out.

No matter what the decision, she could depend on Will's help. She would work hard to stand on her own, but having his faith made it easier.

"Put her in charge of the budget for the whole place? That's a lot of trust." Rebecca's tone hurt, but Sarah understood that they had to be careful. Putting someone who made the wrong decisions in charge could hurt the shelter beyond repair.

Unfortunately, most of the town would suspect her of bad behavior no matter how squeaky clean she lived for the rest of her life.

"It would save us the cost of posting the ad. And the time. And get her suitcase out of this office," Jen grumbled. "There's no way to get around how easily she's changed our opinion, either. The first day we walked in here, I wouldn't have put her out if she was on fire."

Sarah crossed her arms over her chest and reminded herself she knew exactly where that hostility came from.

"And now?" Stephanie drawled. "Please tell me you'd go for the fire extinguisher."

Jen pursed her lips. "If it was close, within arm's reach, say. Anything farther than that,

I'm not willing to promise." Her lips were twitching. "Let's give her the job. I like watching her work hard."

Rebecca stood and offered her a hand. "Six months. We'll draw up a contract. Effective immediately."

"Thank you." Sarah shook her hand and had to bite back the steady stream of grateful gibberish boiling inside. Since she'd hit rock bottom and climbed out of the pit in six weeks, she was pretty sure she could climb the mountaintop in six months.

"If we're done with that, I want to talk about tomorrow." Rebecca clapped her hands. "Five dozen cookies. Are you sure that's enough?"

Sarah blinked slowly and tried to imagine baking five dozen cookies on her own. To Rebecca, it seemed as easy as could be. "Since I only know of two people planning to attend, we may have extras, but I'll need to eat at least a dozen on my own if this flops."

"Then I better get home." Rebecca waved as she opened the door. "Get some sleep. You look tired."

Sarah tilted her head as she tried to figure out what to say to that.

"We'll go help Shelly." Jen shook her head, one hand clamped on Stephanie's arm to halt her escape. "And we'll be ready to serve tomorrow. I already bought bandannas for the dogs. Hope's is pink. And if you can get more than two people to show up, you're going to be impressed at the way the three of us can work a room. Stephanie taught us everything she knows." Then she pointed at the back of the office. "Move the suitcase." Having delivered her final admonishment, Jen left the room.

Sarah's only consolation was the knowledge that washing the roomful of cats would leave her doused and worn-out.

Relieved to have tackled the largest hurdle for the day, Sarah leaned against the desk. Will was watching from the office doorway. "Thank you for encouraging me."

"I didn't do a thing," Will said. "You did that all on your own."

"That smile of yours speaks volumes. And I needed every word today." Sarah rubbed a hand over her forehead. "As tired as I am."

"Neither one of us are all that smooth, are we? Want me to give Jen a noogie? She hates those and she's little. I could still take her."

"No need. She's going to be washing cats. We're even."

They both fought smiles for half a second, but laughing with him was satisfying.

"Unless you get out of here quick, I'll find a job for you, too." She squeezed his biceps. "Heavy lifting. Or washing dogs. One or the other."

Will checked his naked wrist. "Is it that late already? I have to…go, do something." He motioned with a thumb over his shoulder.

She should let him go. She was just getting her feet under her. Until she was steady, he deserved space.

But she needed his help again.

"I missed you." Sarah stepped forward to rest against him, content with the fantasy that he was hers and would give her all the support she needed. After a second, his hands landed on her back to move up and down slowly.

"Your moods change like the weather around here. One minute you're sunny, then you cloud up and rain." Will pressed his chin into the crook of her shoulder. "I think I missed you, too. Why didn't anyone ever warn me how addicting an exciting woman could be?"

"Probably for the same reason no one ever told me how nice it is to have a guy who'll loan you a computer instead of the keys to his 'weekend' apartment. We wouldn't have believed them."

Will nodded. "I'm afraid you're right. But now we know better. You ought to know… There's gossip around town. About the two of us."

Sarah studied his face. From his tone, he believed this news to be very serious. "Well, sure. I'm a popular target." And used to being talked about. Being connected to Will would improve her standing, so she was ready to laugh it off.

Then she understood the problem.

"Oh. Are you losing clients?" Sarah crossed her arms in front of her, afraid of the answer. Spending time with Will was worth a little gossip to her, but the success of his business, Chloe's security, raised the stakes for him.

Will rubbed his forehead. "Not yet, but…"

He might. She wanted to set people straight with choice words and her best sneer, but she couldn't ignore the worry that this was who she'd always be in Holly Heights. Trouble. For any friend or…more.

How could she stay here?

"I should have told Doug Grant what I thought about his gossip." Will grimaced. "I didn't. I'm sorry."

Sarah rubbed at the ache in the center of her chest as she tried to ignore the disappointment. "If you need to pull back from the shelter, I get it, Will." And she wanted to cry at the thought.

She could be strong this time.

"That's just it. I don't want to." His eyes were locked on hers. "I've missed being here. I don't want more space."

Sarah had to look away to catch her breath.

"But finding the right thing to say to people like Doug and Cece Grant isn't easy." Will ran his hand down her arm to tangle his fingers with hers. "I might need your help."

Sarah stared down at their hands. The temptation to hop a plane to Tampa and leave her worries behind had just disappeared.

She nodded.

"If you have time for one more favor, I need some advice." She stepped back, her knees weak. Telling Will about the envelope was a gamble. She knew what his answer would be: call the police. Turn it in. He wouldn't take the easy way out, not even for a chance at a life of luxury.

But for Sarah, it wasn't so easy. For a step this big, she needed the support.

She needed Will's help.

WILL WATCHED SARAH scramble to answer the phone and nodded when she held up one finger. He had time to check on Chloe.

And recover the feeling in his fingers. As soon as he'd said he didn't want his space, they'd started to tingle. Probably because he'd been holding his breath.

Her answer had been…unemotional. Deciphering it would take some time.

Following the string of giggles coming from the storage room was easy. Believing his eyes when he got there was harder. Shelly and Jen were wrestling a big tomcat under a faucet while Chloe giggled at the long string of made-up curse words Jen was muttering.

Yeah. No way did he want to be involved in that. Will eased away from the door as his own cell rang. Sarah trotted past and held up one finger before she stepped out into the play yard.

Will retreated to Sarah's empty office and perched on her dilapidated chair.

"What's up?"

Answering the phone like that would send Olivia into lecture mode.

That's why he did it.

"You know I hate it when you do that. Civilized people follow an established routine. Hello. How hard is it to say hello?" From the breathing and synthesized music, she was either running on a treadmill or doing aerobics in an elevator.

"Who is this?" He waved at Chloe, who had squeaked up to the front counter for something.

"Jerk. How is everything?" Beeps indicated she might be slowing down.

"Great. Same as two days ago. And like I said then, I'm not bringing her back to Austin until next weekend. I know she needs new clothes, and I understand you want to buy them, but this is important. She needs to stay through the weekend." Will clenched his teeth to stop the offer but it rolled right out. "I'll meet you halfway after work one day next week. Okay?"

"I had my doubts you two would make it a week, much less the summer. I miss her. Charles bought enough steak to invite the whole city to the welcome-home dinner."

"Good for Charles. He can start cooking this weekend and it'll all be ready by Wednesday."

Olivia muttered something under her breath. "Are you doing this to get back at me for something?"

Since he'd been the chess piece caught between his mother and his father until he was old enough to remove himself from the game, he had no intention of playing with Chloe's life like that. "No, but the animal shelter we've both been working with is having a big day tomorrow. She won't want to miss it."

"And I guess *Sarah* needs all the help she can get," Olivia said. How much had Chloe told her? "It's definitely time you got a date, Will. I don't love that Chloe seems to think Sarah and her aunt Jen are capable of saving every cat in the world, but...I'll allow it. Let's meet halfway on Sunday. Compromise. We're supposed to do that."

He wanted to argue because he wanted every day he could get with Chloe.

"We're also supposed to discuss things like adopting cats, and you went ahead and did that without me." Olivia usually reserved this tone to remind him of all the special events he missed because of work.

He'd have been livid if she'd done something like agreeing to adopt a pet without letting him know. "Sorry," he mumbled.

Olivia's chuckle was a relief. "Yeah, yeah. Chloe tells me you've been leaving work early, taking her on cat shopping trips, researching cat carriers with her. She needs time with you. If it takes a cat, you go ahead and adopt twenty more." Olivia cleared her throat. "Do not adopt twenty more, crazy cat man."

"Thanks for giving us this summer." He and Olivia would argue, but only because they both loved Chloe.

"We're still a team, Will," Olivia said.

"All right. Where and when?" Shoving aside Sarah's neat stacks, Will grabbed a pen to write everything down on his hand. "I'm going to miss her."

"Yeah, I know, and if you'd moved to

Austin..." The silence stretched. Finally, she sighed. "Holly Heights is close. We can make this work. We'll make sure she has the security we never had. We can do it."

Will had to swallow hard to clear the lump in his throat. They'd been unable to make marriage work, but he was reminded again how he'd appreciated Olivia's friendship. "See you Sunday."

After he hung up the phone, he started to restack all the files. The heavy envelope buried under the paper begged to be opened. Since the flap was loose, he peeked inside.

Cash. A lot of cash.

Why did Sarah have an envelope filled with money?

"Are you snooping through my desk?" Sarah asked from the doorway. "I didn't expect that."

"I *did* want to borrow a pen." He held out his hand to display his notes. "My ex called and I needed to write something down. To find one, I knocked everything over."

Sarah looked over her shoulder and shut the door behind her. "That's what I wanted to talk to you about. I think that's from my father. The lights in the parking lot at midnight? Somehow they're connected to that envelope."

"What are you going to do with it?" Will carefully sealed the open edge and placed it squarely in the center of the desk.

"My father wants me to buy a plane ticket." Sarah dropped into the chair and covered her face with both hands. "Hollister will confiscate it if I call him and all I can think about is all the things I could pay off, set up, the life I could get a start on, if I just…kept it. Here."

"It's a lot of money." Any normal person would consider doing the same thing, keeping the money. It was a gift from her father. Did Hollister really have a right to it?

Big Bobby Hillman's victims might.

"So, you don't want to make your getaway?" Will tapped the corner of the envelope. "I bet your daddy has a lot more of this." He watched her intently while trying to appear disinterested.

He thought Sarah would stay. She was doing good things and making impressive progress on a real, authentic life, one she built for herself.

And he wanted her here in Holly Heights.

"For so long, I was running in place, waiting for him or hoping for a chance to get my old life back." She leaned forward. "I really had convinced myself he was innocent."

Giving in to impulse, Will grabbed her hand and tangled his fingers with hers. "I'm sorry. It can't be easy when your hero lets you down." He'd been there. Through every divorce and shuffle, he'd become a little more cynical about his own parents. "You should be proud of everything you've done *without* Bobby Hillman."

Sarah studied their hands. "You'd think less of me if I just…kept the money. Forget the plane ticket. Forget Hollister."

The answer should be yes. Giving it over to the police was the ethical thing to do.

Why didn't that answer roll off his tongue?

Maybe because he understood that she had to make the decision. "You don't have any doubt anymore—you know that you can save yourself, don't you?"

She studied the ceiling. "Even better. Now I know there are good people in the world who will *help* me save myself."

Will squeezed her hand before he pulled away.

"You aren't going to tell me what to do, are you?" Sarah let out a huff.

Had he finally learned the lesson his sister had been trying to get through his hard head for years? He could tell her what he'd do, but she had the right to make up her own mind.

She'd impressed him with all the decisions she'd made lately.

"Sorry. That's the thing. This life in Holly Heights? Now it's all up to you." Will eased around the desk. "One more day, then the finish line. You've got a choice now. Which life will you choose?"

Will pressed his lips against hers, savoring her taste and the perfection of having her in his arms, while he crossed his fingers and hoped this wasn't the last time he'd see her.

"Are you two ducking your chores?" Chloe said from the doorway. "Aunt Jen and I have a lot to get done this weekend. She wants my opinion on her new house before I go home, and we don't have much time. She's promised to come to Austin to show me the floors she picks, but we can't put every decision off." One hand was propped on her wet sweater, while her sneaker squeaked in rhythm as she tapped it. "We've got a lot of animals to bathe, people, and these cats aren't going to brush themselves."

"Think she has a future in shelter management?" Will asked as he slowly slid his hands to his own hips.

"Perhaps military officer training." Sarah ran her hand down his arm before she winked. Just for him. "Either way, she's going places." She spun around and held out her hand. "Put me to work." Without hesitation, she and Chloe trotted away.

So Jen was now a part of the visitation cycle. As if they were a real family. Will realized that nothing had worked out as he'd intended, but it was going perfectly, anyway.

CHAPTER SEVENTEEN

THE NEXT DAY, Sarah was doing her best not to panic over the second biggest Saturday of her life. Rebecca, Stephanie and Jen had made it clear the community support was critical to them. Sarah didn't want all the work she'd done to save Paws for Love to evaporate.

But fund-raisers needed people with funds to show. Had she done enough social rehabilitation?

By the end of the day, she'd know whether she'd jumped the next hurdle or tumbled headfirst into the track.

No pressure or anything.

That uncertainty had made it twice as hard to make her first phone call of the day. Leaving the message for Hollister had twisted her stomach in knots, but even after examining the issue all night long, she knew there was no way to justify keeping the money.

As soon as Hollister brought her father back,

the people of Holly Heights would understand the truth.

And Will might not be forced to choose his business or her.

Before Sarah had finished letting the second group of dogs into the play yard, Rebecca was calling out from the lobby. "Cookies. Come get the world's best cookies!"

"Set them on the counter for now. We'll move them out to the refreshment table right before the open house starts." She yanked the knife out of the washing machine door and moved the load of dog blankets to the dryer. Even on special occasions, the animals came first. She carefully set the knife behind the detergent box. All she needed was a kid skewering some rich guy's leg.

"Bandannas." Jen held out six different bandannas in a variety of colors. "My assistant and I will match them to the right dogs, according to color." Chloe waved a hand from the doorway. "And she's determined to try brighter collars with these cute name tags—" Jen swung a handful of thin collars and bedazzled tags "—on the cats. Says they need their own bling." Jen shrugged. "We got these and a whole lot more over in Austin last night."

Chloe clapped and dug into her purse. "Also, a digital camera. There was a camera place right next to the pet store, so Aunt Jen said we should pick one up. The first open house will be captured in pictures."

Sarah slapped Chloe's hand in an exuberant high five. Jen held up a fist for Sarah to bump, but she surprised them both by wrapping her arms around Jen and holding on tight for an awkward hug. "Your ideas rock."

"First my dad. Now you're all lovey with Jen. Should I warn Brenda to be on the lookout if she wants to avoid being squeezed until she squeaks?" Chloe asked as she sorted the collars.

"Nope. You're next." Sarah made grabbing motions until Chloe shrieked and ran away.

"The shrieking. I'd forgotten that part." Jen cupped her hands over her ears. "And watch the hugs."

"There'll be more today. I feel huggy."

"The suitcase is out, right? Office is clear?" Jen waved the bandannas.

"All clear. I'll be a legitimate renter tomorrow and I won't even have to ask Will for help moving." Sarah held her breath, certain she'd hit the missile launch button.

Jen let out a breath. "He's taking Chloe home tomorrow. Buy him dinner." Then she disappeared down the hall. The barks of ecstatic dogs filtered from the dog room and Hope's happy howl was easy to distinguish. Hope would be pretty in pink. The bald areas where Les had had to cut the collar off would barely show.

And the crowd would eat their hearts out because Hope was spoken for.

"Are you ready?" Rebecca asked from the doorway. Stephanie and a handsome man, who had one arm draped over her shoulders, hovered behind Rebecca.

"No. Yes. No. Yes." Sarah shook her head. "Yes. We're ready. We've done everything we can."

"Meet Daniel." Stephanie tugged Daniel forward. "He's not great at pressing donors for cash, but you've got us."

Daniel gave Stephanie a long stare. "Not sure about that introduction, but I know better than to complain." Daniel held out his hand. "It's nice to meet you."

Sarah tried not to shift nervously under

Daniel's stare. He was in Peru, saving lives, while his sister was giving a fortune away. What sort of star had the Lincoln kids been born under?

Saving a bunch of cats and dogs was...

"Thank you for everything you're doing here," Daniel said. "I admire anyone who'll stand up for animals who have no voice."

Sarah blinked back tears and cleared her throat. Admiration. That was new. She'd had envy and jealousy and spite and anger and even friendship and love. Admiration was nice.

"I hope you'll be able to keep Rebecca and Jen on the right path once we head back to Lima. We all know that Stephanie is the voice of reason in this group." Rebecca rolled her eyes behind her brother's back. "Stephanie's science in the schools program is taking off, but leaving them here unsupervised is dangerous."

Stephanie slid under his arm again, and the look they shared was enough to make a cynic's heart gooey. "Hiking in the Andes will be a vacation compared to house shopping with Jen. You've saved me, Daniel."

"I can imagine what that sounds like. Jen

and Rebecca owe me and South America big-time."

She fluttered her eyelashes at him, and his deadpan head tilt made them all laugh.

"It's go time, boss." Shelly stuck her head around the corner. "Tables are set up. We put out the cookies and the bottled water. Shady awnings are in place. The chairs are on either side of the fashion runway and Les is on alert, the digital camera locked and loaded." She grinned. "This is going to be awesome."

Sarah returned her thumbs-up and watched her bustle away.

Then she retreated to her office, tickled Bub until he stood up to stretch and pulled him down across her lap. "We did it. Now all we can do is wait to see if anyone shows." He rested his chin on her chest and blinked up at her.

Dinah was the first one through the door, followed by Brenda, Sue Lynn and five other business owners she'd approached to ask for employment opportunities. Bub immediately assumed the position of Head Dog and greeted each one with enthusiastic tail wags. His payment, pats on the head, kept him loitering around the front door for the next

visitors. Sarah tried to make a list of everyone who visited, because she wanted to send
thank-you notes with a discreet request for
donations.

The contractor, roofer, fence guy, the salesperson who'd walked her through the fright
of buying a computer and the parents of all
four high school volunteers arrived in the
next wave.

Before she could greet them, a reporter
from the Holly Heights newspaper pulled
her aside and Shelly asked where the list for
businesses with donation stations was, because she needed to add two more, the repair shop that had replaced the van's battery
and a day care.

Shelly, Jen, Rebecca, Stephanie and Les
were each running tours through the shelter,
answering any questions that might come up
and leading people out to the repaired second play yard.

Will floated on the perimeter. She lost
track of him and then got a happy jolt when
he crossed her line of vision again. Sarah
shook herself free of the reporter to find that
he had been cornered by Cece and her husband, Doug. Since they were also his clients,

Sarah hesitated to free him. Doug offered his hand and, after a hesitation, Will shook it. Whatever he'd decided to do about Doug and his gossip, it looked as if they'd be working together.

Relieved Will was keeping his clients, Sarah went through the cat room to make sure every single cat was collared and tagged.

Then she hit the dog room, closed the door and let one group of overexcited dogs out into the play yard. "Les, get the camera!" The dogs, sensing the need to put on a show, were in fine form, romping in their bright bandannas.

Until Meatloaf got too excited and threw up his breakfast and whatever else he'd eaten in the past week. At that point, her volunteers were suspiciously absent.

"That's all right, Meatloaf. I've got it. The show must go on." She shooed him back into the yard and hurried to the storage room to grab the scoop. She didn't want a close encounter with bodily functions to put anyone off their donation game.

"Sarah, honey, I can tell how hard you've been working." Sarah turned as Cece shook her head sadly. "It shows all over your poor hands and face. But really, this is quite a cute party."

Torn between the urge to take care of Meatloaf's mess and schmoozing a potential whale of a donor, Sarah said, "Thanks, Cece. Go enjoy the party. I saw you talking with Will. Smart decision."

Cece's eyes lit up. "Not as smart as yours, honey. Will just made it very clear he's your number one fan."

Sarah tugged on her shirt as the heat of a blush covered her cheeks.

"A man like that, one who'll pay your electric bill and defend your honor..." Cece shook her head. "How do you always land on your feet?"

Pay my electric bill?

Sarah watched the people milling around the play yards as she processed that. She'd thought he'd gotten the lights back on by pulling strings. Instead, a guy who'd hated her had spent his own money to help.

And he'd done it without handing her a bill or asking for anything in return. He wanted to be with her.

She must have been born under the luckiest star in the sky.

"Make sure to try Rebecca's cookies. I know how you love your desserts," Sarah said. Then she gave herself a mental slap. Sure, she could trade hidden insults with the best of them. That wouldn't win her any big donors.

"I've got to run outside. Wait for me?" She checked over her shoulder as she walked to make sure Cece was waiting, then hustled out to pick up the mess as best she could.

She dumped the scooper and turned to see an impressive grimace on Cece's face. They walked outside. "Please, Sarah, don't you have people for that?"

"She doesn't need people," Jen said from her spot in the play yard. "She knows how to work."

Gratified that her biggest critic was defending her, Sarah cleared her throat. "And that's what this event is all about, Cece. Getting more people, more help. You've got such a generous spirit. I'd love to hear any suggestions you might have on how you can help Paws for Love."

Cece stepped carefully around the spot Sarah had just cleaned up, her high heels as out of place at an event like this as Sarah had been in her own life lately.

Until today.

Then Cece dodged Jen's glare twice as carefully. "Well, you know," Cece said as she waved a hand at the refreshments, "I've always had a knack for flower arrangements. I could help the next time you have an event like this."

Jen's snort made her opinion on the offer clear.

Sarah's lips were twitching when she said, "Uh, Jen, let's go ahead with the show. You're on."

Jen stared at Cece and then nodded. "Got it."

"Let's get you a good seat," Sarah said as she motioned Cece forward. "This should be fun."

Sarah stood under the awning, next to the bottled water, and watched her dogs prance on their leashes. Every kid holding one was grinning and some of the dogs were, too. The little redhead kid who'd demanded his soda loudly claimed that Meatloaf was going to be his dog.

Given the way his helpless parents followed the boy, Sarah wondered if she should have set up a separate table to run adoptions as soon as the show was over.

Jen and Hope were the final pair on the runway and everyone who knew Hope's story was sniffling by the time they made a graceful turn and swaggered back down the aisle. Her brindle coat was shiny, the bare patches in her skin were filling in and she'd gained fifteen pounds. Hope walked with a certain step that made it clear she was right where she was supposed to be.

And as soon as Jen rested her hand on Hope's head, the dog sat beautifully, as if she'd been trained her whole life.

"Not tears again." Sarah pinched her nose. She didn't have time for this.

"You should be patting yourself on the back, not pinching your nose." Will's whisper in her ear made her shiver.

"Happy tears." His hand on her shoulder steadied her and made it possible to clear her throat.

"And now, we'd like to introduce you to the woman responsible for keeping Paws for Love open, Sarah Hillman." Jen and Hope stepped aside and Sarah was nearly certain that if she didn't step up, Jen would make her.

So she did.

"I'd like to thank everyone for coming…" Her words faltered when she noticed Hollister standing outside the play yard. He didn't wave. His face revealed nothing.

"I haven't done this alone. Shelly and Les taught me how to take care of these animals. Rebecca, Stephanie, Jen and Will gave me the confidence and most of the cash to keep the doors open. And you, all of you, who took time out of your weekend to see what we're doing here, will be the ones to take Paws for Love forward. We need volunteers to help day in and day out. Fosters take the dogs that need one-on-one care. And donors keep the lights on and the food coming. Please, whatever help you can give, let me know. These animals deserve it."

The light applause that followed her as she stepped off the runway faded as she walked over to the fence. "Meet me inside. I have something to give you."

Hollister nodded and headed for the front door. As she turned to follow, she was relieved to see that Will was behind her.

Will shoved his hands in his pockets. "You're really going to give that money to him?"

"You don't think I should?" Sarah stepped closer. "Come on, don't give me that. Especially now that I've done the hardest part!"

He wrapped his arms around Sarah and squeezed her tightly against his chest.

"I need to see my father, Will. I don't want to worry about him hurt or alone. He made a mistake. I'll never understand it, but I love him. Hollister will bring him back. Then we'll figure out the rest." Sarah closed her eyes, afraid her father would never forgive her but certain it was the best decision.

"You're doing the right thing. Good for you." Will leaned down to press a kiss on her lips. "When it's time to make the tough call, I know I can count on Sarah Hillman."

Those words coming from this man were enough to make her weak in the knees.

Will whispered, "I'm proud of you."

Sarah closed her eyes and took nice, even breaths because she was half a second from ugly sobs.

"Will Barnes, I never stood a chance." She

pressed her forehead against his shoulder. "I'd have to be a fool not to love you."

"And we both know you're smart." He rubbed circles across the small of her back. "Thank you for blackmailing me with a large brown dog. I almost missed out on a good thing."

A small group had gathered around. Shelly and Les. Chloe, Rebecca, Stephanie and Jen were all glued to the action.

The kids who'd hated her with a passion had grown into friends. Somehow.

It was a dog shelter miracle.

Everyone—all the people she'd hired, the old friends who'd come to see the trouble she'd gotten herself into and the new friends who were convincing her every day that life was good—they were all watching the show.

"Hollister is waiting." Sarah glanced toward the door. "But I've got a very important question. Can a cat man love a dog woman?"

Will pursed his lips. "I don't know. I only like dogs that do tricks, like howling on command."

Sarah wrinkled her nose. "Then I should definitely get to work teaching Bub that trick."

Sarah glanced over at Chloe, who had knelt

in the grass next to Hope. She had to dodge Hope's flying tongue now and then but she was definitely interested in the conversation.

"You should invite me to dinner, and I really think Chloe and I should spend some quality time together. At a mall." She winked at Chloe, who mouthed, "Anytime."

The small wave of chuckles that swept through the crowd reminded them all they had other business to attend to.

"Who would like information on adoption?" Shelly asked, waving both hands. "Follow me." A few people in the crowd drifted off.

"You. Miles. Come talk to my brother." Jen pointed at a balding man standing next to the cookies. "My real estate agent stands to make a chunk of change. He should be ready for investment." Jen raised her eyebrows at Will. "Make it snappy. My interior designer is heading your way next."

She marched off, Hope trailing behind her, tail wagging in delight at being with her person.

Will caught the high five Chloe gave him before she darted off after Jen. Will turned to Sarah. "I thought you liked being in control of your own life. We don't have to be so old-fashioned. You can buy me dinner."

"Your sister suggested the same thing," Sarah said. They both grinned. "I'll make you a peanut butter sandwich. Bub loves them or thinks he would if I ever gave him one."

"He deserves a little something for pulling this whole thing together." Will pointed at his feet, where Bub was sitting, his fluffy tail flipping slowly across Will's running shoe.

Without Bub, she might never have taken that first step, the one that had put her on the path to getting the best life, a life she'd never dreamed of. "Never underestimate the power of a big brown dog."

* * * * *

YES! Please send me **The Montana Mavericks Collection** in Larger Print. This collection begins with 3 FREE books and 2 FREE gifts (gifts valued at approx. $20.00 retail) in the first shipment, along with the free first 4 books from the collection! If I do not cancel, I will receive 8 monthly shipments until I have the entire 51-book Montana Mavericks collection. I will receive 2 or 3 FREE books in each shipment and I will pay just $4.99 US/ $5.89 CDN for each of the other four books in each shipment, plus $2.99 for shipping and handling per shipment.*If I decide to keep the entire collection, I'll have paid for only 32 books, because 19 books are FREE! I understand that accepting the 3 free books and gifts places me under no obligation to buy anything. I can always return a shipment and cancel at any time. My free books and gifts are mine to keep no matter what I decide.

263 HCN 2404   463 HCN 2404

Name	(PLEASE PRINT)	

Address		Apt. #

City	State/Prov.	Zip/Postal Code

Signature (if under 18, a parent or guardian must sign)

Mail to the **Reader Service:**
IN U.S.A.: P.O. Box 1867, Buffalo, NY 14240-1867
IN CANADA: P.O. Box 609, Fort Erie, Ontario L2A 5X3

LARGER-PRINT BOOKS!
GET 2 FREE LARGER-PRINT NOVELS PLUS
2 FREE GIFTS!

◆HARLEQUIN®

super romance®

More Story...More Romance

READERSERVICE.COM

Manage your account online!

- Review your order history
- Manage your payments
- Update your address

> ### *We've designed the Reader Service website just for you.*

Enjoy all the features!

- Discover new series available to you, and read excerpts from any series.
- Respond to mailings and special monthly offers.
- Connect with favorite authors at the blog.
- Browse the Bonus Bucks catalog and online-only exculsives.
- Share your feedback.

Visit us at:
ReaderService.com